# Of All Possibilities

*Joe Butler*

Text Copyright © 2021 Joe Butler.

All characters appearing in this work are fictitious. Any resemblance to real persons (or multidimensional versions of them), living or dead (or other), is purely coincidental.

All rights reserved. No part of this publication may be reproduced, distributed, or transmitted in any form, or by any means, including photocopying, recording, or other electronic or mechanical methods, without the prior written permission of the publisher, except in the case of brief quotations embodied in the critical reviews and certain other noncommercial uses permitted by copyright law.

www.writelikeashark.com

Of All Possibilities: First Printing 2021

Cover by Bex Glendining

Typesetting by Alex Laurel Lanz

Edited by Jaclyn Arndt

| | |
|---|---|
| One | 9 |
| My Troubled History, Part One | 13 |
| Two | 39 |
| My Troubled History, Part Two | 44 |
| Three | 74 |
| My Troubled History, Part Three | 78 |
| Unforeseen Consequences | 104 |
| Second First Time Around | 134 |
| Four | 136 |
| My Troubled History, Part Four | 140 |
| Five | 162 |
| My Troubled History, Part Five | 168 |
| Six | 196 |
| My Troubled History, Part Six | 200 |
| A Brief Interlude | 214 |
| Seven | 230 |

| | |
|---|---:|
| My Troubled History, Part Seven | 234 |
| Eight | 246 |
| Jess's Troubled History | 248 |
| My Troubled History, Part Eight | 266 |
| Nine | 290 |
| My Troubled History, Part Nine | 292 |
| Ten | 306 |
| My Troubled History, Part Ten | 310 |
| Eleven | 322 |
| My Troubled History, Part Eleven | 326 |
| Twelve | 344 |
| My Troubled History, Part Twelve | 350 |
| Thirteen | 354 |
| Acknowledgements | 356 |
| About the Author | 358 |

*Creatures of a day! What is anyone?*

*What is anyone not? A dream of a shadow*

*Is our mortal being. But when there comes to men*

*A gleam of splendour given of heaven,*

*Then rests on them a light of glory*

*And blessed are their days.*

*—Pindar, Pythian 8*

*"Neither by ship nor on foot would you find*

*the marvellous road to the assembly of the Hyperboreans."*

*—Pindar, Pythian 10*

# One

**Now**

A philosopher named Gottfried Leibniz once said that we must live in the best of all possible worlds. Just so you know, that is absolute horseshit. I have seen the empirical proof that the world we currently inhabit is not the best version of reality. It's not even close. Look around and you can see how far we have fallen through the choices we've made. Just look at the fucking people in charge. They are actively choosing to shape this world into what it is. This reality is so deep in the shit that all we have left at this point is optimistic bumper-sticker phrases and internet top ten lists.

I've been to universes where we've cured cancer because big pharma never came into existence. Where we've solved the renewable energy question because oil companies failed at covering up the fact that they were skull-fucking the planet into an apocalypse. Even ones where we've settled on other planets. *Other planets.* Already. Bright, chrome-covered sci-fi realities that the dewy-eyed optimists of the '50s dreamt up, where other, better versions of ourselves have been brought into being.

But even they aren't that many steps away from the dystopian reality I find myself in nowadays.

The best description of what the infinite space between realities looks like is an endless glass of Coke.

I'm being absolutely serious.

Each bubble represents a universe, connected to the next by a diaphanous web of dendrites. They shimmer-shake as all realities twist and press gently against each other. An endless layering of liminal worlds, interconnected and tethered together by simple convergence and divergence, possibility and outcome. Branches and branches of what might be, all linking back to a single point where the universe burst into being and spread like a burning root system across the void outside realities. The truest rendition of the mythical tree Yggdrasil, the sacred centre of the cosmos, as described in Norse mythology. A tree, it is written, that connected all nine of the Norse realms.

The first time I saw the place in-between worlds, the pure sensory input was overwhelming to the point of being incomprehensible. When I see it now, I am still utterly scared, flattened by off-the-scale levels of existential anxiety.

Why don't I just go live in one of those amazing, shiny realities, you ask? Well, that's a complicated question.

I can't travel that far from my own reality—not for long, anyway. When I drop into a different reality, I start to feel sick, my head starts to hurt. One universe away and it's bearable, but unless I come back to my starting point and go again from there, it only gets worse. If I travel, say, two universes away—as in, go into one and from there drop into another one—I get nosebleeds, tremors, migraines. The further I go, the worse it gets. The farthest I've been is five down. You ever had Ebola? I imagine it's a little like that, and it's certainly not something I wish to repeat, let me tell you.

So, you probably want to know: What does a man who can slip between universes do for a living?

What do you think? I work for an organisation called the House of August. After everything, I ended up a henchman in a shady little operation called the Atropos Project, and I help shape the fate of this reality.

And before we get into morals and ethics, I didn't actually directly kill people. I just dropped them off in a place where no one could ever find them, at the same time excising them, their histories, and their possible future influence from our timeline. There's a little version of reality that I've been using for just this purpose since I was six. We call it Purgatory.

# My Troubled History, Part One

## March 12, 1985, The New Sunrise Project

I am six and my Grandfather is dead. I remember being woken up by the sharp, desperate cry of my Mother calling out his name, followed by the sounds of people running past my room. Watching the dark breaks in that delicate thread of amber light that filled the uneven gap between the floor and door.

I was up and out of bed, covers thrown back, silently padding to press my ear to the cold wood of my bedroom door and listening to the low voices on the other side. I could hear people talking urgently, someone sobbing on the verge of wailing, hissed whispers. Then, furtively poking my head from my bedroom out into the dimly lit hall, I saw a cluster of adults standing at the doorway to my Grandfather's room. Some of them were shaking. Their eyes glistening, noses running, shoulders drawn up as they buried their heads into other people's chests. The light from inside the room cast the group's tremulous shadows into some monstrous inky creature that slipped along the patterned wallpaper of the hallway.

I crept quietly down the corridor to them, floorboards cold against my bare feet, and pushed myself under the arm of my aunt to see.

"Eli, no!" she exclaimed with a dramatic flourish, throwing her arms up and head back. She pressed her meaty hand into my chest, a chipped nail catching a loose thread and pulling it away.

It was too late—I could see my Grandfather. It was the first time I ever saw a dead body, and the

details of what I saw lived with me in nightmares
for a long time afterwards. He was spread out naked
on top of the rumpled peach-coloured bedsheets,
half in and half out of his bed. His skin, waxen and
papery, grey in places and mottled with patches of
pale purple. Mapped with reddish stains, loose coils
of blue veins twisting and sticking up from his skin,
the limp curl of his penis against his inside leg, feet
dangling down, toes just grazing the carpet. His face
was slack. Eyelids half open to reveal frosted
glimpses of rheumy eyes. His thin lips pulled back
to show a pink line of empty gum. The liver-spotted
knobs of knuckles, riddled with arthritis. Long,
bony, wand-like fingers stretched down past his
hips and stick-thin arms laid by his side, one hand
held in my Father's own.

It was hard to believe the things I'd later learn
with this image in my mind. To know what he had
accomplished and how I would only pale in
comparison.

On the bedside table next to his body was a
thick paperback he'd never finish. It was opened
with pages down, cover up—a James Clavell novel.
I scanned the bookshelf and found the empty space
it had once occupied. Next to the book sat a pair of
wireframe glasses and a dirty tumbler containing his
dentures, as if the process of taking him apart had
already begun.

My Father, perched silently on the edge of the
bed at his father's side, dripped spats of water from
his wet hair onto the old man. His head was down,
looking at my Grandfather's body. My Mother
stood behind him, her trembling hands clutching his
shoulder. She had turned and caught sight of the
commotion I made as I had pushed through, then
leant forward and kissed the top of my Father's
head. After I had been pushed back out of the

room, she came out into the hall, a sad smile playing across her face.

"Eli," she said, kneeling down beside me. She hugged me gently, pulling me into her. When she pulled away, I could see she was crying. "I'm afraid Grandad Bill has gone."

"No, he hasn't—he's there," I said, pointing into the room and not really understanding.

She smiled, then let out a small laugh. "His body's been left behind, that's all. But his spirit has gone on."

"Oh," I said, loosely grasping the concept. My Father's speeches always seemed to revolve around death in one way or another. That and the agents of darkness who always seemed to be moving against us, always just one step away, one move behind.

She kissed me and led me back to my room. After she pulled the sheets up to my chin, I lay there for a long time, eyes wide, until I saw the sun kissing the cold glass of my bedroom window.

My Grandfather had the same ability as me. He was a Key. The key to the door of creation, he used to say. A key that could open a special door between worlds. His grandfather was one, too. It always skips a generation, he'd said. Though I didn't understand the ramifications for me, then. That night is the last time I remember feeling truly whole.

▽

The New Sunrise Project was made up of six families including ours. We lived on a three-acre stretch of land just north of London and just outside a town called Scratch Hill.

The living quarters was a ring of connected houses that met on either side of a wooden stave church at the westernmost end. The original main house within the ring was an ancient cottage constructed from hand-laid slate. Low, smoke-scorched ceilings, a few rooms with small, square windows. Silver blocks of light cutting at just the right angle to slowly bleach the old photographs on the granite mantle. Two armchairs set just so, facing the fire and a ticking clock, which faithfully passed the time in the always soupy-aired room. Time somehow seemed slower in there than any of the other buildings. The rest of them were modular in some fashion or another, attached by a long corridor that held them all together, like a length of silver chain on a bracelet. Some were new, but none of them really matched each other in any kind of coherent way.

The stave church was simple yet ostentatious when judged against the rest of the compound. Two storeys of heavy timbers laid against one another. A few generations back, they added a tower room that gave the best view of the compound and of the surrounding countryside.

In the centre of the ring of buildings was the stone dais we used for our rituals. On it stood the Great Stone Door—a dolmen composed of three solid grey stone blocks resting on one another. Our very own mini Stonehenge. According to my Father, it was the site of a significant divergence, and the doorway to Purgatory. An apocalyptic place to which the offerings, as we called them, were sent.

"We have to cut away the weeds to help the flowers bloom," my Grandfather had told me once, his breath smelling of cherry-flavoured cough sweets, watery eyes smiling at me as I held onto his finger.

Aside from that, we also had a bunch of storage buildings, a greenhouse, and two barns dotted around the land, surrounded by crop fields and finally an enclosure of wooden fencing topped with razor wire.

The town of Scratch Hill is small and allergic to the sort of change that might bring foreigners or tourists. It's one of those places where everyone takes pride in the fact that they know everyone else's business. Small enough so that most everyone knew me as *that creepy cult kid* and the rest of my family as people to generally avoid. There were urban legends and rumours of course—there always are when you live an isolated life. I've been told we were what kids were threatened with when they wouldn't go to sleep. *The creepy Clarkes will come and take you away*, they would say, and the kids would scream and run back upstairs to bed.

The site of the compound used to be farmland until our family settled there in the 1800s. I was told by my Father that his great-grandfather had been instructed to settle his family here by his father, so they bought it off the farmer who lived in the original cottage and took over the land.

▽

We buried my Grandfather next to his wife, in a quiet spot behind the church at the western end of the compound by a patch of small white flowers. We left no gravestone or markings, just a mound of hard turned earth, a thin skin of glittering ice covering it. Loose white powder racing upwards in the swirling wind, up towards the blank sheets of grey cloud.

We sung happy songs and my Father spoke about my Grandfather's life, the work he did and how much he had achieved. Then we all laid yellow and red flowers on the place where he lay. I don't remember the words, just the feeling of needing to pee. That, and how cold my knees were.

Afterwards, we had what seemed to my six-year-old's mind to be a bit of a party. I couldn't understand why everyone was so happy. We gathered in the larger of the two barns, which was full of tables laden with all sorts of food. Everyone was drinking and eating cakes and telling each other stories. Warm laughter slipped between the men and women like a wave. I played with the other kids, tugging at the older ones, who shooed us away as they tried to look cool to no one in particular. One of my uncles sawed out a jaunty tune on a violin, which made some of the younger kids cry.

My Father held my hand and led me out into the freezing night, the sound of merriment and music following behind us through the half-open door, a slice of warm light thrown across the frozen ground. The snow had begun to fall again in the night. Fat white feathers drifted lazily down, illuminated by the sodium white of the security lights. We crunched around the side of the main building and found our way back to the grave. I stood there on my own for a while, listening to the wind through the chain-link fence, the skeletal clack of tree branches, and the sound of muffled laughter. An owl hooted and I spun around, heart hammering in my chest, but couldn't see it.

Death was still something of a mystery to me. I had been told my Grandfather was gone, and we had buried him, but he was there, right beneath my feet. I still didn't understand the concept of forever.

My Grandfather, like the rest of the family going back for generations, was a religious man. The Book of Yon—our interpretation of the Christian Bible written by one of our ancestors around 1512—refers to the other realities as Arks. In my Grandfather's diary, he wrote that the simple answer to the logic problem in the Old Testament's story of Noah's Ark—aside from how on earth he gathered up all those animals in the first place—was the existence of a doorway to another reality. Through this door and the infinite numbers of others, my Grandfather saw the simple solution as to just how Noah fit all those creatures on one little boat. Christianity, Yon had concluded, had got it wrong and completely misunderstood the real, tangible magic of the universe. Well, the *universes*. As such, people have spent a lot of time and effort misinterpreting the word of God. Or the God In-between, as we referred to him in the New Sunrise Project. While we knew a lot of that supernatural stuff in the Bible wasn't true—I mean, for one, there's definitely no magical afterlife or "heaven." Death is presented as a permanent and inevitable outcome of the timeline. Although, we still believed that the God In-between weighed our work and judged our efforts, and we all sought a place in his garden.

My Father bent over me, his face so close that I could smell the booze coming off him in thick warm waves, red eyes shining and fixed on the cold bare earth. He rested a hand on my shoulder and squeezed.

"Grandad was a special man," he said, eyes having trouble meeting mine. "He had a gift. It's something you have but Daddy doesn't. Skips a generation. Always has, always will. I was supposed to get something too. Supposed to, anyway."

He squeezed my shoulder again until it hurt and I shouted and twisted away. He let me go, held up his hands, eyes wide and shining.

"I'm sorry," he said, shocked. Shocked that he had hurt me or shocked that I had shouted, I wasn't sure. "I wanted to wait until you were older. I really did, but we have a purpose that we cannot turn our backs to. You'll learn. You'll learn the burden soon enough."

He lifted me up and carried me back towards the ring of buildings. The view of the grave bobbed and shifted, distorted through my tears. We went through a doorway back into an empty part of the living quarters. A moment later we had passed through a couple of more doors and were out into the central garden. The stone dolmen at the centre, set on the dais, was eerily beautiful in the snow. Lit by pools of bright light from the ground lights, it threw its angular shadow at us, an inverted image with a square of white it its centre instead of the empty black of the real thing. The falling snow blew through the framed space between the door's standing rocks as if there were nothing there but air.

He stopped and put me down facing that gap. It wasn't my first time being so close to the door, but it felt different somehow. I noticed, as if for the first time, the bright seams of quartz running through the slabs, like silver-grey varicose veins.

Until my Grandfather died, I had never been part of the rituals. I had never witnessed the excision of an individual's history. I had never seen Purgatory, nor the actual doorway to it. We called them devils, the people we cut away from the timeline for the betterment of the world. Called the ritual an exorcism, pulling the old language from the Bible, twisting it to fit our doctrine.

"This is the doorway to the place in-between," my Father said. His voice was powerful, filled with conviction. "It is a place where a great divergence took root, and your great-, great-, great-, great-grandfather steered the world from the path of destruction. Everything we have now is thanks to him."

I could see it now, feel it with all my senses. That dark, empty space at the door's centre scared me. It radiated a sickly warmth that smelt of burning metal and distorted the air. It gave off a flat buzz of static that grew in pitch in relation to my diminishing distance to it. The noise seemed to exist in the very centre of my head. It made my teeth itch, my fingers buzz, the hair at the back of my neck prickle, and my scalp tingle. I tried to take a half step back, but my Father held me firmly in place.

"Hold my hand," he said. "Imagine it: a doorway to another place, right here." He pointed a finger at the space where I knew it was.

"I can't," I lied, scared of it, the growing noise and feeling of it, coring my bones, needling my perception.

He lowered himself so that his eyes met mine. "You *can* see it. I know you can," he said, teeth gritted. "Otherwise, you wouldn't have tried to get away from it."

"I can't," I cried. My Father's grip had begun to hurt again, his large fingers digging into my soft, pudgy shoulders.

He slapped me once across the face, hard, and I was stunned. Eyes wide, brimming with tears, lips quivering. He held up a finger to silence me, and I stood there just looking at him and trying to hold off the wave of bawling that was coming, and a feeling of something new—betrayal.

"This is your purpose. Your responsibility, and you want to run away from it?" he growled, his teeth bared. "I thought you were my son, but I see now that you have the darkness in you."

"No!" I cried. I'd heard the insult before and knew what it meant. My Father hated people who didn't pull their weight, didn't want to face their responsibilities. He saw laziness as a blight on the soul, a darkness.

"I'll do it," I said, and his grip eased a little.

"Good," he said. "You do see it, don't you?"

I nodded.

"I knew it," he exclaimed, pressing his hands to face. "I knew you were ready to be a Key. Our work must continue."

He rose up to his full height again and looked down at me, beaming with pride. Snow began to settle in his hair.

"Now," he said, pointing at that unsettling space between the stones, "you have to imagine the door opening. You have to really imagine it. Picture it in your mind's eye."

I did, and the floor and the stones lilted and lurched, drunkenly swaying in my vision. I felt a wave of nausea wash over me, part motion sickness, part terror. The static grew and then receded, like a distant but powerful wave gathering all its strength just out of sight, promising to become a tsunami as we edged closer and closer. The doorway flickered and flared and then spread like an ink spill in mid-air, filling that empty, ancient space between the stones. My Father couldn't see it, but he knew it was there from my expression. He closed his eyes in reverence of it.

"Good boy," he said, ruffling my hair gently. "Now, take me through."

My hand, grabbed roughly by my father, became slick with sweat as we took a step towards the glittering space. The tidal wave of static finally rushed back and broke over me, began to roll my mind over with its force. I staggered as a thrill of oceanic noise filled my blood. I looked up at my Father, who was mumbling some verse from the Book of Yon.

"I'm scared, Daddy," I said.

"Don't be scared," he said, giving my hand a gentle squeeze and driving away the ghost of the pain in my shoulder. He smiled. "This is your purpose."

His face was close to manic then—eyes wide, sweat beading on his forehead. As he pulled me a step closer to the door, I resisted a little, then just closed my eyes. We lurched forward. The wave hit us and we fell into it.

Formless space followed.

I became keenly aware that my eyelids were gone, along with my eyeballs and the rest of my body, and yet I could see in all directions. My Father, too, was gone. We were reduced to raw consciousness, but somehow more than that—our unfettered inner selves interlinked, my fear overridden by the sudden intrusion of my Father's awe followed by his fears, anxieties, hopes, disappointments. A triumphant leer emanated from the shared entity that we had become. We careened along a channel of pulsing energy, the endless spread of wobbling realities bright as stars around us, crowding us, and yet utterly impossible to reach. I suddenly saw everything with the clarity of an adult, and knew that it was my Father's mind acting as some sort of filter.

Pockets of light and dark strobed and rippled as we chased an invisible and unknown trajectory. Finally we arrived at what appeared to be a flat terminus upon an infinite plane. I felt an impossible burden drop away as we momentarily hung there in the dark space between all realities. It is what I imagine being a God feels like. Then, without warning, we plunged along a shimmering line of divergence, chasing a distant speck of light that exploded into view, like racing behind a runaway train that's suddenly upon you. Everything filled with white light, static, and the smell of burning metal.

▽

## 1985, Purgatory

My Father and I arrived, like everyone who travels between worlds, utterly changed.

Disentangled now, only a ghost of our connection lingered in my senses, like an old wound. The sickness that has written its message all over a survivor's face and body. Somewhere inside I still felt old—could think and reason as an adult from within my six-year-old's mind. It was disturbing to see the world once again through a child's eyes, and even more disturbing that I was suddenly aware of this fact. I was suddenly in possession of my Father's vocabulary, his articulation, his fervour. Some of it faded, his memories mainly. But some of it stuck, lodged permanently in my brain like a tiny sliver of meat between my teeth that I couldn't dislodge or stop thinking about.

Later, I would compartmentalise it, put it down to the trauma of the event itself. The fact that it was my first time through the doorway. It was only years later I realised that I was actually feeling the weight of my Father's disappointment in himself for not possessing the gift he wanted so badly; he was not the Seer that he told everyone he was. That, and his greedy resentment toward me for my gift, and his overwhelming grief over his father's death—a man who saw him only as a disappointment, a break in the chain. Through the shades of his consciousness, I understood the finality of my Grandfather's death then. While my Father's mind had fled mine, the bits that remained behind burrowed deep within my psyche, waiting for just the right moment to come back.

And there's the true rub of being a magical, mystical Key—whenever I take someone out of our reality and into another, our inner minds merge, smashed irrevocably together. Thoughts and feelings, fears and desires, are shared between us, and we each leave an indelible mark on the other.

I saw it in his eyes, how much he hated me for knowing his deepest held secret, the one he kept from everyone in the New Sunrise. All the pacts he had made with himself. He was supposed to be a Seer, because the gift was passed down through the men of our family, just like the gift of being a Key. The way it works is this: The ability of the Key travels down the male genetic line, skipping a generation. My Grandfather was a Key, and so I am. In the gap between is born a Seer. The Seer, also always male (don't blame me, I didn't make the rules), has the ability to seek out the future and isolate a person who needs to be struck from this reality. My Father was the Seer for the New Sunrise back in '85, and if I have kids, my firstborn son will be one, and his son will be a Key. But he was just a false prophet. He had no gift.

He wept and shook as we stood there, a reality away from where we had just been. Freezing air drifting from our open mouths, caught on the icy wind and spiralling up.

I knew then, as I knew all his secrets, that my Father had never travelled to another reality before that night. I saw a string of memories of him begging his father time and again to take him, but being told no. As time had passed, he had begun to lose faith, had begun to doubt his own father and the work he did. But now that the old man had died, I had opened up the route again. Trembling and sobbing, looking out upon the bleak angles of shadowed landscape, he believed again, utterly. I felt his reverence coming off him in waves.

We would never speak of our experience together in Purgatory, not really. We never revealed to the rest of the group what had happened, which meant that, until after the first official ritual, I more or less hid my newfound cognitive growth. I had grown just wise enough to know that playing dumb was my best hope for making it through this strange new world I had inherited. My Father, for his part, stopped meeting my angry gaze, my knowledge of the secrets he had kept between his father and him too much for him to bear. I often thought about how he knew that I knew, could see how I'd changed, how my knowledge had grown, in the way that I looked at him. I often think that was why he treated me like he did for so many years—I simply knew him too well, and I've never been that great a liar.

▽

### October 31, 1985

Halloween. Samhain. All Hallows' Eve. We could see the bike lights of kids cutting blades of ghostly white through the line of trees as they cycled into or out of town on the way to trick or treat.

It was a big day for the New Sunrise Project, too—my first ritual as Key.

On this night, instead of wandering the streets with an old sheet on my head, collecting bite-sized versions of my favourite sweets, I stood idle while my Grandfather's mantle fell to me.

It was bitterly cold, and the clothes I was dressed in—a simple brown canvas robe that smelt vaguely musty, brown leather moccasins, and no underwear—was not adequate protection from the icy wind that screamed down from the north and straight up my robe. I may have been six, but I now possessed my Father's reasoning, and when I questioned the purpose of the robe, I was told that it was tradition.

The family stood in a loose circle holding hands and praying, their eyes closed in reverence, wind snapping at their loose shifts, skirling through the Great Stone Door. The ghosts of those who had passed through was held in the memory of the stones.

I remember feeling the power of it. The sudden realisation of my power, my purpose. I was in control, and I had a distilled sense of my Father's duty still fresh in my brain.

I wasn't afraid like the first time—I was eager. Curious, hungry even, to know another being so completely as I had briefly known my Father. It seemed I had taken some of that from him, too. I have always wondered what I imprinted in him. Wonder itself, maybe.

My Mother led me out into the garden, the wooden door clattering to a close behind us. My hood pulled up about my face, but desperately trying to whip back. She looked a little sad, and it pained me then that she might never want to know the feeling of slipping between universes, and that I may never know her true thoughts. She was so often a quiet woman, never one to make much of a fuss, and never swayed from her belief in our purpose.

She let me go and stood there, swaddled in grey fabric, like a slender pillar. From the centre of the dais, I looked out at the ring of people dressed all in granite coloured robes. Their eyes shone in the dark, lit by the burners filled with dried flowers, candles, and oil dotted around the garden in a concentric pattern. Tongues of fire spat glowing sparks up into the dark. The faces of my family adorned with blue paint in various patterns and symbols.

My Father followed behind. The circle broke apart and reformed into a corridor. Behind him emerged a figure bound at the wrists and neck by a thick length of rope, a hessian sack over his head.

"This," he proclaimed, "is the offering."

My Father dragged the captive down the centre path towards the stones. The family hissed and spat as he passed. The man staggered to a stop before me, halted by my Father's forearm across his chest.

"This is the offering we make to God," my Father bellowed. He stepped forward, knelt on one knee, and held out the rope in offering. "Just as Abraham was willing to give his son unto the Lord, so, too, do we offer this sacrifice to Him."

"Amen," I said, and the family repeated it back. He continued. "We must cut away this weed from the garden of His design, for surely we are the arbiters of His will, and it is our duty to ensure that the flowers that bloom are not tainted by the evil of some men. That this world is kept free from the impurities of the sinner's influence."

I took the rope from my Father's outstretched hand and gently wound it around my own. Then I turned to face the doorway. I was unafraid this time, feeling the warm honeyed waves of static radiating outwards, washing over me. I felt that unpleasant lurch again, like a lift suddenly dropping a few floors. Sweet-scented embers from the burners scattered around the cold stones and passed through the space at the dolmen's centre.

"Now," my Father said. He raised his arms triumphantly. "Strike this offering from the history of our world and make bloom His garden again."

The noise of the family's praying grew louder and louder, almost outweighing the growing roar of static that was coming at me from some distant, invisible point. I looked over my shoulder at the painted face of my Father. A single blue cross starting at his hairline ran down to his chin and crossed over his eyes. They were bright white against the blue and the night that surrounded him. They were fervently pushing me onwards.

I saw the doorway expanding. Filling the space. The smell of burning metal filled my nostrils.

The chanting reached some kind of apex—an orgiastic zenith of religious fervour. I could no longer pick out individual voices, just noise. They were projecting their energies towards us, me and the offering, and it was infectious. I found myself unafraid, empowered. I felt my divine purpose in that moment. I was a scalpel, finely cutting away sin, ushering our world towards becoming the best of all possible worlds.

I paused for effect at the foot of the doorway, grabbed the offering's bare wrist with my free hand, and gently pulled him through and together we became wanderers bathed in starlight.

▽

Once again, I felt the sudden loss of my physical body, but this time I basked in it and the utter freedom it granted. Then our consciousnesses bled into one. A new feeling of unimaginable terror. Terror and pain and loss. I knew clearly that the man who was our sacrifice was not evil or full of hatred. It felt wrong. I had braced myself to experience a flood of violence, but all that pervaded my consciousness was loss. He missed his family with such a terrible urgency that I felt my own brain being entirely overwhelmed by grief. His inner mind spoke in a different language to mine, but in the spaces between universes, conventional languages are meaningless. Frantic, I did my best to project to him the place we were headed to in an effort to calm him.

*Olga.*

The name sounded out over and over again as we chased the tremulous line of light ahead of us.

*Olga.*

With every repetition, love and loss erupted across our interlinked minds, the sound of the name breaking our shared heart. We loved her equally then, and I knew her as intimately as the man I was conveying to a new reality did. Could smell her even though I'd never met her. Could remember the taste of her even though we'd never kissed. I could recall some loose approximation of her face, even though I had never seen her—proud eyes, good teeth, nose slightly longer and more bent than she'd have liked, but we didn't mind that. She was a bright remembrance shared between, like a flare in the dark.

*Olga.*

Where did we meet? Walking next to the Moskva River, the smell of the frigid air lifting from the frozen water. The two of us bathed in the orange of the streetlights, offering no warmth but lighting the edges of jutting ice lifted from the water. It shadows her eyes, and when we smile at her, she looks wary.

Meeting friends near the Pushkin Museum of Arts and had gotten lost, is what she says, as the old furs pulled up past her pale neck shift to reveal a simple silver cross gleaming in the ambient glow. We walk her to meet her friends, even though every step feels like giving her away.

I tried to push out the memory, but couldn't—more of him rushed forth to fill the gap that was being created in me, or was I rather just making more space? Allowing him to fill the empty parts of my mind.

We decide to brave rejection and tell her that we'd like to see her again. She smiles on the steps of the museum, standing over us as she gives her address in Lyubertsy and makes us remember it by repeating it back. Tells us to call by next week. We feel a flutter in our chests, a rush of potential.

The permanence of the feeling that lived from then on in the space we hadn't known was there.

I pushed back, drowning in the memory, focusing forward as the pin light of the destination expanded. The dark space fragmented and the bright line unfolded into a reality.

▽

The journey was instantaneous but felt like decades, and as our minds decoupled, the man's memories began to take on a dreamlike quality. Soon only the feeling of loss remained. That and whatever indelible mark he had received upon his own mind.

He pitched forward, dropped to his knees, and started to retch inside the bag fastened around head. I watched him convulse for a moment, collecting myself and wondering what I needed to do next. A tiny pinprick of pain started to blossom in the back of my head, signalling that my own bout of nausea wouldn't be far behind.

The man began to cry. I knew he had gotten a sense of what this place was from me. Six-year-old me still didn't know much about it beyond its name, but something deeper knew its purpose: it was a place from which people do not return, and, from our interlinking, he knew it too. He angled forward and pressed his head to the ground as if in deep prayer, his shoulders shaking. The air was terribly cold, the sky clear.

The reality in which we had arrived was what I knew as Purgatory then. I would never know the reason why, but there were no signs of any people. It was clear they had been wiped out. In the place where the compound had just been a moment before was a rough square of hard, untilled earth, pale grass that grew to knee height. The patch of land hemmed in by low, rough rock walls that marked the perimeter of the field. A partially collapsed farmhouse sat near a copse of thin, bare trees. The roof was half-gone, leaving a frame of barely standing walls and empty windows clogged with weeds. Moss-spotted and rotting lintels angled skyward.

I knew that my reality was still there, just beyond my sight. Somehow overlaid, like a photographic error. I could almost feel my family, like ghosts moving at the periphery of my vision.

In the distance, I saw the shape of a town. Black and grey fingers of ancient towers and their roofs clawing dark silhouettes into the pitted sky. I followed those jagged lines up to the moon, which was smashed into five or six jigsaw pieces. Each luminous section appeared huge against the black canvas of the sky, the reflected light obscuring the stars. Replacing them was a scattered spray of lunar debris that sparkled in the reflected light— trillions of particles of dust lit up like distant, winking fairy lights.

My heart was racing and my breath caught in my throat as I began to panic at the horrifying thought of being a witness to the aftermath of some great celestial crime, danger still lurking. The moon was a constant, too large to ever change, just like the sun. Like the earth—but that too had changed. I only had to look around to see it. But it was dark, and I could convince myself that it was the same as the one I had just left behind. My fingers tingled as I began to hyperventilate. I started to cry.

It was the man's laboured breathing that snapped me out of it. I knelt beside him, gently untied the sack, and pulled it from his head. He was breathing hard. Vomit speckled his chin. His eyes tilted skyward and I saw the terror in them, and that was almost as bad as feeling it. He screamed, rolled onto his back, and tried to crawl away.

"What is this?" he cried. His accent was thickly Soviet, as I knew it would be. Images of Ostrovskogo Square alighting in my memory. The statue of Catherine the Great dressed in snow and lit by the muted light of a waning winter sunset. The loose powder shifting in the wind, a sound like fabric moving against skin. Olga smiling, her face peeking out from a ring of fur, the new coat we had bought her. *She has such a wonderful smile,* we had both thought. *Such a shame it has been so long since we saw it.*

"Purgatory," I replied, my voice quavering. "And you are going to stay here now."

"Please. I have a family," he said. "I miss them so much. I have a little girl."

I knew it was true, too, but tried to ignore it. The words my Father had hissed at me as he dressed me ringing in my ears. "Be strong, Eli. The devil has his tricks." I thought this man must be especially bad if he was trying to make me believe him so desperately.

"I know," I said, and he nodded solemnly at me. The weight of the bond that had formed lay heavy between us, but unacknowledged.

"I'm not supposed to talk to you," I said, rising and backing away. "You are the devil."

"No," he exclaimed. "No, I'm a scientist. My name is Vladimir, Vladimir Petrikov." His accent was thick and hard to understand. "The government did this to me, to silence my work. You know this.

Please, you must know this. You are making a mistake, such a terrible mistake."

My Father had told me to kill the man, so that he could not be returned. To tie him up to starve or to stab him in the belly and leave him, but I couldn't do it. Not after seeing his life. Not after *living* his life. I wondered how my Grandfather did it.

"Devil." I whispered, my voice hoarse from crying. "In that building over there," I said, pointing to the ramshackle farmhouse and trying not to make eye contact, "there's a knife that you can use." Vladimir craned his neck to see where I was pointing, his eyes bulging in their dark sockets.

"Wait. Please wait. I need to talk to you. Don't go. Just talk. Stay, please. My child needs me."

His child had appeared in his thoughts with the same frequency as Olga, burning just as brightly there. Incandescent in the dark.

I wanted to stay. In my heart, I knew that I could just stand there and that, by doing so, it would all play out in whatever way he wanted it to. I knew that if I listened, he would convince me to take him back. I was weak before I was strong, and strong before I was broken and remade.

He scrambled to stand, but his feet slipped behind him and he fell back onto the cold earth, began crying again.

"I need to go now," I said, as devoid of emotion as I could manage.

"No," he screamed as took as step towards the spot where the doorway home stood. "Don't go. You mustn't."

I stopped to hear him say one final thing before I stepped through.

"Please," he said, broken, dragging the word out into some grief-stricken note. My eyes flicked to his for a brief moment before I had to look away. "Remember what I said."

I pushed through the doorway and fled along those bright, rippling lines and back home. It was instantaneous, and yet the moment spilled out over itself. In my sadness, I almost revelled in the disassembly of my being as I was pulled through the nexus of realities and back home. Then my pure senses were transmuted, once again, into physical form.

▽

My family was waiting. Some were praying. Others were silent, their eyes focused on the place where I had returned. They had completely forgotten the person I had taken through, but the ritual had been planned in advance, and so they still stood there, awaiting the return of the Key, trying desperately to discern the doorway that linked their reality to another. I was not to take anyone from the family through. That was the rule. Only the offerings went through with me, and only I returned.

They greeted me, wrapped me in their arms, and sung to me. My sudden appearance before their eyes reconfirmed their beliefs and they gasped and clapped, and praised the God In-between. In the throng, I caught my Father's gaze as he retreated towards the house, escaping the celebration. Then I was ushered into the church, swept down the centre aisle, and led over to the Book of Names, a big, black, leather-bound tome. One of my uncles pulled it open to where the names stopped, and, in a child's hand, below my Grandfather's neat script, I wrote the name Vladimir Petrikov.

# Two

You ever heard of the Mandela Effect? It's a social phenomenon where a bunch of people believe that Nelson Mandela was killed in the late '80s. People who believe this version of events often recall vivid memories of watching his funeral on television and widespread international mourning. What about the *Berenstein/Berenstain Bears* thing? The kids' cartoon about the bears: there were two versions of it, and some people remember it differently from the rest of us.

Where I work, we simply refer to it as a reality overlap. It happens when a kind of unconscious bleed effect occurs between our world and a version of reality that exists in extreme proximity to this one. Somehow, ideas and facts from there end up being stitched into the fabric of the universal unconscious here.

This sort of thing happens all the time, and you barely notice it. Maybe a slight shift in the quality of the light for no reason. Maybe a faint flutter in your chest that you put down to anxiety, or a mild feeling of déjà vu. A headache that suddenly blooms behind your eyes can indicate a convergence of realities. You are simply experiencing the feeling of subsuming another version of you until a dominant reality is established. Maybe you feel inexplicably tired or angry, or maybe you just go about your day feeling undeservedly happy.

It's not always exact, and sometimes the version of you that is left after a convergence event is the one that existed in a timeline where Mandela was killed in the '80s, but now you are living in one where he wasn't. It's nothing to be concerned about for the most part—it's just an imprecise overlay.

▽

The target leaves his home. A very nice detached house in North London. The swanky Crouch End part, not the dingy Finsbury Park end. He crosses the road and gets into a modest comet-grey four-door and starts the engine. The lights cut two yellow-white gouges into the darkness of the street as he rolls forward and pulls away. I wait a moment and then follow behind him at a reasonable distance. There's not a lot of traffic, which is good and bad. It makes tailing someone a pain, because if they take too many turns, it becomes somewhat obvious, but at least you don't have any issues keeping tabs on them. I let a Mini slip between us and then trail him north, heading towards the M1 via the main roads.

So why do it, you ask? Why work for the government?

Well, for a start, I didn't really have much of a choice. There's not a lot of work for people with my skill set, so the idea of a purpose or a guiding principle for people like me is pretty important. Otherwise we'll go right off the rails. The problem is, once you have seen the fabric of reality itself—have not only seen behind the curtain, but seen the stuff the curtain is made of and drifted freely across intangible planes of existence—well, you can't just work as a barista in an upscale coffee place after that, right?

When everything was said and done, I still wanted to fulfil my purpose. From the moment I realised my gift, it never felt like following the path laid out for me was a choice. Like, you read about writers and artists who, when asked why they do what they do, simply reply, *Because I have to.*

Look at Luke Skywalker. He kinda *had* to become a Jedi, because his Father was one. Sometimes, when the family genes are that strong, freewill takes a back seat to destiny.

Plus, the pay is good—phenomenally good, actually. Comes from all that cash the government can't really account for, as well as the not inconsiderable amount that people like me pilfer from other versions of reality. It gets filtered through the cracks and through reality and into departments like mine at the House of August. And we *are* a bona fide department. My great-grandfather, seeing the First World War on the horizon, made a deal with the British government and set up the Atropos Project to influence its outcome. The Nazis tried the same thing in the Second World War, but they failed at it. My great-grandfather's department kept running afterwards—for clearly good reason—and so, in '97, after much deliberation, I signed up.

You see, I am not the only person with a gift. I'm not the only Luke Skywalker on the planet. That would be insane. Granted, I *am* the only person with *my* gift. But the other agents at the House of August—they can do some pretty weird stuff, too.

I'm lucky because, unlike a lot of the people I work with, I don't have to deal with my gift at all times. At this point, I can see doorways almost everywhere I look—but I don't *have* to go through. I don't even have to materialise them if I don't want to.

And the work that we do? Well, there is a war on—always—and we are part of an ongoing battle to remove controlling elements to help guide our universe towards its best possible version. We stop military coups that will destabilise regions of the world already on a knife-edge. We insert people into power who are predicted to be good, or, at the very least, the lesser of evils. We disappear the people who could lead us all down the wrong path, and sometimes just the lesser-evil guy's opponent.

Yeah, we have a self-interested interventionist government paymaster. Is what we do morally shady? Hell yeah it is. But it's better to be on the inside of that than watching from the sidelines of a game you aren't even aware is being played. I've been doing this my whole life—for my Father, for my family, and now for the government. At least it pays. Plus, I've seen the changes that I've made. I know the cost of what is cut away to make the world better, because those pieces that are smashed out of it are the ones that fill the constantly made fractures in my psyche, pushing out all those small slices of me to accommodate someone else.

I know that I am doing the right thing. I also know what I am doing *right now* is all kinds of off the books. And if I fuck it up, I'll be done. But if I can pull this off, I will bend the future toward its best possible version. Besides, you should read this guy's history—he's a complete asshole.

I indicate left, drop into the middle lane, and settle behind the target car.

Mill Hill rolls past, along with the first motorway services. We are heading somewhere north, and I know that before we get wherever we're going, the motorway will take us past my old home first, and I brace myself for all the shitty memories that'll shake loose.

# My Troubled History, Part Two

**November 1, 1985**

My Father and I were sat in the kitchen next to the heat of the stove, the occasional plume of smoke floating past the window. He was leant over the table, hands supporting his face as he read the James Clavell novel that I had seen by my Grandfather's bed. I was sat opposite him, a half-empty glass of milk in front of me, practising my writing at the kitchen table. Outside, it was getting dark, only the loose amber strands of a fading sunset left in the sky. I placed a finger on the cold glass and covered the moon visible through it, making it appear like a ghostly halo around my fingertip. The sight of it forced the memory of Vladimir to bubble to mind.

*Olga,* the voice in my mind cried, screamed, and I caught that frigid smell coming off the Moskva River once again. I jerked, kicking at the air. My Father looked up from his book, creasing the corner of the page with his thumb.

"Daddy, can I ask you something?" I asked.

I could hear my Mother moving around in the living room, but, unusually, we were alone. I remember my legs dangling in the air below me.

In the same way I had taken from him, I'd taken on a portion of the man I had brought with me to Purgatory the night before. I had realised the change in me even then. I'd taken from him some measure of scientific abstraction. Objective rational observation. My Father's shame was still present, but this was joined now with a sense of curiosity. I was still a child, but the words in front of me, written on that practice book in bright, friendly colours, seemed so inane. I had already started to thirst for more sophisticated material.

"Okay," he said, his eyes narrowing. I look at myself now and see so much of that version of my Father's face in my own features.

"What am I?" I asked.

He tried to smile. Forced the edges of his lips into a thin unconvinced line. "We call it a Key. As is written in the Good Book."

"A key, like for a door?"

"Yes, but for many doors. More doors than you could possibly enter in a lifetime. And only you have the gift to journey between worlds, to remove the influence of evil men and women in this world."

He closed the book and slid it to the edge of the table nearest the window.

"Why only me?"

"Who can say? Save that, our family line has been chosen to be the keeper of this beautiful universe. My Father was one, his father's father, and way, way back down the line, we have been the keepers of His garden."

"Grandad took bad people away too?" I asked. The red crayon rolled off the edge of the table and cracked in half on the stone floor.

My Father nodded. "The world will never understand what that man did for it. The stories he told me of a history he—*we* averted. The sacrifices

Of All Possibilities | 45

he made…" He trailed off and looked at me—into me. He appeared taken aback by my comprehension of what he was saying, but then he seemed to remember that it was artifice in a way. Nevertheless, I had not been that way before. He never admitted it to me, but I always suspected that, after that first time, he saw me as someone, some*thing*, else. An uninvited stranger in his son's skin.

"Did it change him?" I asked.

He didn't answer for a moment, just looked out the window at the stones lit by the moon, the quartz seams glittering like rivers of frost.

"Yes," he said finally. "And it will change you too."

"That man…" I said, struggling to articulate exactly what I wanted to say. "The man I took away."

"The sacrifice? The devil who sought to fill His garden with thorns?" he replied.

"He wasn't a bad man," I said. "I saw into him, like I did with you when I took you there."

I saw the muscles in my Father's jaw flexing. He raised a finger up and jabbed at the space between us.

"You don't ever speak of that again," he hissed, voice low and urgent so my Mother wouldn't hear. "It was a mistake to have done that. I can see it got your mind all confused. And as for that man, the devil will do his best to try to convince you not to cast him out, but you have to be strong." He leant forward, resting his forearms on the table. "You tell me now: What lies did he tell you?"

"He told me he missed his family," I said. The feeling was still so vivid inside me, it felt like a flare burning in my guts. "He has a wife named Olga." It hurt to say her name aloud, my throat closing up as I did.

"These people we deal with," he said, his glare burning into mine. "Those *things*, they might not even know how bad they are, but I promise you, they are. The names we mark in the Book are stepping stones to Eden. Now, these men"—he spat the word—"these devils do not always see the evil they do, they cannot foresee, as we have foreseen, the Hell they would see come to pass."

"But you can't foresee it either," I said, weighing my next words carefully. "Why don't you ever talk about him? About your brother? Henry *could* see, couldn't he?"

He was rising from his seat, leaning forward, his knuckles white as he gripped the edge of the scarred table, the black lines cut deep into the surface over the long years just beneath his palms.

"Do not speak that name in this house," he snarled.

I tried to push myself away from him, knowing I should be quiet, but unable to stop myself.

"*He* could see it. He was always Grandad's favourite, and that made you feel bad. I saw it inside of you."

My Father rocked back as if stung by a blow, teeth clenched, eyes pinched shut. Then he slammed his hands down on the table. My glass jumped and rolled on its side, a white pool spreading from it, like moonlight, towards the edge of the table.

"You've got that damned devil in you, boy," he growled. "I can still see him in your eyes!"

He lurched forward and grabbed my arm. I yelled and screamed as he pulled me through the house, kicked my bedroom door wide, and threw me into my room. He slammed the door behind him.

I was so scared, but I stood there.

"I don't think you are a failure, Daddy," I said, my throat trying to squeeze shut and keep the words in.

"I'll have to beat the devil out of you."

Then, he did.

He slipped his belt off and wound it round his open hand. He recited the Book of Yon as he did it. I still remember the passage he kept whispering over and over: "And for fear of my own earthly soul, I must seek to cleanse the unholy, wicked ghosts from my spirit. I must suffer to see clear the design that He has laid before us, the wickedness in my heart fled before His glory."

"Daddy," I whimpered when he'd finished and was looping the belt back through his trousers.

"You aren't my son anymore," he said, and closed the door.

▽

The next morning, my family moved me into my Grandfather's old room. Not the one he had died in, but the one he had lived in for most of his life. It was situated at the very top of the tower of the church. The high-vaulted prayer room was directly below mine. A cold, wide space filled by two rows of pews, a lectern at one end in front of a huge bronze disc, golden lines radiating off it, representing the sun. On either side of that were two glass cases. One held the Book of Names and the other the Book of Yon. We gathered there every evening for prayer and stories. My Grandfather told the congregation of the worlds he had seen, the brutal histories he had averted. He would pluck names from the Book and tell us of the secret missions he undertook with the Atropos Project. I remember the day he told us why that name was chosen—for the Greek Moirai, the weavers of fate. Atropos was the Fate who chose the destiny of men and women, and who, wielding the Abhorred Shears, cut their lives.

He'd clear his throat, push the bridge of his wireframe glasses up to his brow, and squint as he ran a leathery finger along the page. "Ah, yes," he'd say, and cast his gaze around the room. "Let me tell you about Hans Gourig. Or maybe Fredrick Rosehorn." And we would all sit there, rapt, and listen as he told us the stories of what could have come to pass.

He began living in the church tower after his grandfather had died, and he continued to live there until he was too old to climb the steep stairs and we had to move him to a ground-floor room.

My new bedroom was long with sloped walls on all sides, tapering to a point at the tip of the tower. Lines of dusty cobwebs criss-crossed the space, lit by a single porthole window on the northern side. The walls were lined with wardrobes with sets of drawers built into them. They were still filled with my Grandfather's clothes. Wrapped in white plastic bags with the hangers poking through the top, like a line of strange ghosts. On the far side of the room, under a large square window, was my new bed. Two other rooms were partitioned off from the main bedroom. A claustrophobic study filled with towers of mouldering and dusty books, a dark-green leather office chair pulled under the table. The other, an en suite bathroom built sometime in the 1950s and never redecorated, cracked light-blue floral tiles rimed in mildew, a run of brown rust at the seams of the leaky faucets. The ancient plumbing creaked and rattled and gurgled, as if crying out in protest, and the shower always shook violently for the first minute or so. Everything was layered in a thick coat of dust, or stained, or faded, or just slightly broken. The ghosts of a life lived ingrained on every surface. The window had a gossamer net of cobwebs across it that gently moved in the breeze like a spirit sail. On the curved stone sill lay the husks of spiders, flies, and other bugs.

Generations upon generations had lived and died without ever escaping the confines of the room. My Father nonchalantly held my hand as we climbed the creaking stairs, as if he hadn't used that same hand the day before to beat my body black and blue. Bright-pink notches in the shape of the eyes of his belt still clearly marked my legs and stomach.

He smiled brightly at me as he turned the long brass key in the lock and the door creaked open. Then he turned, knelt, and placed the key in my palm.

"This is your room now," he said and planted an awkward kiss on my forehead. I flinched, and he held me in place by my shoulders.

"It's scary," I replied, poking my head around the doorframe and taking in the apocalyptic quality of the décor.

"We'll clean it up for you, of course," he said. "But just think about all the wonderful prayers that will float up through here on their way to God."

"Okay," I said. I wonder if I had started to doubt the religious aspects of what we did then. Whether my Father's own creeping doubt had been the catalyst. Or maybe Vlad's logical influence on my thinking was the cause. I didn't doubt our mission, just the alt-Christian rhetoric that sat behind it.

He pushed me gently into the room and we both stood there, the silvery daylight touching the faded floorboards and curled rugs, creeping over the pale edges of the framed photographs hung from rusted nails. My Father stopped in front of one and studied it intently. He seemed lost in the image of him and his father standing by a newly built fence. I recognised it as being the one near the farmhouse. He was wearing thick gloves and had an elbow crooked over the end of a shovel, a wide, careless smile on his bearded face. My Grandad had one muscular arm stretched over my Father's shoulders, and he was looking off somewhere, head angled up at the sky, eyes half closed and smiling.

I felt my Father's sadness as keenly then as I had the day we had intermingled, and I realised that the price of my gift was that I would forever carry an active piece of each person I moved between worlds. I wondered if they would each take something from me until I was completely gone. Of course, I couldn't really articulate my fear at the time, but I felt it. I was still reeling from the instant maturing effect that the imprinting of two adult consciousnesses had had on my own fragile, still developing one. In that room, bathed in melancholic light, for the first time I felt an acute sense of ennui, and a state of helplessness. I felt life's stream pulling me in a direction that I could see might destroy me, but I was powerless to stop it. I was only six and no one would listen to me, no matter the sophistication of the words I expressed myself in. My Father swiped at his face, coughed, then turned and closed my hand around the warm key before leaving me there in the room, alone.

▽

The beatings happened after every scheduled ritual, whether someone was taken through or not. So that it became a ritual in itself. Joyless and mechanical for him, full of fear and eventually dissociation for me. It would go like this: if there had been an offering, I would arrive back through the Great Stone Door, and everyone would praise me and congratulate me as I added the latest entry to the Book of Names; for victimless rituals, they'd simply watch raptly as I walked up to the dolmen, did an about-face, and walked back. Either way, the evening would be a celebration, full of prayers and stories. I was seven when I started telling the stories myself. Then, late at night, my Father would climb the creaky stairs up to my room and stand in the square of light, his features cloaked in darkness.

He'd ask me if the devil was in me, and I would always say yes. It became transactional. I had to ask him to do it. I was always too afraid to say no.

"It's the remedy for the evil that lurks in you," he'd whisper in my ear as he slipped free his belt.

Post-violence, red faced, sweating, and tearful, he would sit on the bed next to me and gently stroke my hair. I remember so clearly the weight of him on the mattress, making it impossible to escape his gravity as he pulled me into the crook of his arm, the smell of sweat, and most times alcohol, filling my nose. His near incoherent ramblings as he tried to rationalise his cruelty with quotes from the Book of Yon. He would tell me how much he was helping me. The sacrifices he was making to keep those devils from the door. All the while, those new parts of me that I had gained from each new sacrifice screamed in unison, but I remained silent.

"I see so clearly your burden, and I am sorry that you have to bear it on your own. I wish I could help you more than I do. I wish it were mine."

And that was the rub—because he really did wish it were his. He desperately wanted the power he thought he deserved, the one he told everyone he had. He needed to be special. The strength of his belief demanded it. I had felt that desperation in him, and he knew it.

I don't know why—maybe because of the traces of Vladimir in me—but my own beliefs started to drift from the doctrine of the New Sunrise. Yes, I sang along and prayed with the others, but whenever I met my Father's gaze, the words tasted bitter, rang hollow.

I *did* believe in God, but my thoughts started to rebel. Even now, I can't say that I'm ruling Him out completely. That type of hardwiring is tough to shake—doubly so when you have an actual, real superpower. Have coursed along the raw electrics of reality itself, witnessing first-hand the true scope of an infinite multiverse. I mean, once you've seen behind the curtain, subjective opinion kind of goes out the window.

For a month and a half after taking through Vladimir, there were only two more offerings. I turned seven in mid-December.

▽

**December 25, 1985**

The year 1985 was particularly hard for my Father, as it was the first without his own father. It was obvious for all to see that the loss was still incredibly painful for him. On the wall of the church, he'd hung a large photo of the man next to the painting of his great-grandfather. The composition was similar, too. He was facing the camera, but focused on someone or something just to the left of the shot, and behind him loomed the Great Stone Door. Within its grey frame, a setting sun reduced his features to shadows. The painting was more formal, but the details were too similar to be an accident.

While we didn't recognise Christ in our beliefs at the New Sunrise, we still had a kind of Christmas. My Father begrudgingly allowed a holiday from outside our own doctrine to infiltrate the walls of the compound under pressure from the rest of the family and to generally lift the spirits of everyone, especially the kids. He did, however, stipulate that the purpose of the holiday would be to focus on appreciating the world as it was and as it might be. To the other kids and me, it was still all about the presents. We had a Christmas tree in the church just in front of the lectern, and while it was bereft of any ornamentation, at the base of it there was always a pile of presents.

That non-Christmas, there was a morning prayer led by my Father, who remembered my Nan and Grandad. Then my Mother spoke about her parents, who had both died when she was a teenager. I wasn't even able to comprehend that kind of loss occurring to me then. My Mother remembered them fondly as good, kind people who had been snuffed out in a horrible accident and consoled herself with the reality that, in another universe, they were still alive and happy. We kids all listened with a restrained impatience, since the presents were next. Each of our names was called and one by one we'd go down and open the one package with our name on it in front of my Father. I don't even remember what I got that year. I just remember sitting in front my Father and staring at him as I tore the wrapping paper off.

In the afternoon, we played games as the adults cooked three of the chickens that, a few hours before, had been casually pecking at grain in the cold garden. We all sat together in the largest barn, which had been temporarily converted into a dining hall. At its centre was a long wooden table lined with benches. The adults sat at one side and the children sat at the other. I was at the head of the table, my Father and Mother to my left and right.

A couple of my aunts and uncles entered the room and placed big plates along its length, filling the table with food. Piles of carrots and parsnips, steaming heaps of mash potato, the chickens carved up into a big pile of pale slices, and several jugs of thick, rich gravy.

I still remember that smell—musty air, old hay, and animal piss soaked deep into the wood and then the hearty fragrance of that food. My Father raised his glass of water and wished us all a happy day.

"Eli. My boy. The right hand of God," he said, and looked at me. There was pride there, grief still, and a hidden measure of envy. "You should say a prayer for us on this day. Your Grandpa did on occasions such as these, when he was well enough."

I was nervous. Obviously, I had only just turned seven. So I just riffed on the prayer that my Father had said for the previous night's dinner. Scanning the expectant faces of my family, I found little support. It felt like a test. The laughter had gone now and only the sound of the creaking barn remained. The weight of their listening weighing heavy on me.

"Thank you for the blessings you have bestowed upon us, God," I said and looked around. Some of the family were nodding, all looked deep in prayer. "For you have blessed us with these gifts, which we are about to receive, and again for our part in your divine purpose, without which we would be merely a part of the burdensome flock. The inheritance of your work, O Lord, is a perfect future for those who believe and act in your name. An unparalleled cataclysm, built brick by brick upon the foundation of inaction and disbelief, is recompense for those who ignore your word. Thank you, finally, O Lord, for granting us the responsibility of shepherding this world into the shape of your glorious kingdom. For permitting us to divine your ultimate purpose and knowing, without question, that what we do is for the good of all."

My Father looked up and fixed me with a rueful gaze. I looked into his watery blue eyes and nearly froze, but some wicked rebellion in me pressed me forward.

"And protect the souls of those we have delivered unto you, O Lord, for they know not their wicked trespasses against you."

The family repeated my final sentence and the room turned cheery again, the icy chill of their expectations melted away. They congratulated me, slapping me on the back, amazed at my speaking abilities. I told them that I had been practising with Daddy, and they turned their attention on him, and clapped again.

Gravy was spilt, the other children laughed and whooped, and the adults gesticulated at each other, threw their heads back, and laughed. Plates and bowls of food were passed around. I found myself smiling and joining in every now and then, but I'd catch my Father glowering at me, returning the icy feeling to my guts. The promise of future violence written in his look.

In one such stare down, my Mother broke the space between us, and I was surprised she didn't burst into flames.

She kissed me on a ruddy cheek. "Well done, Eli," she said. "That was lovely. Wasn't it, Abe?"

My Father's gaze melted from mine and met my Mother's. He smiled a predatory smile.

"Certainly was," he lied. I knew I would pay for that last line of my speech, but it was worth it.

My Mother was a quiet woman. Nice to a fault, and only saw the best in my Father and me—and the rest of the family, for that matter. She absolutely believed in our purpose and refused to accept the evidence of what my Father was doing to me, even when faced with it.

I remember the reedy winter light through the kitchen windows, dull rainbows of condensation running down the glass. I was washing my hands in the sink next to her as she peeled vegetables, pressing them down with a thin hand and chopping them up. My T-shirt must have ridden up, and she must have caught sight of the purple and blue bruises that clouded the pale skin on my back, because she pulled my top back down to cover them up. She didn't say a word, but I saw how the sight of my abuse translated into her twisting expression.

She still bathed me, which itself was a bizarre experience, being intellectually fully capable of taking care of my own cleanliness. But I still *looked* seven, and so she helped me. And when she did, she would take great care as she ran the bath sponge over my skin, apologising if she pressed too hard on a bruise. Delicately ran soapy hands over the constellation of welts left by the metal rivets of my dad's belt. I would gaze up at her, my expression piercing the facade that we had constructed around each other, and she would just look away, guilty.

"He doesn't mean to hurt you," she said once. "It's what's inside you that he hates."

"There's no one inside me, Mummy," I replied. She kissed me on the forehead and wiped away tears with the damp sleeve of her dress.

I fantasised about the both of us escaping under the cover of darkness and living a life together on the lamb, away from the clutches of the New Sunrise.

Back at the Christmas party, I quickly ate my food. I smiled, talked with the adults, and then, under the pretence of wanting to play with the other kids, I excused myself from the table and slipped out into the frigid night air.

Orange light spilled out in front of me from the wide, red door onto the icy ground. The dolmen stood there ominously, inert to everyone's eyes except mine. I heard the gentle static rolling from it like waves crashing on a beach, could feel a subtle compression in the air radiating from it.

My intention was to go straight to my room and try to go to sleep. Hopefully, I figured, given enough time, my Father might soften or forget about the night's proceedings. But I kept seeing the white flash of his teeth. The fixed anger in the greying curve of his chin. I wanted more than anything to leave the compound, but the gates were locked. As I approached it, the shimmer inside the Great Stone Door seemed to grow in step with my increasingly desperate impulse to escape.

I had never gone alone before, and I was worried that I might not even be able to, for some reason or another. So it was a bit of a shock as I fell through without resistance and was subsumed into the infinite. The experience of going through is traumatic, even now. I worried about radiation, the invisible killer. I had seen something on my aunt's

TV about radiation bombs. I had asked her about it, and she said it was a sign of the end times, and that if it did happen, it was because the God In-between had desired it to occur, so that our futures may be brighter.

It felt strange travelling alone, a single neuron firing in the dark. A lone spark in rippling space. I found that I could halt my progress along the connecting line to Purgatory, could stop and contemplate the scale and shape of what I was seeing—the membranous walls just beneath the surface of reality. I saw that the Coke bubbles, with their universes within, were swaying gently, like a field of grass moving gently back and forth in the wind.

$$\triangledown$$

The icy cold was a shock as I suddenly found myself standing in a thick layer of glittering new snow. From east to west, a sharp wind howled through the skeletal trees, gusting across the length of the field, whipping up flurries of snow that animated the moving air with angry ephemeral poltergeists.

The smashed moon lit the ground a ghastly shade of supernatural green. The glitter of dashed lunar debris obscured the stars even more than last time with its fractured web of ghostly light. In the near distance, I could make out the outline of the slate farmhouse. I slowly made my way there, my legs disappearing up to the knee in the snow with each laboured footstep.

I became worried that I would find Vladimir, or more so that he would find me and attack me, even though I hadn't got a sense of violence from him at all. But I couldn't be sure what this world might have done to him in the meantime, if he was alive at all. What type of madness might be hanging in the corrupt air of this place, I couldn't know. My Father had spoken of lunacy before, and my uncle Geoff always seemed to comment on full moons, joking that that the lunatics would be out. I didn't realise it was a joke, and that to the people who lived outside our compound, *we* were the lunatics.

The cottage creaked and moaned in the wind, the parts of the structure that still stood sounding as though they would stop doing so at any minute. Gleaming points of icicles jabbed down from windowsills and from the slanted edge of the sagging roof like a row of rotten teeth, the sick light shifting along their twisted shafts. Terrified as I was, I approached the building.

I went to the place where the knife had been—where I told Vladimir he would find it—and it was gone. I breathed a sigh of relief and wondered how he was. I had a fleeting thought that maybe I could rescue him, take back some of the harm I knew I had done. Find him, or maybe the woman I had brought through the week before.

Aside from her quick rasping breaths, she had been quiet as my Father led her out into the garden, the hessian bag tied loosely around her neck, hands bound behind her back.

Then, when we entered the place between all things, she thought only of hatred and violence, any gleam of hope fled by thoughts of revenge and injustice. She didn't even soften in the face of the infinite or at our intermingling. She wasn't chastened by the sheer scope of it, or what it meant. She simply existed.

*Chanthavy.* That was her name.

All at once, as our consciousnesses meshed, we felt the wet warmth of a jungle again. Dark fronds rubbing against our forearms and rustling like fabric moving against itself. Could smell freshly turned earth, cow shit, and gun smoke. Leaning against an abandoned car with burst wheels. The comforting weight of a machine gun gripped in our hands. Then moving slowly as the bright morning sun creeps over the rough horizon, blinding us. Watching with abject horror as our dead friends are rolled into a ditch dug by their own hands, their eyes rolled back and the backs of their skulls yawning white and grey and open liked cracked shells. Large, dark birds circling impatiently overhead, two screeching from a lilting pylon.

When we arrived, I was possessed of a blistering anger that I had yet to experience. It was all encompassing. Even the balled-fist rage I had felt after every beating paled in comparison to how I felt then—raw, red, and lethal.

On the other side, she said nothing.

She simply lay there in the snow, her almond-shaped eyes angled up to the dislocated moon. No awe or wonder or shock in them. Just impassive. Snow drifted down and settled on her eyelashes. They hung there, suspended, unfurling into droplets when she slowly blinked. Somehow, that made my anger worse, and so—dizzy with rage—I screamed at her to move, to stand up, to do something. But she just continued to lie there, staring up at the sky. I told her about the knife, about a man named Vladimir who might help her if only she'd move. A part of me hoped that what she had left permanently behind in me wasn't the anger—because I knew I wouldn't be able to exist with it, burning in me and making me sick with fury. But the smallest sliver of me hoped that it might be what stayed. That it might motivate me to escape. But it didn't. It lessened, leaving only scorch marks in its reckoning.

Back on my own in the cold of that broken building, I felt a sudden swell of fear bloom in me. A fear that Chanthavy rather than Vlad might be out there waiting for me, as she had been waiting the day her friends were massacred. I felt the electric thrill of the possibility of my being caught. My heart clapped in my chest, applauding my sudden fear. I wanted to have the courage to continue on and explore this ravaged version of the world. My head had also started to pulse with pain, and I could feel the blood worming along a vein in my temple. I was an interloper in this reality, in Purgatory, and the pain brought that fact into sharp relief. I turned and walked back through the doorway.

My uncle Tim stood at the door to the barn, looking out solemnly towards the place where I had returned from. He jumped in fright when I appeared.

"Eli!" he exclaimed. "What are you doing?"

"Uncle," I replied, my voice high from my own shock, my hands itching from the sudden temperature change. The pulsing behind my eyes had grown suddenly worse. I held my head for a few seconds, fighting the nausea. "I was just, well. The place in-between is very peaceful." I was struggling for a lie, grabbed one quickly and blurted, "The space in-between is close to God, for only he could have filled that space and used it to create all of life."

My uncle's eyes lit up. He closed the barn door behind him and waddled over. "I would very much like to see that place," he said. My uncle (well, I called him that—I called them *all* that—but he wasn't actually a real uncle) looked back to the barn. He was a simple man who loved his family. His wife had killed herself and left him with their only child, now a teenager named Steven. He said that he had felt utterly numb until he met my Father one day and found God, although he would always say that God found him. Both he and Steven were absolute devotees. They had seen the proof of my Grandfather's powers, and now mine. They, like the rest, were all in.

"I can't, uncle. I'm not allowed. Daddy told me not to."

"Oh," he said, dejected. "Never mind, then."

"Maybe one day, uncle," I said.

He stood there, his hands resting on the cold grey stone of the dolmen. The smell of the stove wafted out from the barn, and Steven soon joined us. Steven, with his blonde mullet, olive eyes, and good looks. He was allowed out of the compound on errands with my Father and some of the other adults. He went to a normal school along with Sally and Jenny, two of the other family members. The rest of the children were too young.

"Hey, Eli," Steven said. "Grace was really cool."

"Thanks," I said.

My uncle Tim huffed and rolled his eyes. A big puff of warm smoke drifted from his lips and floated away into the frigid air. "Speak properly for pity's sake, Steven. All this 'cool' and 'wicked' talk. It makes no sense. You sound like a moron."

"Whatever," Steven said with a sneer.

"Why can't you be more like Eli?" Tim said.

Despite my sneaking away, my Father remembered to come up to the tower room that Christmas night. It was just past midnight and I was woken up by the heavy thunk of his boots on the stairs. Panicking, I jumped out of bed, thinking maybe I could hide in the bathroom or the wardrobe. I was hoping he would think I was sleeping with the other children somewhere else. His shadow moved under the door and I could already imagine the sour stink of alcohol on his breath, feel the anger that had brewed in him as my words during grace stirred his temper. I turned, opened the bathroom door, and took a quick step back: before me was a doorway. This one was far more subtle, less affected than the door to Purgatory. Only gentle waves of static rolled out at me, and I found I had to really concentrate to make it more real. The bedroom doorknob squeaked as it turned, and, in panic, I squeezed my eyes together as hard as I could and stepped forward.

▽

On the other side was my room. Snow gently drifted past the darkness of the window. In the bed that had become mine lay my Grandfather. The first thing I thought was that I was once again looking at his corpse, and a sudden rush of fear coursed through me. It hadn't occurred to me that he would be alive in another version of reality—but of course he was. I let out a strangled yelp and his eyes snapped open and he sprang up like a mechanical toy. Of course this only made me scream again, except louder and higher pitched. He shrieked back this time and bicycled his feet up the bed.

A second later he squinted at me, snatched his glasses from the table, and flicked on the bedside lamp.

"Jesus fucking Christ, Eli. What the hell do you think you're playing at?" As annoyed as he was, it was still good to hear his voice. I thought about the mound of turned earth in the garden.

"I'm so sorry, Grandad," I stammered, hands raised, fingers spread. His angry stare turned my cheeks red.

"Eli? What are you doing in my bedroom? You scared the hell out of me."

I needed a good lie, but none was forthcoming.

"I'm from…" I struggled, pointing hopelessly towards the doorway linking the two worlds. His face immediately softened.

"Oh," he said, eyes downturned, fixed somewhere between my feet and the dresser. "You've taken my place."

He sighed, swung his legs over the side of the bed, and sat up.

"Let's get a look at you then, lad," he said, some of the old friendliness returning. I was afraid to look at him. Seeing him sprawled out on his bed had left an afterimage like a swollen sky after a flash of lightning, and when I looked at him, I saw him naked, dead again, laid out for all to see. I felt a fresh spasm of loss and a pang of inarticulate grief. He was there in front of me right then, and yet I missed him so much. I also missed my life from before he died—before I had become what he was.

He pressed a knotted finger into my cheek and pushed me this way and that. "You look like you've been to Purgatory a time or two," he said.

I nodded.

"I take it that means I'm dead where you're from?" he asked, matter-of-factly.

I nodded again.

"And your Father, is he okay?"

I paused for what felt like far too long, but the lie passed. "He's fine. Grandad, where's Nan?"

"Oh, Matilda. Sorry, Eli, she's not around anymore. Not for a while, lad."

"Oh."

"Is she…" He paused. "Okay with you?"

I shook my head.

"I miss you. Daddy does too."

"I'm know he does. Maybe one day I could visit. I'd like that." He shifted uncomfortably. Under the sickly orange glow of the lamp, he didn't look well. "Listen, Eli," he continued. "You need to know something, about our—" He searched for a word.

I automatically went to say "gift."

"—curse." He looked over his glasses at me. "You need to understand that when you take someone through to the place within places…"

"A piece of them gets stuck inside you?"

My Grandfather's face drooped a little. "That's right," he said. "That's exactly right."

"I know. I met a scientist called Vladimir. He was so sad."

"Was he? I expect you were told that he was bad?"

I nodded. "But he didn't *seem* bad."

"I know, Eli. I know. When we say 'bad,' it doesn't necessarily mean that the person is a bad person—just that his ideas or something that he will do might upset the balance of the world. That's what we do, you and I. We keep the balance"—he raised his upturned hands, mimicking a perfectly balanced scale—"just so."

"Daddy says that the devil is in me when I talk about those things," I said. It felt like the most beautiful betrayal of my Father. The secret of my abuse was told and he would never find out.

"Well, the thing about your Daddy is: he will never understand. No one does, nor will they ever."

I looked into those eyes, the ones I had seen rolled up and glassy not so long ago. "Daddy was supposed to be a Seer. But he isn't, is he," I said.

My Grandfather look shocked, then nodded.

"That's right. Our family lost that gift after your uncle Henry died. I'm surprised your dad told you." He stopped cold. "Did he... did you take him to Purgatory?"

"He made me," I said, looking at the floor.

"You are *not* supposed to excise family, Eli! It could have caused a catastrophic divergence," he exclaimed. "You must never take family members through a doorway, not ever. Have you learned nothing from my diary?"

"What diary?" I asked.

His eyes went wide and he pointed at the floor.

"That rug there—lift it up. Under the loose floorboard."

I slid my fingers down into the gaps and lifted the pale wood. In the revealed space was a thick, battered leather journal. My Grandfather told me to take it back to my reality and to read it, but to keep it hidden from my Father. I told him that, inside me, I shared the mind of a scientist. While I couldn't comprehend *how* I knew or understood certain things, I could. So, when I returned home and found my Father gone, only the ghost of his whisky stink remaining, I hid the diary in the same place my Grandfather had kept it. When I pulled the board up, I was half expecting to find my own Grandfather's diary in that space, but there was nothing. He must have moved it when he switched to his room on the ground floor

The next day, I started to read it.

Of All Possibilities | 69

▽

In the new year of 1986, we ended up getting one offering a week for the first six months. On the nights we made the offerings, I would wait in my room to be called. Someone would paint my face with blue lines above and below my eyes, a large circle in the centre of my forehead. I would sit on my bed and watch the cold white of headlights cutting through the dark as the van that brought the offerings to our door navigated the bumpy and twisting road to the compound.

After each one, my Father came and visited me in my room. He would help get the devil out of me by beating me with his belt while whispering prayers from between his gritted teeth. There was a Haitian woman named Rosalie who believed in God and the devil, and when she saw the shattered moon, she howled that she was in Hell. She was so loud that I got scared and left her tied up. I ran back through without telling her about the knife. My Father asked me what she said to me, what I had learned about her. When I told him, he said that she was right: she *was* in Hell—exactly where she belonged.

When he left, I would retrieve my Grandfather's journal from under the floorboards. Sometimes I just held on to the cool leather for comfort and cried. Other times I would lay in bed, skin stinging with pain, and pore over the old man's intricate cursive. There were dates, names, events. The details of offerings stretching back forty-five years.

I dismantled each page, each paragraph, each sentence, each word, and tried to make sense of them. I knew the individual meanings of the words but could not discern the context. I lacked so much history. Things I hadn't learned yet, things that had no longer occurred because of my Grandfather's work. Things about my Grandfather's and great-grandfather's work that I didn't understand. There were references to the Atropos Project and to the House of August, but no further explanations given. I would read until my head began to grow so heavy it would loll, and I would feel myself drifting into sleep. Then I'd carefully hide the book back under the floorboards, crawl back into bed, and dream.

The first night after I take someone through, I dream of them, of their lives. All the things both remembered and forgotten. Their childhood memories, embarrassments, regrets, first loves, and heartbreaks. An entire life lived in a single night. When I wake up, the ghosts of those lives have fled with the dark, and only the feeling remains.

▽

*Miller, let me tell you about Hans Gourig. Born in Frankfurt in 1888 to a middle-class family. He fought at the Battle of the Somme, where he was wounded but still held a position for three days by propping up his dead comrades along the front wall of his trench. Then, when his position was overrun, he lay among the rotting dead until nightfall. He slaughtered a dozen men as he fell back to friendly lines.*

*He watched the injustice that was wrought upon his homeland in the wake of the war and quickly rose to prominence as an outspoken nationalist, blaming the Jews and the rest of Europe for the depression in Germany. In 1920, Gourig's mother and father died of exposure, homeless and destitute, their business seized by the banks, who cast them out into the streets. Gourig then followed a similar trajectory that Hitler eventually would, rising to power and enacting his own version of the Night of the Long Knives, but much, much more brutal and a lot earlier in his career. Where Hitler played games, vacillating and appeasing his way to power, Gourig tore through his enemies, invading Europe and annexing Czechoslovakia early on. He was popular because he lifted Germany from the depths of despair and made it a powerful and united country again. He refused to pay reparations for the previous war, instead funnelling money into his own war machine. The Maginot Line was still a half-formed idea when Gourig's army stomped out of the Black Forest and spread like a deadly virus. By 1939, Germany had almost won the war on all fronts. The US entered the fray when they saw what was happening and how it was likely to spread to American shores, but were beaten back in most engagements. The Japanese saw to it that the Americans could not further engage the Germans, and not long after that, the US supplicated on the condition that it would not be invaded.*

*In the spring of 1940, Gourig and his advisers visited England to arrange for the formal surrender of the United Kingdom. It was pointless showboating and arrogance on his part, but Gourig respected the country's former glory and decided to attend the meeting personally. Churchill, seeing the bloody writing on the wall, had decided to concede to the Germans. Gourig was met by an entourage, including Churchill himself, and me. As he was being given the grand tour of Buckingham Palace, I took the man by the elbow and gently pulled him into another reality. And, just like that, Gourig's influence was instantly excised from our timeline, replaced instead by the similarly horrendous Hitler.*

*The war was changed. Hitler instead rose to power, extolling the same rotten agenda as Gourig. But he wasn't the same man, and, by 1941, was on the back foot with half of the casualties Gourig had killed. It wasn't the best of all possible results, but the world was changed for the better all the same.*

*By the time we had our chance at him, Hitler was already dead and his body had been burnt by the Thule Society. It is presumed he was taken out by Himmler to ensure that the timeline couldn't be changed and that Hitler's influence into the future could not be excised.*

*January 9, 1947*

*William Clarke*

# Three

So, the thing about cults is, they love rituals—and we were no different. In fact, in order for the family to be able to witness the miracle of the offerings, we had a regular uninterrupted schedule of rituals at the same time every week, no exceptions. If we only did them when actually needed, when there was an offering all ready to go, it would be impossible for them to occur—because after the sacrifice's removal from the timeline, the members of the New Sunrise would have no reason to attend any ritual, as the offering had now never existed to them. And so they'd have no reason to be standing there to see me miraculously pop back into reality via the Great Stone Door. Cool so far? Days when I was failed to pop back through the door meant that no offering had been made. Of course, they wouldn't remember the offering when there was one—but that's what the Book of Names was for.

I, as the Key, retain all memories of the actions I have taken. They are unchanged when I remove someone from the timeline. This effect is not limited to me, although back then I was unaware of that fact. Some places, like the House of August, exist in spaces that are immune to the effect. Some people are, too. Individuals with strange powers exist all over the world, and a good few of them remain unaltered when the timeline changes. Seers, for example, have the ability to view and unpick meshed realities.

We're about twenty miles out from the compound. It's not there anymore. Well, it is, but it's been fenced off and the ruins boarded up. Thick brambles have grown up around the base of the fence and neat rows of bristling razor wire like steel shark's teeth are pinned to the top. It looks worse than it is—you can get past all those jagged bits of metal with a long bit of carpet and a ladder. At various points along the length of the fence, plastic signs read: *No Entry. This site is under constant surveillance by Panther Security. Violators will be prosecuted.* In case you didn't already guess it, Panther Security is a government shell company. No one is watching the compound, or the hole in the western end of the fence.

Have I been back since I fled? Yes. I've spent time there. I went back for the Book of Names and my Grandad's diary as soon as I could, but both were gone. So was his body. I stood at the rectangle-shaped hole, the air spiced with night-scented stock, and examined the machine-made excavation into the cold earth, the one that had allowed them to pull a man's body from the ground.

The car I'm tailing drops into the left lane and indicates to come off at the next set of services. It's a manoeuvre used to try to shake a tail or, at the very least, to expose one. I've employed it myself a couple of times. The turnoff comes up, but the car stays in the lane until the exit passes. Then the indicator goes off and the car slips back into the middle lane. I stay exactly where I am, and my target slides back into position just ahead. My training tells me that if he is still paranoid about being followed—you know, the old limbic system flaring up, telling him something dangerous is stalking him—then he will most likely actually pull off at the next services.

I breathe a sigh of self-satisfied relief. I can't lose this fucker.

The radio fuzzes out and I switch to a different station. It's another '80s-only station, and they are halfway through the Cure's "Close to Me." Man, I love this song. I remember the first time I heard it. I was at school, obviously. My parents would never let me listen to good stuff at home. I didn't even know electric guitar existed until I was finally let out into the world.

All the music of that period brings me back to Jess. I didn't really want to get into that quite yet, but, you know what—if I'm going to do this, I'll need to get to her at some point.

She had this bright-red Walkman. Long, liquorice-black cable to a big set of over-ear headphones. A thin slice of orange foam over the speakers. I can still see it as if the thing is sat right in front of me. Can still hear the first words she ever said to me.

On the steering wheel, I tap out the claps on the song: boom, clap-clap-clap.

"Hey. You're that kid from the creepy cult, right?"

I say it aloud. Emulate her voice. Her relaxed cadence. There's no malice there, just curiosity and not giving a fuck. I can see the young version of her. That dark-skinned girl with her long, black hair scraped back into a tight ponytail. Hot day, long after school has closed. She's sat on the scratched-up aluminium bike racks by the side entrance of the school. Seagulls scream and fight over thrown-out lunches, chips, crisps, crusts from half-eaten cheese sandwiches.

She pulls her headphones off and I hear a tinny version of the Clash leaking out. Joe Strummer singing, *Should I stay or should I go?* I remember nodding to her, rolling my eyes, and preparing for yet another round of taunting.

"Cool," she said.

And that was it.

Five miles farther and my target indicates to come off again. We both slip off the motorway towards the neon lights of the services. The rain distorts the bright colours and the wipers smear the image across the curved glass.

# My Troubled History, Part Three

**1991**

I was, of course, home-schooled until secondary school age, and then a council person came round and told my Dad that I had to go to a normal school. My parents were furious about it and complained repeatedly, but to no avail. I, however, was secretly very excited about leaving the compound and meeting other kids.

Scratch Hill is an old rural town surrounded by farmers' fields and wild countryside. The town's secondary school, Old Hill Secondary, is just on the outskirts of town and sat a good three-mile walk from the compound. It managed that magical feat of feeling like it was uphill going in both directions. Back then, ancient woods lined the long stretches of narrow, single-lane roads, which eventually got wider the closer they got to the town proper. Until I was old enough to walk to and from school myself, my Father drove me in the truck. It was an old beat-up transit van, with the back part of the roof cut off and a trailer attached.

I'd sit in the passenger seat, my head against the window, and watch the fins of daylight falling in through the interlocked copse of oak and beech trees like bright predators scouring the dark ground.

Countryside slowly blurred, dreamlike, into suburbs with good roads, streetlights, and wide pavements. Thick clots of people were everywhere: parents dragging their protesting kids in tow, a red-faced man dressed in a rumpled suit with toast jammed into his mouth hurrying to work, builders and labourers leaning against the wall of a building site, smoking cigarettes, and laughing among themselves, stopping only occasionally to leer at women walking past.

At the end of a long road canopied by cherry trees was the school, an imposing three-storey, red-brick building crowded on one side by a small cluster of newer buildings: a sports hall, a brand new steel-and-glass science block, and some ancillary huts used for form rooms.

Every morning as my Father and I arrived at the gates, often just as the bell was ringing and the other children were running in, he would turn to me and say, "You must never tell these people what you are. Remember that."

He would make me repeat it every day. No "I love you." No kiss on the forehead or whatever. Just the cold mantra of: We must operate under the radar, or our existence as we know it will end. You are a liability to the mission.

The other kids treated me well enough until about six weeks into my first term, when word got around that I was one of those cult members. My initial enthusiasm for school suddenly dried up. At first, they were intrigued—they wanted to know what it was like to live at the compound, what my parents were like, what we believed. But that intrigue soon melted into suspicion, fear, and hatred. I was the creepy kid with the weird clothes who did secret magic on people. According to the fairy tales told by other adults and then recounted by my multitude of tormentors, I could talk to ghosts, kill people if I looked at them hard enough, and curse a person's entire family. One kid said he had seen me walk through a locked door, and it started a minor frenzy among the other kids.

Eventually a few teachers got the class to wave it all off as nonsense, but even they still wouldn't look me in the eye when talking to me. I got worried that that particular rumour would get back to my Dad, and he'd think I'd been walking between worlds on school grounds and then he'd go ahead and kick the shit out of me.

It all quickly turned into me getting beaten up by a few of the bullies as a fairly regular event. I had no friends. Who would want to associate with a pariah of the lowest kind? So that made me easy enough prey for the assholes of all castes. The big names didn't really bother me that often, unless they were having a particularly dry day. Despite my celebrity status, I was still too low on the food chain to bother with, because of the lack of challenge. In some ways, the mid-level bullies were *much* worse. They had to be crueller and more cunning than the higher-tier kids if they were going to move up. Aside from the beatings, I would often have my pencil case emptied out into the toilets, my clothes hosed down with piss, wet tissues thrown at me, food trays emptied into my bag—you know, the usual. One time someone threw an actual piece of shit at me from the second-floor window of the science block. It missed, but the point had been made. I was regularly turned upside down for money, even though I had none, a fact met with disappointment and violent rebuke. The bruises they gave me intermingled with the ones gifted to me by my Father. I tried to fight back once—managed to bite one of my attackers on the arm and then get him into a kind of headlock—but that only ended with his friends falling in on me and loosening one of my teeth. Of course, my Mother just waved it off as kids being kids, and I settled into a rhythm of near constant abuse as I hatched endless escape plans.

▽

## July 29, 1993

The end of the last day of school before summer holiday. I remember it was sunny and the air smelt like sumac, dandelions, and melting macadam. A few days later, the surface of the playground would sag and collapse, creating a deep bowl in the centre of it, and they had to get the whole thing resurfaced.

In the empty corridors, the phantom odour of hundreds of sweaty, unwashed teenagers seemed to leak from every wall and scuffed wooden floor. The place felt abandoned suddenly—all the kids had run screaming straight into the arms of summer. Six weeks of carefree running around, forgetting the trauma of funky-smelling classrooms and weirdo teachers like Mr Bryant, who, rumour had it, liked to shine his shoes so he could see up the young girls' skirts. I had hidden in the third-floor staff bathrooms as soon as the bell rang. The bullies would be stalking the playground and car park looking for their prey. The last day of term was almost entirely free of any kind of consequence for beating up other kids.

The year before, I had been caught by Ronnie Green as I was leaving. I remember how happy I had been in that moment—temporarily escaping from at least one of the shitty environments I was forced to endure. I was actually even looking forward to spending some time with my family.

He caught me by my rucksack and pulled me into the toilets, where his little gang was waiting. They all took turns beating me up, laughing as they did it. Accusing me of cursing their families, killing their pets, being the reason one of their parents was out of work. When they had finished, my eye was puffed shut and my little finger broken where Ronnie had stamped on it. My screams had shocked them, and they ran laughing from the bathroom. They had thrown my backpack and shoes in the urinal. After they were done, my Mum thought I'd been hit by a car. My Dad, who had been waiting for me in the van outside the gates, told me I needed to pray for the boys. He instructed me that I must not, under any circumstances, attempt to fight back and advised that the Lord's judgement would be rendered unto them in the fullness of time.

Ronnie would eventually go missing one autumn day. Somewhere, in another version of reality, another happy little Ronnie Green suddenly found himself with a doppelgänger.

Back to me hiding in the staff bathroom, with its large toilet bowls and quality toilet paper. When I thought it was safe, I slid out of the strange, weird-smelling toilets and into the empty corridor. It was spooky hearing just the squeak of my shoes and the echo of my footfalls on the varnished wooden floor.

I pushed open the door and headed down the stairway, flashes of afternoon light cutting bright squares onto the cold stone stairs. I heard a door open and then close somewhere on the floor, so I quickened my pace, my heart beating hard in my chest and the illicit thrill of adrenaline suddenly dumped into my body. The stairway smelt vaguely of school dinners mixed with the antiseptic fluid they kept in big blue drums locked up in the cleaner's closet.

I shouldered the door open and lurched out into the blinding day. There was no one around. Gulls picked at discarded chips, hawing and crying at each other. I smiled smugly to myself at my successful escape—just a short sprint to my Father's van and I was away, unharmed. The air was fresh and I caught the faint aroma of a barbecue drifting over the back fences of nearby houses. To my right, someone coughed and I screamed a little, almost wet myself. She was perched on one of the stainless-steel bike racks bent into an N-shape. The untied laces of a pair of black Converse dangling in the empty space where a bike should be.

"Hey. You're that kid from the creepy cult, right?" she said, taking off her headphones. The Clash tried to fill the air between us. A bee buzzed against the wire mesh covering a window.

I nodded, wide-eyed.

"Cool," she said.

It seemed she had waited back, too, maybe hidden in some other place in the school. I wondered if it was her I'd heard on the stairway, and if there were others like me, waiting in the building for their shot at a pain-free introduction to the summer holidays.

Jessica was one of only two black kids at my school and, as such, also endured an onslaught of near constant bullying.

"What's it like?" she asked.

"Umm, okay, I guess," I said. Through the gaps in the metal fence, I caught the shape of my Dad's van, could see the grey-black smoke curling up from the exhaust.

"Is it?"

"Is it what?" I asked.

"A cult, genius. Is it really a cult?"

"I don't even know what that means."

"It's like a bunch of people who do crazy chanting and shit? Think the end of the world is going to happen?"

My eyes grew suddenly wider, my brain moving through the catalogue of things that we did. I considered an answer, but it was too late.

"No fucking way. Do you do, like, rituals on people and stuff?"

I was half-tempted just to tell her everything, but there was no way I could trust her then. I also felt like I was squandering my chance at a clean getaway. At any second, all of the worst bullies might suddenly explode from the exits like vicious poltergeists and drag me back in, back to the toilets where they could beat me all summer long.

"I don't really want to talk about it," I said, but that only spurred her on.

"Is it like devil worship?" She hopped off the bike rack and closed the distance. I felt a rush of heat on my neck and cheeks. "My dad was watching this thing about Satan and stuff, and this cult in America was, like, killing kids and animals."

"We don't do that," I said. I thought about the dozens of people who had been left in a dead world with no civilisation that I was slowly repopulating. "We just sing and pray and stuff."

She looked mildly deflated.

"That... actually pretty dull." She pointed a finger at me, closed one eye as if trying to visualise something in the far distance. "Eli, right?"

"Eli." I said. I was switching between looking at her and at the truck. I wanted to escape, but she was the first person in school who hadn't acted like a complete dick to me.

"I'm kinda disappointed, Eli. Still pretty cool you're in a cult though, I guess," she said. "I'm Jess."

"I know, and I'm sorry," I said. "I'll ask my Dad if we can kill a chicken or something next time."

She laughed, then spotted my Dad's van. "That ride for you?"

"Yup. Going to take me back home just in time to—" I drew a line across my throat with my thumb, then did a stabbing motion in the air.

She laughed again, then shooed me away with a hand gesture. "Go. Be free, Eli. Go kill a goat in the name of our Dark Lord."

I looked back just in time to see her retake her seat on the bike rack and slip the headphones over her ears.

"Have a good summer," I stammered, but she didn't hear.

▽

The start of the summer holiday was good. We had one offering in the first week (a Polish business analyst who had a minor cocaine addiction and lots of salacious information on his former employers, a huge banking firm). Then I was clear for the next three, baking-hot weeks.

I spent an inordinate amount of time thinking about my meeting with Jess. I had extended our little meeting in the playground into some fantasy where she invited me to get together with her and we spent the holidays hanging out. In the evenings, I would sit in my tower room and stare out the window, hoping I would catch a glimpse of her riding down the hill on a bike. The rest of my time was taken up with attending family prayer sessions, playing with the other kids, and reading my Grandfather's journal.

I had put it aside after reading it through twice shortly after I'd received it, understanding next to nothing. He talked about government operations, missions, and kidnappings. All way over my six-year-old's head. So, I had hidden it again until I felt I had a decent understanding of things—you know, as a totally mature fourteen-year-old.

When I came to it for the third time that summer, I found that I was finally ready.

The diary started out hopeful. In 1932, my Grandfather was doing his part for the war. An accord had been struck between our family and a government agency called the House of August just before the start of the First World War, leading to the founding of the Atropos Project under my great-grandfather, and that my Grandfather later became one of their most powerful assets. I didn't know what the project was exactly, but I'd worked out that our family worked closely with the British government. Frankly, I was astonished our family secret had been kept from the public, and even some members of our own family, as long as it had.

I read about Nazis who had dabbled in the occult. Walter Neuhaus, a German veteran of World War I, who started an organisation called the Thule Society referencing something called the House of Night. While the organisation was primarily concerned with the occult, it incorporated a great deal of Nazi doctrine alongside its various mystical elements. It attracted a large following of obsessives—but this was not Neuhaus's primary goal. His only desire was to assemble a group of individuals with certain unique abilities, and to use these individuals to bring about total domination. Neuhaus was an art student with the unusual ability to see "short stretches of possibility," as he called it. He found the ability both confusing and inspiring. He also had a second gift—for location. He could find anything that he set his mind to. He didn't know the words for people like him back then, but he was both a Seer and a Seeker.

Along with dozens of useless hangers-on, Neuhaus eventually recruited ten people with the abilities he sought: Dietrich Eckart, Erik Jan Hanussen, and Heinrich Himmler, all Psychics—with the ability to filter and identify an individual's thoughts from the vast network of thoughts in the universal unconscious. Ludwig Straniak, a Seeker, an individual capable of identifying objects of power. They were joined by Wilhelm Wulff, a Seer, able to parse future timelines. Karl Krafft was a Speaker, someone who can commune with individuals across realities. Finally, Rudolf Hess, a dual ability holder like Neuhaus himself: a Psychic and an Influencer—someone who can push another's behaviour to the limits of their own moral extremes.

When Neuhaus had finally gathered together his choicest cronies, the rest of the followers of the Thule Society were almost immediately thrown out of the gang. Under Neuhaus's instruction, this core group went to work tracking down others like them and, in classic Nazi style, experimenting on them. Hess came into contact with a nervous kid named Adolf Hitler and tutored him in public speaking while pushing various aspects of his personality into a shape that had been designed by Wulff, the Seer. In a turn of events you might be familiar with, Hitler's rise to power after their meeting was dramatic. He kept Hess in his council until the late 1930s, when—according to the information my Grandfather, with the help of the rest of the House of August ,was able to get out of Hess—Hitler got too big for his boots. Hitler started to divest himself of the cult, despite some of its members' predictions coming true. He foresaw a power struggle and, drunk with his own ego, sought to take out Hess and the other Thule members behind the scenes. In actuality, the Thule Society was letting it all play out, so they could manoeuvre in the large shadow Hitler cast, without too much trouble or attention being brought on themselves.

The Seeker Straniak spent his days searching for objects of supernatural power under the intensely watchful eye of Neuhaus (a feeling I found myself sympathizing with). Neuhaus, you see, was obsessed with finding the location of Hyperborea, a mythical "perfect" land originally described by some ancient Greek guy called Herodotus. After reading Herodotus's writings, Neuhaus had come to believe that another ancient Greek guy, the poet Pindar, was a person with the ability to traverse the multiverse—a Key, like me—and that his poetry was meant as a guide for other gifted people to locate Hyperborea.

My Grandfather discovered that years before starting the Thule Society, while on a trip to Greece in 1905, Neuhaus had come into possession of a book of predictions recovered from a hidden chamber in the tomb of Šuppiluliuma II. Nearly three decades later, he entrusted the inner circle of his Thule Society to finally read it. Hanussen was the only person in the group able to decipher the Greek. In ritual ceremonies, he would translate the prophecies from the book for the others.

It took ten more years before Straniak was able to locate the Spear of Longinus, an object that Neuhaus believed would allow him to access Hyperborea. The spear is believed to be the same one that pierced Christ's side—more often referred to as the Spear of Destiny. It's also discussed in the Book of Yon. My Grandfather's last diary entry on the Thule Society ended:

As we know, thanks to Wulff's diary (which was found near his burnt corpse back in 1943); Straniak eventually found Neuhaus his coveted spear in Constantinople. Neuhaus immediately set off to finally use the Spear of Longinus to gain access to Hyperborea, which he had interpreted, via Herodotus, to be located within the Arctic Circle.

But Neuhaus did not need to go that far (or perhaps, more correctly, that close). Because what he really needed was a Key—he just couldn't find me.

I also read about how my great-grandfather had started the Atropos Project as a way of influencing the outcome of the Great War, the same way my Grandfather would go on to influence the outcome of the even greater war that followed: using supernatural means to ensure that the good guys won. Under the command of the House of August, their official responsibility was extracting designated individuals to remove their influence from the timeline. Nowadays we call it supernatural rendition, but back then it was just called extraction. Like what a dentist does with rotten teeth.

But the most mind-blowing things I came to realise thanks to the diary had nothing to do with war. What can I say, when you're a kid, the personal is a lot more important than the political, no matter what way you slice it. Children are selfish.

One, my extended family of aunts and uncles were not, in fact, related, but were initially part of the government agency that my Grandfather co-founded and had been tasked with protecting us. They eventually left the government and joined us permanently after witnessing my Grandfather's abilities first-hand.

Two, I learned that there were other people in the world with powers comparable to mine.

Throughout the journal, my Grandfather recorded the names and accounts of people he had removed from this universe. One hundred and twenty people in total. Most of them were German, Italian, Russian, Japanese, but some were English, American, Swiss, and French. I carefully transcribed the list into my history exercise book and snuck downstairs in the middle of the night to look for them in the Book of Names. I couldn't find them anywhere.

The entries in my Grandfather's journal about these people were disturbing, depressing, and sad, and as the journal continued, I saw that his world had become coloured by the people he had extracted throughout the war. He grew less optimistic and more cold, calculating, and brutal. He detailed one encounter with a British intelligence officer who was secretly spying for the Nazis. He had been forced to shoot the man as he tried to escape through a graveyard, and he recalled the feeling of pulling the trigger with a subtle excitement. Watching the plume of blood spill from him as he tumbled forward and lay among the rows of the dead. Then, the thrill as he pulled him into another version of our world that was nothing much but smouldering ruins, the sky poisoned and dark with bomb smoke. *Look around, this is what you would have wrought upon your own people*, he had told the dying man. Then he recounted how, before the man could answer, he shot him again and again until his revolver ran dry.

It was difficult for me to reconcile the two versions of my Grandfather: this man who found joy in brutality, and the one who would smile easily and gently hold his wife's waist and dance with her to old songs on the radio. I understand it now, of course. But, at the time, I could only wonder which version of him was the real one.

▽

A couple of claustrophobic weeks into the summer holiday, I begged my Father to ride with him and Steven into town when they went on their supply runs. Steven, who I had just discovered was not even related to me, was the eldest of the children in the group. He had blue eyes and dark hair pushed into spikes. It now seemed so obvious to me that all those people were just government imposters installed to make sure my real family did our job properly. They were not my blood, even if they had taken the family name. I liked Steven, looked up to him in some ways, but at the same time, I now loathed him.

It felt good to get out, even if it was with my Dad. He had softened a little, too, as summer wound on. The gap between offerings seemed to have made him a bit more relaxed, and our private exorcisms, as he had taken to referring to them, hadn't occurred since the night of the Polish analyst. Steven played with the radio and, despite my Dad's initial protests, was allowed to listen to some of the pop songs that came on. There was no chance he would've let us to listen to anything like Iron Maiden or Alice in Chains, but cheesy pop was grudgingly permitted. Kate Bush came on and my dad tutted and turned the radio off.

Scratch Hill town centre in the early '90s consisted of a Woolworths, a Blockbuster Video, two butchers (one at either end of the main street), a cinema, a Chinese takeaway, and an Italian restaurant run by a man called James, who was originally from Cricklewood. There was also a supermarket and a collection of ever-changing random shops. They would pop up—a sweet shop, a curiosities shop, an antique shop—and then, one by one, close six months later. In 1993, two of these little shops were derelict. Dead insects lined the sills of the papered-over windows, unopened letters piled up against their front doors, and half-ripped posters covered their walls.

Off to the east was the rough part of town, with its council estates, numerous Irish pubs (each one taking turns to have boarded-up windows after football matches), a snooker hall, and an arcade. South of the arcade was the rubbish dump, at the centre of a tract of scrubby hinterland surrounded by a strip of untamed woods filled with brambles, stinging nettles, and old fridges—the sort the government was terrified children were going to hide inside of, get stuck in, and die. There were a couple of dumped cars reduced to burnt shells, stacks of tyres, and debris pretty much everywhere. I'm sure from the air it look as though a rubbish bomb had gone off, with the dump being ground zero and the surrounding miles of forest a zone of shitty shrapnel.

The old milk-line train used to run through there, but after the war, the rails were pulled up and the second station on the line became the first. Kids used to play down in the streams and on rope swings that had been there seemingly forever. After a few kids went missing in the late '90s, the council put up a metal perimeter fence. It didn't stop all the kids, but for the most part, it worked. The rubbish dump is gone now, replaced by a retail park—all those tyres, fridges, and other unwanted crap covered with a layer of tarmac.

On the other side of town, the good side, my Dad pulled into the supermarket car park and chose a spot at the far end where only a few other vehicles were. Steven got out and walked around the back of the truck. I went to follow, but my Dad pressed a hand to my chest and pushed me back into my seat.

"Stay here," he said.

"But why?" I asked.

He didn't answer, just shot me a look, then climbed out.

I watched them both walk across the car park and disappear inside the supermarket. It felt like they were gone for ages. I watched as the shadows of the branches overhanging the car crept slowly across the peeling paint on the bonnet like gnarled fingers. My Dad had left the keys in the ignition and the radio on, so I spun the knob until I found something that sounded vaguely pleasing to my ear. I think it was the Kinks or something, and just as I'd started to get into the song, bopping my head and air drumming, I saw Jess being chased by two boys along the alleyway that ran the length of the car park. She was on her bike, riding as hard as she could, but the boys were catching up. I recognised one of them: Ronnie Green.

I grabbed the ignition key and jumped out of the van. By the time I had covered half the distance between us, Ronnie's sidekick had gotten close enough to Jess to unseat her with a hard kick to her back wheel. She wobbled and then collided with a wooden fence post. She came off the bike with a yelp, then hit the ground and rolled to a stop. Ronnie and his pug-nosed friend jumped off their bikes and stood over her as she tried to get up.

"Why don't you fuck off back to your own country, eh?" Ronnie shouted at her.

"Yeah, you monkey," his obnoxious little compatriot added. "My dad said you lot come over 'ere and gave everyone AIDs."

Ronnie kicked her, not hard, but hard enough to make her jerk away. I could see she had skinned her palms, and blood was already bubbling on her grazed chin.

She seemed more angry than scared.

The two boys were so absorbed that they didn't hear me coming until I was on top of them. I barged Ronnie's friend's elbow first from behind. He let out a high-pitched whine as he tipped sideways and cartwheeled over the low fence into the carpark.

"You!" Ronnie exclaimed.

He drew back a fist and punched me just above my eye. It remains one of the top five of all the many times I've been punched in the face. I wasn't ready for it at all. A flash of white light and explosive pain took my breath away, made me close my eyes and stagger backwards until the back of my legs hit the fence and I sat down on it, awkwardly perching on a post. He followed up with a kick that sent me tumbling backwards towards the hard tarmac. I heard a crack as my head hit the pavement and another flash of pain lit the blue sky above me. Ronnie's friend was on his feet again and he stood over me, a rotten sneer flowering on his face.

I heard Ronnie say, "Fuck him up, Jon."

And then some distant part of me exploded in pain as he stamped on my hand and began kicking me in the stomach.

I can't tell you how long it went on for, but it felt like years until the pain finally stopped. I saw from below a vision of Jess swinging her bike from right to left in a wide arc, hitting Jon across the face with it. He let out a cry and lay on the ground tangled up with it. I rolled over just in time to see her punch Ronnie directly on the nose, snapping his head back and sending him reeling. She stalked forward and kicked him full in the balls—wound her leg right back to do it, too. Like a footballer taking a corner kick. The noise that came out of the little "O" of his mouth was heard only by dogs. Ronnie dropped onto his arse and started to cry.

Jess stood over me and offered her hand.

"Nice try, hero," she said. Blood from the cut on her chin had started to soak into the neck of her white T-shirt.

I groaned and we both walked over to my Dad's truck and sat down in the flatbed.

"You okay?" I mumbled.

She nodded. Her lip had begun to swell.

"You?" she asked.

"It hurts, um, everywhere."

"Yeah, they beat the shit out of you pretty good. Why'd you do that?"

"I wanted to help." I gingerly ran a finger over the indent Ronnie's sovereign ring had left in my forehead. It was quickly rising into painful lump.

"By using your face as my shield?" she said, and we both laughed a little.

"I just don't like to see people getting bullied," I said.

"Yeah? Well, wanna come and deal with my dad, too?" she said. "That asshole hits much harder than these fucking idiots."

I saw the instant regret in her eyes at telling me that. She grimaced, sniffed, looked out towards the place where Ronnie had been sat. He was gone now. A car alarm went off and an old man fiddled with his keys to get his car door open.

I wanted to tell her the truth of it then. I knew exactly what was happening at home, because it was happening to me too.

"Hey!" I heard my Father shout. "You—get away from my son."

"That's my Dad," I said. "You should probably go."

She nodded and jumped down from the flatbed. "Thank you," she said, and kissed me on the cheek. "Even though you did literally nothing." She turned on her heels and walked over to her bike. Jon made a half-hearted effort to hold on to it, but that fight was over and she yanked it out of his hands and started riding away.

"You're welcome?" I said, mostly to myself. My lips were tingling as they swelled. I could taste blood.

"What the… what is all this?" my Father said when he reached me, gesturing to the boy lying prostrate on the ground nearby.

He held out his hand, and I reached into my pocket to get the van key, but it wasn't there. It had clearly fallen out during the fight. That was the last time I went with them on shopping trips.

▽

Jess's mother died shortly after giving birth to her and her dad had never remarried. Sometimes he'd tell Jess that her mother was a horrid bitch and he was glad she was gone. Just a typical nagging woman that he was planning to leave anyway. Then he would get drunk and see how much of his dead wife's face lived in Jess's eyes and lips, in the bend of her neck. He often remarked how little of him he saw in her and how angry that made him, as if he were incapable of leaving a mark on anything other than his daughter's skin. Most nights she tried to stay out as late as possible and then sneak in when her father was passed out drunk.

Sometimes there would be women living in the house. A few lasted a couple of months before rushing out the door, palms pressed up to a fresh black eye. Other times, they would be prostitutes, and Jess would catch them as they slunk out of the house, pockets full of her father's dole money. Sometimes, she would find her bedroom door open and her things gone.

She told me that her mother's engagement ring had disappeared from the small jewellery box she kept hidden in her underwear drawer. She came home and found the house empty, her room torn apart, and the contents of her drawers strewn all over her bed. The only other item she had from her mum was the small silver cross that she wore at all times. I remember catching sight of it just a few times in the couple of years that followed. She didn't tell me about it until I had finally seen it with my own eyes, felt the tiny, priceless weight of it with my own fingers.

After the showdown with Ronnie and his friend, I didn't see Jess again until we were back at school. The hazy warmth of the summer had dissipated like the memory of a dream. The playground had been replaced, and freshly painted white and yellow lines marked out a new five-a-side pitch and a basketball court.

In my room, I had played the fantasy scene of me seeing Jess for the first time after the holidays over and over in my head. She would approach me, sometimes surprising me by yanking on my arm, and I would turn around and say, all cool like, "Hey, how's it going?" She would tell me that she'd missed me and couldn't stop thinking about me since the fight in the car park. Then we'd hang out and gradually get closer until some kind of relationship bloomed between us.

What actually happened was this: My Father dropped me off at the schoolyard gates, his sad smile partially lost under his beard. I slowly walked in, a cold sweat prickling the skin on my back as I realised that, once again, I was swapping one violent tormentor for another. The playground was filled with other sad-looking children, unhappy at the prospect of returning to education after such a wonderful time of doing nothing except hanging out with friends.

Then I saw her, running towards the school block, pushing through a cluster of kids who shoved out of her way. I followed the grumbling wake after her and finally caught up with her just outside the science building.

"Hey. Jess," I said, and she spun around, her face a picture of hurt and anger. Her lip had been split and her left eye puffed shut.

Of All Possibilities | 99

"What?" she demanded.

"Are you okay?" I asked meekly.

"Are you fucking serious right now?"

"I just saw you running…" I looked at my feet. "Who did this?"

"Who do you fucking think? That shithead Ronnie and his stupid little friends. God, I fucking hate them!" She kicked the wall a few times. A small boy with big hair looked at us, then ran off. "I wish he'd just fucking die."

"Yeah, me too," I said. "I don't see anyone missing him."

"Not even his mother," Jess said. "After he was born, the doctor must have slapped her."

I laughed, and she tried to smile, winced with pain, then went back to kicking the wall.

"Wait here a sec," I said, and ran off. I brought back some wet tissues and handed them to her. She split the wet mass and pressed half to her eye and the rest against her lip.

"What are your parents going to say when they see that?" I asked.

"Ha," she barked. "Like my dad gives a shit. He'll probably just think he got drunk and did it himself."

"Really?"

"Yeah. I don't even know why I bother coming to school anymore," she said. She spat a wad of dark blood and it landed on one of the newly painted white lines. "No one gives a shit about me."

"Hey," I protested. "I do."

"You hardly even know me."

My heart was hammering in my chest all of a sudden. My spit was hot and I wondered if I was about to be sick. "I'd like to."

And that was it. For the next month we hung out at school. That consisted solely of meeting in the canteen at lunch and talking about the myriad ways in which we would murder Ronnie Green. Then we would walk the perimeter of the field and tell each other jokes, new swear words. Jess would talk about music she loved, and I would just listen, because I wasn't allowed to like those types of bands. She asked me about the New Sunrise, and I was evasive, disclosing only what I thought was safe. I told her about my Father, and so then we talked about how we would murder our parents, too.

"How about we push them all into a massive hole and just fill it in?" Jess suggested.

We were in that snatched moment after the bell had rung and school finished but before I'd climb into my Dad's truck and watch Jess shrink behind us.

"Too easy," I said. "I thought you wanted Ronnie to suffer. Besides, what if he just comes back as a zombie or something?"

"Then I'd shoot him in the head." She extended her index finger and pointed it at my face. "Pow," she said.

"Okay, so, mass grave, zombie headshot. Not bad," I said. A young gingered-haired girl ran past us and careened into a teacher, sending a stack of exercise books flying from his hands.

"Sorry, sir," the girl said and then just took off running. We laughed until the teacher shot us a stern look.

"Okay, now you," she said.

"Umm, sharks?" I offered weakly.

"Sharks? That's fucking lame."

"I mean, taking them to a planet where there is no land because there were all these floods, and now only massive sharks live there, and they're always looking for food. I would take all three of them and just drop them there and they would get eaten."

"Eli, that's a totally spasticated idea. I wanna, like, destroy them."

"I'm sorry. My Dad always told me to turn the other cheek because all people will be judged eventually."

"Urghh," Jess said, rolling her eyes. "Karma is for lazy people who lack the motivation for revenge."

"Okay, okay," I said. "How about... if I could just erase them from reality altogether, and then we would just totally forget them?"

It was a delicious confession of sorts. As we grew closer, I wanted to tell her about what I could do so much that I figured it was safer to tell her in a hypothetical way to avoid just blurting out the full truth. It felt electric—everything that I was suddenly out there in front of her. She stopped and looked at me, wild-eyed.

"You mean, like they never existed?"

"Yeah. So as if no one had ever cared for them or even knew about them."

"Total fucking annihilation?" she asked, a cruel joy in her smile.

"Total annihilation."

"Holy shit, that is dark. I love it. Eli, you are truly evil, you know that?"

"I serve only our Dark Lord and master, Santa."

"If *only* we could do that. I have a whole list of people on my naughty list."

"Oh yeah? Tell me."

As we walked towards the double doors that opened out into the playground and then the street where my Dad was waiting for me, a sinister idea began to take root.

Of All Possibilities | 103

# Unforeseen Consequences

Ronnie Green was a terrible, horrible little shitbag. I knew it at the time and I know it now. He would never have amounted to much. Maybe I should have contented myself with that reality instead of intervening, because, in the end, he cost me a start. Assholes like that are the glue that hold the good people together.

As luck would have it, I got my opportunity two weeks later. It should have struck fear into me, but when my Father told me he wouldn't be able to pick me up from school for a couple of days, as he was going to be out of town, I almost wrung my hands in malicious delight. I had been hatching secret plans to disappear Ronnie since the conversation with Jess, but apart from trying to escape the compound, I could see no way of creating a window to do it without being caught. I pretended to be put out by it all, throwing my weight around and decrying my Father for being selfish, but it was all just a ruse.

That first day, I walked into town with Jess. She was going to hang out with some of her friends from outside of school by the Blockbuster, so I went with her some of the way. She made me listen to Jesus and Mary Chain and the Pixies as we strolled the long road away from the school. After she had forced Iron Maiden's "Number of the Beast" on me, I handed her back the headphones.

"Whatcha think?" she asked.

"Pretty cool," I said.

"They're English as well. I've got all their albums, and my friend said he could get me into one of their concerts easy."

"Oh, that's really wicked."

"If he can sort it out, you wanna come? We can get alcohol and everything."

"I don't think I can. I don't even know how I'd be able to get out."

"Jesus. Is it really that bad?"

She kicked a pebble and it pinged off a parked car's tyre and skittered across the road. An elderly woman pushing along a tartan trolley filed with shopping looked at us and shook her head in disappointment.

"What?" Jess protested. "It was an accident." She turned to me conspiratorially. "Fucking old bitch. I hope she gets hit by a bus." Then she started laughing.

"I wish Ronnie would get hit by a bus," I said, turning the conversation to our favourite pastime: disappearing the lives of people we hated.

"Jesus. Did you see him outside the maths block this morning?" she asked.

"Yeah, I saw from registration. He jammed Jamie's head through the bars of the metal fence and put a bike lock around his neck so he couldn't get out."

"What an utter arsehole."

I grimaced. "Do you know where he lives?"

"Yeah, he's actually not too far from my house. My dad used to talk to his sometimes. Why?"

"I was thinking that we maybe, umm, throw a brick through his window or something."

"Yeah!" she exclaimed. "Or we could collect up all the dog shit in the park and leave it in his garden."

Then she was off talking about the myriad things we could do until it turned into a fantasy, and we were both flying a fighter jet and blowing his house up, murdering everyone he loved, and finally shooting him down as he tried to escape.

She introduced me to her friends—a group of punks a good few years older than her, with their noses pierced with safety pins, wild hair pushed up into spikes, and leather jackets collaged with band patches. They laughed when I said I was into Green Day, so Jess told them to fuck off, and then everyone was laughing.

I waved goodbye to her and started on my way home, making a detour towards Ronnie's house.

The street he lived on, one over from Jess's, looked ominous. Battered cars lined both sides of the road. The front gardens were littered with old ovens and fridges, piles of tyres, and car batteries. In one garden sat a rusty transit van missing all of its wheels. The rear window was covered in loosely attached clear plastic that snapped and rustled in the evening breeze. The streetlights flicked on and buzzed. A few of them didn't work, and upon walking underneath them, I saw their bulbs had been smashed. A dog barked and then another one that sounded streets away barked back. The call and response went on like that for several minutes. I could feel a doorway nearby—that sense headache began to prickle in the centre of my brain. It set my teeth on edge and the hairs on arms stood to attention. Then I saw it, just hovering there in the centre of the street, the gentle waves of static rolling from it.

I approached it, then froze as a group of three or four kids whipped past from behind on their bikes. One of them passed straight through the doorway and carried on down the street. I scanned the windows around me for curtain twitchers, for anyone walking by who might see me, and when I thought it was safe, I jumped through.

▽

On the other side, the street was just as dark. The friendly face of a yellow moon peeked up over the town. I even saw the kids as they raced down the hill. On the surface, at least, everything appeared to be the same. It wasn't a flooded world inhabited solely by giant man-eating sharks, but it would do. I turned on my heel and stepped back through.

▽

I had just twenty-four hours to pull off the rendition of Ronnie Green, and I spent the entire day with my stomach in knots, my hands sweating, and a very real feeling that I was going to get caught. I also felt like I spent entirely too much time just staring at Ronnie. In class, at lunch, during PE. I couldn't take my eyes off him—I didn't want to lose him somehow. He caught my gaze a few times and informed me that I was gay and that he would punch my head in later. I just smiled at him; his words felt empty at that point. I just kept thinking, Oh, you'll fucking see me later, but this time it's going to end with *you* in tears.

Being a teenager, my skills at keeping covert consisted entirely of what I had learned from my own and other kids' experiences of trying to evade bullies at school, as well as what I had taken from those people I had taken to Purgatory. Needless to say, my skills were not great. I watched, my heart in my mouth, as Ronnie swaggered out of the school gate, flanked by his little lackeys, and made his way home. The small gang harassed a couple of girls until they ran off, threw a can of Coke at a passing car, nearly causing the driver to hit a cyclist, and bumped into everyone who looked like they wouldn't put up a fight. It made me furious to watch as they flung themselves into an old lady, knocking her into a hedge, then pretend to be sorry, only to bust out into peals of laughter as they walked away.

It was getting dark when Ronnie finally made his way home on his own. My legs ached, and I felt sick—sick from hunger, sick from nerves. I couldn't stop my hands from shaking. I detached myself from behind a brick wall, blew a big breath to steady myself, and walked confidently towards him. He was approaching the doorway and was about to walk straight past it when I called his name.

"Ronnie. Oi, Ronnie!" I called just loud enough for him to hear me. He turned and grinned that stupid fucking grin. My hands were pins and needles, the blood in my chest boiling.

"It's you," he sneered as he flexed his shoulders. "I didn't think they let you out on weeknights. Must've got someone else to fuck, eh?"

I was close. Nausea burned in my guts—either from the thrill of what was about to happen or from the proximity of the doorway now. As I strode up to him, jaw set, I checked the surrounding windows. The dog barked somewhere. We were all clear.

"Yeah," I said confidently. "Your mum."

He looked confused for a second, but then his features began to shift to something more sinister. I pushed him towards the doorway with everything I had and held on tight.

---

The worst feeling in the world is when you hate someone—and I mean absolutely despise them down to the very fucking marrow in their bones—and then all of a sudden you can't hate them anymore. Then you realise too late that you've done something irreversible and are going to regret it for the rest of your life.

His mind was obtuse but filled with jagged thoughts. A dull approximation of understanding flared dimly in his mind, a lonely light in the unending darkness.

He thought about his dad. There was fear and finally a sense of optimistic relief. Was what was happening to him a final escape from his abuses?

His memories were brutal. Yet another string of tragedies held together and vividly punctuated by paternal abuse. At once, I felt something approaching guilt—I was just another shitty thing that had happened to him. Yet, more strangely, I felt a sort of kinship with him, the same kind that Jess and I also shared. I understood emphatically what it was like to be beaten, to have a fistful of my hair yanked back and be forced to stare into the frothing mouth of someone who was supposed to protect me as they tried to break me. I just went a different way than he did, refused to turn that abuse outward.

▽

There was a couch, lunar craters of cigarette burns scarring its brown surface. A hand, limp at the wrist, its fingers squeezing a smoking Superkings between two tattooed letters, hanging over the armrest. The forearm attached is muscled, a cartography of blue-grey veins just below the surface and purple-pink scars cut into the thick hair. A badly rendered tattoo of an eagle on the bicep, a leopard tearing into faded red skin on the opposite one. Stained T-shirt with the sleeves ripped off, a gut hanging over the black leather belt.

"Where you going?" the figure's voice slurs. By the man's feet, crumpled beer cans and bottles of cheap but lethally strong booze. His face shadowed and lit by the strobes of ghost blue from the TV. A laugh track plays, but Ronnie can't hear it, really. His ears are ringing from the burst eardrum this man gave him clapping him round the head.

"Out," we say, and swallow down a fear that a fifteen-year-old shouldn't ever have to experience.

"Get to fuck are you," the voice growls.

"But, dad," we protest, but are stopped short. "I thought you said I could."

"Changed my mind. Now fuck off upstairs." He closes his unoccupied hand into a fist and we instinctively shrink back.

"Okay," we say and creep quietly upstairs.

We hear our mum return with armfuls of shopping and it's not long before an argument starts. The screaming makes our heart hurt, but the silence is always worse. Because it means that they've stopped arguing and he might be strangling her, or punching her. We sneak from our room and sit on the stairs. A cry comes from the kitchen and our mother falls backwards into the living room. Staticky light falls across her face as she back-pedals across the carpet, trying to get away. She hits one of the cans and beer spills out in an amber pool underneath her. The shadow of our father looming over her.

"No, dad," we scream, and then we stare into his wild, drunken eyes. They are sick with a rage that we can only fail to comprehend.

Then he comes for us.

▽

"Oh, fuck you!" I screamed at him on the other side. I was crying big wet heaves as the fear of that memory slowly dissipated. "You don't get to make me feel bad for you now."

His eyes were wide, glassy with disbelief. The dog was barking like crazy at the fact that the other dog streets away was not barking back. Orange haze settled above the roofs of the houses. Nothing seemed to be different here than to where we just were. At the top of the street, I saw another version of Ronnie slowly walking towards us.

"What just happened?" said this one, rocking on his heels like he was about to pass out.

"Fuck you, Ronnie," I repeated, and disappeared.

▽

The street was empty. The dog still barking, orange sunset, the night leaching the warmth out of everything, the low hum of a plane cutting a single white line across the dark, underlining a row of blinking stars. A crow called from the top of a telephone pole as I passed by on my way back home.

He was gone, and I couldn't believe it, even though I was the one who had done it. My hands still shook, and even though there was no chance I could be caught, I felt on edge for about a month after that night in fear that the police would come knocking. I've spent a lot of time between that day and this one wondering if it was worth it. I don't think it was.

I got home later than I'd ever been before and my Mother was sitting in the kitchen waiting for me. Luckily, my Father hadn't returned yet, but the look in her eyes made me feel far worse than my Father could have. I told her I had been with a friend, and she began to soften. She was inquisitive and I told her about Jess, about how we had become friends.

"Oh, well," she said, laying an empty dish in front of me. "It's good you have a friend at least."

I agreed with her, and we sat looking at one another for a moment. Something passed between us then that at the time felt like pity, but I know now was actually closer to envy. Aside from the people in the compound, my Mother had no friends. She never left, and I wasn't sure if she was even allowed to.

"Mum," I said, unsure of how I was going to continue. "What would you do if someone was bullying you?"

"Well," she said, leaning forward on her chair and closing the distance a little. "Bullies are normally people who have been bullied themselves. My Mother always told me that we should always try to be kind to people, because you never know what they are going through."

Of course she was right. She so often was.

"But what if this person was really mean? What if they won't stop?"

"Well, my mother had another piece of advice for that," she said, with a wry smile. "Kick them in the goolies and run away." She laughed at that, and so did I.

She went over to the stove and came back with some beans, three sausages, and a few vegetables. I ate everything except the mushy white cauliflower, which I tried to hide with sauce and the cutlery.

"Are you okay, Eli?"

I was taken aback by the question. Hadn't really considered my position on my general well-being.

"I'm fine. Why?"

"It's just that—" She stopped for a second, scooped the remains of the meal into the big bin next to the sink. "You are still so young to be doing, well, what we do. I just want to know you are okay."

It was the first and only time since I was six that she had asked me if I was okay being the Key. In hindsight, it could have been that she was starting to examine our life and had realised that I was rarely offered any kind of autonomy, to the point where I had just become an object, an icon to be directed and not offered any choice. Or it might have been the fact that my Father wasn't there. I suspect it was probably the latter by the way she jumped when she heard the door close, followed by the sound of his voice.

"Tabitha?" he said, as he walked down the long hall towards the kitchen.

She looked at me conspiratorially, then aimed a tired smile towards the door.

"Ah, there you are," he said. Then his eyes moved from my Mother to me. "Good evening, my boy," he said and pulled out the seat opposite me. The legs scraped on the wooden floorboards, his knees clicking as he bent to sit. Then he let out a long sigh. My Mother went to the kettle and started to make him a cup of tea.

"Hi Dad," I said. "How was your trip?"

"Well, we ended up being delayed by a couple of hours because the people we were buying from hadn't received the proper order, so we had to wait around an extra day."

"What?" my Mother exclaimed. She placed the tea down on the table and a little bit slipped over the rim of the cup and left a brown ring on the wood. "They're usually so good."

"I know. It's the only reason I waited, and they gave us a discount, too." Then he turned to me once more. "How was school?"

"Yeah, okay," I replied. "I've got history homework."

He laughed. "History is fluid—it can be changed as easily as *that*," he said with a snap of his fingers. "How can they possibly give you a test on something that can change as easy as the wind?"

"But they don't know that, Dad."

"Obviously. It just makes me laugh that they think they have all the answers when they know so little. They are the flies that believe the room they are trapped in is everything. Imagine if they saw, and read, and believed the Book of Yon, or read the Book of Names and witnessed the sacrifices to a forgotten history of this world? What then? Their whole system of belief would crumble to dust, Eli."

He took a sip of his tea, choked a little, coughed, and then carried on. "They would raise us on a pedestal and worship us, but instead we live like humble men and follow the path as set before us by God, and do as we are bid."

"So, yeah," I said trying to break the flow of my Father's proselytising, "it's on the Great Fire of London. I've got to write about what caused it and what happened afterwards."

"Well," my Mother started. She banged the upturned end of a pot into the bin with the palm of her hand. "Did you know that after the fire, when they were rebuilding everything, people took advantage of the situation and said that their buildings were bigger, wider, longer, that sort of thing. That's why London is such a knotted mess. It's why the streets get so small in places."

"That's what happens when you let the common man rewrite history, Eli. They will do it to serve only themselves."

"There's truth in that, son," my Mother said.

"Of course there is," my Father said, shooting a sideways glance at my Mother. "A fundamental truth about the greed of man."

I thanked them, excused myself, and went to my room.

Still giddy with excitement, I sat on my bed, knees drawn up to my chin as I shivered a little from the effects of the adrenaline. I kept replaying the moment before I'd walked away from him. He'd looked so vulnerable. The whole time I had known him, he'd been an asshole, and the second I got some kind of revenge, he made me regret it.

I hadn't even realised the true consequences of what I had done until the next day at school. It was raining hard, my Dad's windscreen wipers offering very little improvement to the visibility. He cursed and swore a couple of times as he manoeuvred the van gingerly through traffic. When we came to a stop, I watched the grey silhouettes of kids running into the building through the steamed-up window. I jumped out and ran along with them towards the main building. Then I saw Jess locking her bike up, so I broke away from the noisy crowd and went over to her.

"Hey," I said, and she turned to me and stared. Then she shrugged her shoulders. I pressed on. "How was hanging out with your friends the other night?"

"What?" she said, turning suddenly hostile "How did you... Are you following me?" She pointed a finger at my face.

"No," I said confused. Then it hit me. I had erased a part of our history together. Our mean-spirited collusions on the topic of what we would do to Ronnie. Our whole reason for bonding. I spent the rest of the day in a sick, dreamlike daze. Everything seemed as if it were being conducted underwater, my heart crushed by consequences I stupidly hadn't considered.

As kids filed out at the end of the day, I saw her again. She was riding her bike through the crowd, weaving between people. She had her headphones on. The ones she had forced over my ears and used to introduce me to Iron Maiden, and the Jesus and Mary Chain, and the Cure. I remember fighting back tears, a burning lump in my throat, and asking myself how could I be so fucking stupid as I ran to my Dad's waiting van.

I couldn't just go back and get Ronnie, I knew that much. There was no way he would keep his mouth shut, and if our little family secret got out, everything would be ruined.

I got back home and made it as far as slamming my bedroom door shut before I burst into tears. I kept replaying the memories of all the things we had done together that had been lost. The fight with Ronnie and his little henchmen and the kiss on the cheek afterwards. That one hurt. I bit my lip and punched my leg until my brain stopped playing back the moment. The proximity that we had shared that we hadn't repeated after. Her eyes so close to mine, the splashes of gold in the dial of honey brown.

The jokes we had told each other. Falling about laughing in the canteen. Or her screaming, "I'm going to piss myself," as she stood doubled over behind the science block. All gone.

Wracked by a fresh wave of grief, I snatched the rug up and grabbed my Grandfather's diary from beneath the floorboard. Feverishly racing through the pages, I was looking for any reference from his experiences that might help.

$$\triangledown$$

I found endless diary entries focusing on erasing people, but not so many on the topic of bringing them back. None, in fact. And so, I realised, unless I could figure out how to find and return Ronnie—unknown consequences be damned—I had lost her. Well, my version of her anyway. I felt lost, heartsick, and generally broken.

"Eli," my Father said as he pushed the door open. "Didn't you hear me calling you—" The rest of his words locked in his throat when he saw the book and realised I was reading my Grandfather's diary. I snapped the cover shut and tried to hide it. My heart hammering in my throat, skin instantly alive and prickly. I saw his eyes slide from me, to the rug drawn back from the hollow floorboard next to the bed, and back to the diary clutched to my chest.

"Where did you get that?" he growled. I was surprised that he recognised it, and then I realised that there must have been another copy in the house—the one from this reality—and that he must have it. He strode over and snatched it off me.

"How do you know what it is?" I shouted.

"Tell me," he threatened. His face was grey from shock. I could see it had dawned on him that I most likely knew the secret about our "family," along with dozens of other things he never intended me to find out.

"It's mine," I said. I jumped up and swiped at the book.

"Where?" he growled.

"It was meant for me," I said.

My Father rounded on me, taking slow, heavy steps forward. I backed away until I bumped against the bed.

"How did you get this?" He smacked me hard across the face with the back of his hand and I reeled away, falling onto the bed. The hot pain on my cheek was almost immediate, delayed only briefly by the shock of it. I started crying. The doorway in the bathroom seemed to shimmer.

I tried to push myself up, but he hit me again, this time with his palm. I threw my hands up and deflected some of it, taking a lot of the force out of it with my forearms, but he still caught me on the side of the head, sent me reeling with a loud ringing in my ears.

"I burnt this book," he hissed. "Now, tell me." He raised his hand again.

"Grandad gave it to me," I cried.

He took a step back, stunned as the realisation crept over his features that *of course* my Grandfather was alive somewhere in another universe, only a step away. He dropped the book next to my feet.

"You saw him?" he said.

"He gave it to me years ago. He said it was meant for me," I said, some measure of courage returning to me. "I know everything. I know about your brother. I know that Grandad planned to erase you to get your brother back, and the only thing that stopped him was when you told him Mum was pregnant."

My Father looked like a child all of a sudden. Tears crept to the corner of his eyes and he nodded. "How is he?"

"Alive," I said. Waves of static rolled outwards and I could feel the doorway's pull as I focused all my attention on it, willing it to open.

"Can I see him?" he asked, softly.

"You'll never see him again," I screamed as I shouldered him, pushing him back. He gave a roar as his foot went into the space in the floorboards and his ankle twisted. He pitched backwards, clawing at the air, and fell onto his back. I snatched the journal up and ran for the doorway in the bathroom.

▽

My fear, anger, and humiliation were quickly replaced by wide-eyed shock and disbelief. The room was empty, abandoned for how long, I couldn't say. A thick layer of dust coated everything in the bathroom. The tub had a dark stain around its rim, tiger stripes of brown and yellow. Years of dead insects curled up into dry husks. A thick layer of lime scale coated the taps. The mirror was dingy, the light above it missing a bulb. I wiped a hand across the dirty surface and caught sight of my face. My right cheek was red and puffy. I lingered there for a moment longer, overcome with a sense of grief and impending loss. In an afternoon, I had lost Jessica, attacked my Father, and now, faced with this reality, possibly lost my Grandfather, again. So, I just stood there, gripping the edge of the sink until my knuckles turned porcelain white. Looking down at the scattered husks of woodlice like withered rinds, I wheezed a deep breath, trying to build up the courage to open the rotting bathroom door into the bedroom. Threads of golden light spilled through the cracks near its bottom.

I pushed open the door and stepped beyond the threshold. The pictures on the walls were gone, squares of unbleached wall left behind. "What happened?" I said aloud, my voice carrying a little.

Fuzzy grey webs dangled in corners and connected the exposed ceiling joists. Books lay in random piles here and there. Some were open and their pages had mouldered. My Grandfather was nowhere to be seen. I walked to a window, where the curtains had been pulled away and lay rotting in two piles beneath the sill, and looked out at our garden. The standing stones had somehow been toppled and were lying in a loose pile. The two supporting stones were laid flat, and the top stone spanned the short gap between them. A line of moss like a high-water mark crept in an uneven line along the length of the dull rock. Thin vines lashed the blocks to the earth, and here and there along the green tracks small white flowers bloomed. The grass in the centre grew wild, obscuring the dais and creeping up through it. Beyond the fallen door to Purgatory and towards the perimeter of the property stood the tall corrugated-iron fence topped with spools of razor wire, barbs winking dully in the light.

I walked down the creaking stairs and moved through the houses like a ghost. The spectre of a child who'd once lived here and, through some divine machination, had escaped—or maybe something worse. More dust, shelves thrown open, odd items strewn across the floor of the corridors: knives and forks, a teddy bear, piles of clothes blown to the corners of rooms and the edges of hallways. Things dropped in a hurry or looted and discarded. I felt a sick sense of nightmarish foreboding as I navigated the compound. The floorboards protested as I made my way to the central house, then out into the garden. Small birds, sparrows or finches, darted up from below the grass line like a handful of thrown stones. They zigzagged along the fence line and zipped between the rough bramble-toothed whorls of the razor wire, leaving only a feather or two. The grass sighed as I made my way to the standing stones. All around me were the small wildflowers that bordered my Grandparents' graves back in my own reality. Belts of red campion and dog rose bloomed from the sides of the concrete stairs.

A pool of stagnant water had collected in the dais and insects squirmed and writhed beneath the mucky surface.

As I crossed the garden, again disturbing the tall grass and accidentally knocking a couple of honeybees loose from their flowery perches, I wondered what could have happened here. It had been nearly eight years since I had visited here, when my Grandfather had given me the book. The house itself revealed no sign of distress caused by anything other than its abandonment. No scorch marks, no bullet holes, and no real evidence as to the cause of the evacuation. I wondered if maybe my family had just up and left for somewhere else and were now operating elsewhere. I played out fantasies that versions of us were living and working somewhere sun-kissed.

The noise of a car winding through the narrow road heading towards the compound registered and began to grow, so I went back inside the house. My head was starting to throb already. It was partly caused by the argument with my Father, but mostly by the new reality trying to burn itself into my brain. I didn't want to go back home yet, so I went to my old room, the one I had shared with my family before I was moved to the tower room. It smelt of dry mould, rotten paper, and stagnant air. I shook the dust from the bed sheet and lay down. It was a beautiful autumn day here too, and while the room was warm enough, I shivered as if I were running a fever. I remember watching the grey tendrils of webs that hung from the cracked ceiling shake and snap hypnotically in the breeze, moving through the house like a wheezing breath. Thoughts of Jess, then the confrontation with my Father, ran over and over in my head on a loop. I had no solution to either problem, so just went exhaustingly from loss to dread to loss again.

At some point I fell asleep, because the next thing I remember is waking up to the sound of voices. Braying laughter, shouting, whoops that, at first, my groggy brain interpreted as my family, until a boom box starting up and grunge music echoed down the halls. I practically jumped out of the bed and carefully crept to the door. Whoever they were, they were in the kitchen. Someone wrenched a cupboard door off and threw it through the kitchen window—a violent crash that was followed by laughing and cheers.

Another window smashed and someone yelled "Nice!" in an unmistakably teenaged boy's voice.

I didn't want them to see me—I was scared of what they might do to me—so I watched through a gap in the rotten door. Two of them seemed to have split from the group and started wandering in my direction.

"Shitshitshit," I hissed, my eyes darting around the room, looking for somewhere to hide. The windows were boarded up, so no way out there. I didn't want to hide in the wardrobe because it had no escape route.

I heard the sound of Dr. Martens creaking on the wooden flooring close by.

*What would I say to them?* I wondered.

I crept back to the door—they were close now.

"Ritchie, why would you let anyone push you around? You carry, right?" one said to the other. The details of their faces were obscured by lank, greasy hair.

"Yeah, course," the other said. He reached into a back pocket and produced a butterfly knife.

Across the hall, I saw a doorway into another reality slowly start to unfurl like an indistinct flower as I concentrated on it. There was no way I would be able to make it back to my room, my home. I was being forced into making a move that my heart was loudly applauding in my chest. A third member of the group joined the other two, bringing the boom box with him, blaring Guns N' Roses.

I yanked the bedroom door open and dove across the hallway towards my exit. The other reality yawned open.

▽

I found myself back in the house. The boys were still here, except the one with the boom box was still somewhere in the kitchen.

"Shit," one of the two in the bedroom screamed. "It's the fucking ghost."

I stumbled forward. The room I was in was connected to the next one by an internal door, and I could feel the pull of another doorway manifesting beyond it. I staggered towards it, tripped on something and fell, slamming my elbow into the corner of a cabinet on the way down. My arm instantly went fuzzy and numb. The two boys were at the threshold, just behind me now.

Of All Possibilities | 125

"Jesus. It's just a fucking kid."

"I'm going to fucking murder you," the other said.

I got up, ripped the door open, and fell another universe down into a fourth reality.

▽

The boys were gone, but music was playing in the kitchen, Guns N' Roses again. I poked my head around the corner and saw the three of them pulling out the kitchen drawers, letting the contents clatter on the floor. One of them snatched up a butter knife and comically stabbed at the other, who pretended to die.

I stepped out into the corridor and turned to go upstairs, but bumped into the boy who kept the butterfly knife in his back pocket. He loosed a high-pitched scream, which made me panic. In an automatic fight-or-flight response I punched him in the face as hard as I could, sending him backwards into the wall, blood streaming from his nose. Then I turned and bolted back down the hall. The voices quickly turned to shouts. What they said, I have no idea. I sprinted left into the reception area—straight ahead of me was the front door, and to the right, a set of stairs that went up to the second floor. I saw yet another doorway ahead of me, heard footsteps behind. Without thinking about how I would get back to my origin reality, I lunged forward as hard as I could and felt the strange warmth of the fifth universe envelop me.

This time there was no one. No kids. I moved toward a gravel patch where my Dad used to park the van. I slowly turned in the late afternoon sun, a heat haze rising off the ground. The compound was just a long skeleton. The roof beams had collapsed inwards and buttressed the gable at the front of the house. It resembled a hoarding of some kind, a fake front. I half expected it to fall on top of me, the round window cut into it saving me, like I had seen in some black-and-white movie.

Behind the ruins of the house, the grass grew wild and high. Bright, lazy butterflies flitted just above. The huge stones lay there as in other realities, immovable and inert, strangled by the life that crawled all over them.

That was when my head decided to cave inwards.

Not *actually* actually, but the small, niggling pain that was present when I crossed over suddenly bloomed into a nuclear explosion inside my mind. I pressed my palms to my temples and squeezed, trying to stop my brain from bursting open like that guy's in *Scanners*, as I collapsed. My vision shrunk until I saw only white and red pulses, and I think I must have had some kind of fit as each successive reality slammed into each other, cannoning into my brain like a train wreck. My nose erupted in blood, then I started crying, except it wasn't tears—it was blood. Just before I passed out, I vomited. Yep, blood.

I can't tell you how long I was there for, but it felt like an eternity. When I woke up, my hands were shaking so hard I couldn't control them. My lungs felt crushed and I fought for every breath as I flailed about like a landed fish, trying to wait it out. But the pain felt terminal. I rolled onto my side and managed to get to my hands and knees. My entire world vibrated as the crushing weight of realities overlaid each other in a violent mesh. I saw in flashes, like an afterimage, ghostly copies of the boys who had chased me run down an invisible corridor and disappear.

I struggled to my feet. My legs didn't want to work—it felt as if my very cells were trying to tear themselves apart. I staggered up and stumbled forward towards the ruined house, towards the reality I had come from. It enveloped me and as I shot between worlds, I felt a single layer of pain lift.

▽

It became a shade less unbearable.

The boys were gone. I could see their boot prints in the dust. I staggered towards the other doorways and one by one began my return.

▽

It wasn't long until I had arrived back to the reality where I had first encountered the teenagers, and they were gone from here, too. The pain was back to something that resembled a toothache, but the echoes of what I had just been through still reverberated through me. My bones hurt and my joints ached. Even my teeth and hair hurt.

The boy with the boom box had left it by the bedroom door. It was on its side, blaring L7's "Pretend We're Dead." He must have abandoned it as they all fled from "the ghost." I turned it off, grabbed it by the handle, and took it up into my Grandfather's old room and back to my own reality.

▽

My Father was gone from my room. I expect he must have waited but had given up. I had to come back eventually. Surprisingly, he didn't beat me for that little episode. In fact, after that incident, he never beat me again.

I had the sort of skull-crushing headache for the next three days that can only be replicated by downing two bottles of Sambuca, a pint of Baileys, and then getting into a fight with a boxer. Hours after I returned, I was still spitting thick wads of dark blood into the bathroom sink. It took two, very long, days for the shakes to fully subside.

I'd learned the agonising limit of my power.

When she saw the dried blood soaked into my clothes, matted into my hair, and covering my face, my Mother wept. She looked at my Father with something approaching hatred until he screamed at her that he had nothing to do with it. I told her what had happened, leaving out the part about the argument with my Father about my Grandfather's diary. Instead, I told her that I had just gone exploring and ventured too far.

She wanted to take me to hospital of course. I told her I was fine and my Father reassured her gently, telling her that the hospital was likely a bad idea given that explanations would be asked for.

For those three days, she brought my breakfast to my room. She sat at the end of my bed as I ate and we talked. I remember so clearly the liquid quality of the early morning light as it streamed through the old windows, settled on the sheets in warm squares. Lit my Mother's face, so that all the years of worry that had wrestled themselves into her expression were gone.

"What is it like?" she asked. "I can't even imagine."

I thought about it, how incomprehensible it was.

"Like being set adrift in a sea of stars," I replied. "It's beautiful, and frightening."

She closed her eyes to imagine it, then reached out and squeezed my hand in hers. "I'm sorry that you have to carry this burden. I know it is a great responsibility, and what you do is so—" she paused, "—important. But it must be very hard to be the one to do it. And your Father…" She looked away, out the window, maybe to see if she could spot him. "He's just so… He is dedicated to what we do. And I worry that it might be too much for you."

"It's not so much the doing it," I said. "It's what it leaves behind. I remember their lives. I live them in my dreams, feel their influence in everything I do. I worry that I don't even know who I am anymore."

"You are a gift," she said. "A wonderful and special boy."

"Dad doesn't think so."

"Your Father wants to be as special as you, I think, and the fact that he's not upsets him. He sees your behaviour and your attitude and, well, it can make him angry. He thinks you are purposefully squandering what you have."

I sat up in bed, spine pressed against the cold wood of the headboard. This moment felt conspiratorial, but I still didn't mention the diary, didn't mention the revelation my Father so desperately wanted to hide from me, from everyone. What my Mother had said confirmed what I already thought—that he hated me because he was so ordinary. I can see it so clearly looking back at that moment, but then I had felt lost, detached from my family somehow.

"Do you ever doubt what it is we're doing?" I asked.

"Never," she said, even though she would come to eventually.

"And what if I wanted to stop doing it?"

"This world would fall to ruin," she said. "But I would still love you." She smiled. "Now eat your food."

She stood up and went to the door, stopped, and paused there by it.

"How's your friend?" she asked.

I almost broke then and spilled everything that had happened with Ronnie and Jess. It was right there—but instead I said, "We've kind of fallen out."

"Oh," she said. "That's a shame. Is she worth you trying to fix it?"

My voice cracked. A terrible, burning lump in my throat appeared with tears close behind. "Yeah," I managed.

"You should fight for this friendship, then. Relationships are hard, and sometimes they can be doubly hard when they are really worth it."

She was, of course, and as in most things, absolutely right.

# Second First Time Around

I decided to see if I could bring Ronnie back. But in the reality where both versions now resided, he was nowhere to be found. His family had moved away, or maybe they had never lived there in the first place. There was nothing on the news or in the papers about two identical kids finding each other. It was as if he had simply disappeared again. The only person who missed him, was me.

So, I resolved to get Jess back the only other way I could, and I had a game plan. I would use my knowledge of her and the things she loved to win her back. Music was going to be the key.

This new version of her was a little louder, more rebellious, more prominent. She seemed to be that much brighter and, as such, had garnered a few more friends than in our original iteration. A few of the other kids in her year who had never seemed alternative in any way before had started to dress a little like her. She'd even started a punk band with a couple of them called the Rotten Ones. Jess, of course, was the lead singer.

Even though Ronnie had been removed from existence, the natural ecosystem of the school required an alpha-dick to fill the void he had left behind. Unsurprisingly, it was his pug-nosed compatriot Craig who had taken the crown. He was less overtly psychotic, but just as violent and threatening and, towards Jess, just as racist. With Ronnie out of the picture, he too seemed louder. It was strange to witness the reconfiguration of the cloud the disappeared boy had cast when he had been around.

Jess and her friends hung out behind the religious education huts at break to smoke cigarettes and listen to music. So, one lunchtime, I casually walked by. It was Jess and another girl whose name I didn't know. They were listening to Alice in Chains. Her friend smiled as I approached, patted her well-coiffured hair, rigid with cheap hairspray, and took a long pull on her cigarette. Jess looked me up and down.

"You're that creepy cult kid, right?" she asked, and flicked her cigarette into the grass.

I smiled.

# Four

Yeah, I know. It's pretty shitty to manipulate someone into liking you, but, let me ask you this: Is it still shitty if you already know that they like you?

I don't think it is.

I used everything I knew about her to worm my way in, and it was so difficult to not just fucking blow it, to not just unleash all of our lost history on her and freak her out. But, slowly, we ended up spending more time with each other. Thanks to my Mum nagging my Father, and mine and my Father's reconfigured relationship, I started hanging out with Jess in the evenings and at weekends. We instantly bonded over music, and I even got to relive sharing headphones with her as we walked into town together. It felt just as good the second time around.

The weird thing was—she *was* different. Yeah, the new king bully Craig was an asshole, but he was an asshole of a different ilk. He wouldn't target like Ronnie did. Instead, he'd just destroy all who stood in his way and leave the little people to do whatever, as long as they remained outside his sightlines. That meant that Jess and I were left alone for the most part. (Craig ended up in prison at twenty for dealing drugs. I assume he acted the same inside, because a year into his five-year sentence, his throat was cut in his sleep.) I had to accept that the old Jess was dead—lost to a simple divergence in time—and, eventually, I was okay with that.

▽

The M1 services look like a bright, exotic island in a sea of drab, rainy English countryside. I'm parked three cars over and one row back from my target car. The place is pretty much empty aside from a few couples milling about. A young guy stretches his arms and legs, throwing his hands in the air as if in some kind of victory. He runs his fingers through his wet hair as his girlfriend struggles with a baby seat in the back. They are all so blissfully unaware of the nature of things. In other realities, some of these people crashed on the way here. They are sprawled out and dying on the slick road, their bodies banjaxed and split in ways that cannot be fixed. In their final moments, they wonder what they could have done differently, not knowing that another version of them is just blithely carrying on, ignorant of their pain.

I switch off the engine and observe my target walking towards the brilliantly lit building. He pulls his coat up over his head and walk-run-walks in through the entrance. I'm tapping out the drumbeat along to "Blister in the Sun" by the Violent Femmes. Man, it's been such a long time since I heard this song. It was on a mixtape I used to listen to all the time, first on that battered boom box I stole from those kids, and then on a personal stereo I used to carry around with me at all times.

I'm stupid. I know the tricks—well, most of the tricks—and yet here I am. I turn too late and my car door opens. A fist smacks me right above the eye. I manage to turn my head just in time so it misses the socket. I hear the crack of knuckles possibly breaking as I am rocked sideways. I manage to turn my foot just enough to kick out and send my target sprawling backwards into the hatchback parked next to me. He bounces off the car and slips down to his knees. I unclip my seat belt and drop down to the tarmac. He pushes up, grabbing me about my waist, and rams me into my van's side panel. I punch about his ears, but then I feel hammer blows in my stomach.

I drop an elbow into his spine and he budges a little. Another, and he backs up enough for me to slide away. He pushes forward, but I evade and smash his face into the panel, denting it. It's a rental, but I was planning on burning the thing anyway. He tries to turn, but I stamp on the back of his leg with my right foot, dragging the skin with the grip of my shoe, then I knee him in the face with my left. He buckles sideways and collapses. I look around. A couple of people are staring at me. A woman is fumbling in her bag for what I think is her phone. She produces, yep, a phone, and is clearly calling the police. I turn my back to my growing audience, slide the panel door open, and throw in the now unconscious target.

I need to get the hell out of Dodge. I'm not in love with the idea of leaving him just rolling around in the back unsecured, but I can't do anything about that here, so I trust to luck that the fucker doesn't wake up.

The engine starts with a twist of the ignition key, and I'm gone, past the fuel pumps and twenty-four-hour coffee shop. The tall reedy trees fall away and I'm back on the motorway. Five minutes later and I pull over into the hard shoulder to take a second and better secure my guest. He's murmuring something, but still looks all floppy and out of it, so I climb between the seats and check him. At the far end of the van is a toolbox. Inside are a few lengths of rope, two sets of handcuffs, a hessian bag, duct tape, a ball gag, and a box-cutter. I handcuff him, one set over his wrists, and the other I use to cuff him to the passenger rail just above the door. He offers up little resistance aside from dead weight. His head lolls to one side and a thin line of pinkish spit starts to hang from his lips.

In his pockets, I find a phone and his wallet. After I climb back into the driver's seat, I check and see that he's had one missed call. I go through the wallet and find a driver's licence, some loose change, a condom, and a couple of receipts. There's a picture of him with his arms wrapped around the neck of a gorgeous woman. They are both smiling out of the see-through plastic sheath. In the picture, he's a handsome dude. I look at his smashed face in the rear-view mirror and wince. Not anymore.

The radio plays some new song from a band I've never heard of. I turn it off, smack the indicator down, and pull back onto the motorway.

# My Troubled History, Part Four

**November 11, 1995**

The year 1995 was a busy one for me. I remember as November approached, I was pretty much burnt out. The world, it seemed, was on the brink of something apocalyptic. It wasn't as bad as the '80s by a long shot, but some remnants of the lethal Cold War mythology still danced in the zeitgeist of the time. Clinton was in office in the US and John Major over here. There were waves of terrorist attacks, civil uprisings in dusty countries, massacres happening seemingly everywhere. War criminals were crawling out of the woodwork left, right, and centre. Compared to what would happen later, we should have taken it as a lovely break from all the violence, but people could only see the tensions that were rising to meet them.

We'd had an unprecedented number of offerings, each one taking its pound of flesh from me. Each supernatural transaction altering me. I felt fragmented. A hundred, two hundred little hooks in my mind all pulling me in different directions. I often wondered how my Grandfather did it, but then I remembered his faith. Religious faith, and faith in the task itself. He trusted the people in power to lead the mission. Loved his country and fulfilling his God-given purpose.

The money didn't hurt either, I imagine. Piles of it. I'd read in the journal that we had enough money after World War II that the next seven generations of my family would never have to work. I assumed that by '95 we had even more—and yet we lived meagre lives. I wondered what my Father was doing with it. I imagined it must've taken some creative accounting for the government to hide what they had given us.

It was also the year Jess and I both decided that smoking was cool and had taken up the habit in earnest. It was something she and I did on our way home from school, a kind of ritual of our own. We'd share two cigarettes and then eat four strips of chewing gum each as we approached our respective homes.

What were we then? Friends, definitely. What type of friends, however, was a hard thing to define. I fancied her, that much was clear, and I was pretty sure she knew it. I thought she fancied me too, but then she kept telling me about all these guys she liked. Kept getting drunk and sleeping with them. Then she'd go out with them for a couple of weeks, three weeks, a month before it inevitably all went south, and she'd be back—heartbroken, but all mine again.

Around then, she had started seeing this older guy named Paul. He was eighteen, didn't listen to the same sort of music as us, drove a red Fiesta, and had a job in the local arcade, which is where Jess and I would hang out and play games whenever we were together.

"He has this token thing that gives you infinite games on any machine!" she exclaimed, then took a drag on her cigarette. She blew out a cloud of smoke and watched it rise. "That's got to be worth a blowjob at least, right?"

I nearly spat my drink out then proceeded to blush from my collarbones up.

"Wicked," I said, feigning excitement.

"He doesn't give a fuck either," she said, telling me about a fight he had gotten into at a gig she and the Rotten Ones had played on the top floor of the local pub. "The guy just goes down, bam! Then Paul jumps on him, literally jumps on him, both fucking feet, right on his face. It was insane."

"What happened? Did the guy die?" I asked, horrified.

"I dunno," she said, then spat into the treeline. "Don't think so. Anyway, I pulled him away before the police turned up. It was a fucking mental gig. You should have come."

"The guy that Paul beat up, what did he do that was so bad?"

She clucked, shrugged. "He said the dude spent the entire show staring at my tits or something. He was a creep anyway."

Her evenings were always this interesting. Fights, gigs, parties, getting drunk. (I had been drunk three times at this point, and two of those had ended with vomiting.) I envied her nighttime shenanigans. Wandering the streets of Scratch Hill, or taking a train down to Camden Town and causing trouble, going to clubs and hanging out with the punks on the bridge. I always had a horrible, sick yearning feeling when I thought of her having all this fun without me, or when I imagined her in the arms of other guys. Dancing in the acrid streetlights of an empty street to Black Flag, playing in dingy clubs to a hundred drunk punters.

It didn't feel fair.

It was also in 1995 that Jess introduced me to Pantera, Machinehead, Metallica, Fear Factory, Nine Inch Nails. Still some of my favourite bands.

After the death of Kurt Cobain, I had felt listless, musically rudderless somehow. I had sat in the bedroom of the abandoned version of the compound, the one where the kids had chased me almost to my death, and listened to Nirvana's *Bleach* on repeat. Then Jess gave me copies of all her Alice in Chains, Smashing Pumpkins, Pearl Jam, and Cure albums. She also gave me a copy of the Rotten Ones demo, which they'd recorded for £100 in the studio of a friend of a friend in North London. The sound quality was pretty awful, but the songs themselves were great. Hearing her scream those angry lyrics over a wave of distorted guitars made me so damn happy.

▽

I stopped and stubbed out a cigarette with my shoe, shoving my four pieces of gum into my mouth, then continued along the black curve of the path that led to my home. A full moon cut along the road in front, its light filtered through the fingers of the trees in thin, milky slices. Alongside the sound of branches clacking and scratching together like old jawbones, owls hooted and bats trilled shrilly as they looped and threaded invisible vectors in the dark air, seeking out food. Stars pricked the night sky, for once not bleached out by light pollution from the town. I remember thinking how full the night sky actually was, but how empty the spaces in-between made everything seem.

The sound of an engine rumbling behind me made me start. I quickly stepped up onto the scrubby bank that lined the road and carried on, the low branches poking and prodding me. A white panel van passed, its rear lights leaving an ominous red trail. The exhaust turned the smell of night-scented stock on the air sour.

In the distance, I could see as the van slowed to a stop at the gates of the compound, and a few seconds later the horn sounded. I watched from the top of the hill as the gates were opened and the vehicle rolled in. I'd seen that van many times before. I knew what it held. What it meant. I spat into the dark and trudged the rest of the way home.

My Father came out to meet me a minute after I buzzed the gates. Even now, I remember his face—his skin was ashen and he wore a wide expression of concern.

"What's wrong," I asked.

"You better come in," he said. He took my arm and led me through to the kitchen. I flinched at his touch as I had done time and again, and he withdrew his hand. We crunched across the gravel drive in awkward silence. I thought about the versions of the world I had visited. In most, the family was gone, the compound a ruin. I wondered if this was a moment of divergence. One that would lead to that eerie outcome.

"Eli," he whispered through gritted teeth. "There is a man here who wants to talk to you. He works for the government."

"So? Why does he want to talk to me?"

"It's the offering he brought with him. It's different this time. It's a child." My Father stopped outside the front door and put his hands on my shoulders. "We have to do this. It's our purpose, even though it's hard. We can't know what not doing this might lead to."

I thought about the tattered sheets, the broken floorboards. The teddy bear rotting in some dirty corner of another version of this house.

"Why a kid?" I asked.

"I don't know. It's not our place to ask questions. But you know we must do this. We must cultivate the garden that He has gifted—"

I cut him off. "All right, all right," I said. "I get it."

I nodded and went inside, leaving my Father to nervously wring his hands.

At the kitchen table sat a man in a dark-grey pinstripe suit. I didn't like the look of him even then. I remember the greasy little smile he fixed on me, the way his eyes moved slowly over me as if judging my worth in that small moment. My Mum set a rattling cup of tea down in front of him.

"Ah, Eli, is it?" he said. His accent was upper class English, like James Bond or some kind of politician. I can see now how he tried so hard to cultivate that air of superiority, but I didn't see it at the time, or maybe I just didn't care.

He didn't get up, but he did offer me his hand, which I took and squeezed as hard as social convention would allow.

My Mum slipped from the room, casting one wary look at the man sat at her table. I cast around but couldn't see the offering. Maybe outside already, I remember thinking.

"Take a seat," the man said, gesturing for me to take the chair opposite. I sat down and watched as he met my stare with one of his own. He smiled widely, revealing two small rows of bright white teeth.

"I've been looking forward to meeting you, Eli. My name is Johns. I work for the government. I'm the Operations Director of the House of August, and this little project, and I must say, I was rather impressed to hear about your…" He looked me up and down. "Your particular ability."

I shrugged.

"Well, as I say, I'm in charge of the project, and I thought it would be good to come along and finally meet you. Maybe observe you working, eh?"

"Who's the target?" I said, mimicking the cold, professional language of my Grandfather, who spoke of targets and assets, operations and missions in his journal.

"Straight to the heart of the matter," the man said and chuckled. "I like you already." He took a sip of his tea, smacked his lips, and continued. "The *package* is a Tibetan boy named Dolma Nyima. He—"

"A kid?" I asked.

"Yes. One that will eventually lead an uprising in China. The bloodiest that has ever been. It makes

Tiananmen Square look like a good-time street party. The Chinese government is—"

"How old?"

"—going to be in our debt for a long time to come after this," he said. "He's six," he added, with a nonchalant wave of the wrist, as if shooing away a troublesome fly.

"Six!" I cried. "No. I'm not doing it."

Johns leant back in his chair and sipped his tea.

"Really?" he said with a sinister kind of glee. "Tell me, Eli—what is it like on the other side of that door?"

I stared out the window at the tall, dark stones lit by the burners. Someone was milling about in the garden, putting out washing, maybe. Something so mundane given their proximity to another reality where there was no one at all apart from the political targets I had put there.

I imagined the cold, flat square of field and the ruins that lay not far from here. My Grandfather had used a particular phrase to describe the place on the other side of the door, and it took me a short moment to seize upon it.

"Utter desolation," I said.

"Interesting. I would very much like to see what that is like some day."

I secretly vowed to make that wish a reality.

"Still," he said, "the fact of the matter is that I need you to do this, Eli. Not just for me, either. For the country—for the world, even. Your family lacks a Seer, Eli. Your people can no longer see the path that lies ahead of us should this not happen, but at the House of August, I am well informed of the immediate future." He shifted in his seat, placed his cup down, and leant across the table. "Would you like to know what will happen if you say no?"

I didn't answer because it was clear enough, but he finished his threat anyway.

"Your family and everyone you love," he said. "Dead." He silently mouthed that last word and smiled that greasy smile again. I imagined the empty compound ringing with the music of the Dead Kennedys.

So did I do it? Yes, I did.

With tears prickling my eyes and under the curious observation of Johns, I led the little boy to that doorway. My Mother clung to my Father's arm. His baleful expression was fixed on Johns, his hands balling and unballing into fists.

All that was inside the boy was fear and confusion.

▽

On the other side, dead, cold earth under our feet, a phantasmal pulling and tearing at our clothes, and setting a rampike to cackling, rubbing its dead limbs together like malicious bones. I told him to stay where he was and that I would be back. He didn't understand, so I mimed that he should stay where he was and trusted to hope that he would still be there when I returned.

▽

When I stepped back through into my reality, Johns was standing a few feet from the doorway, eyes squinting, as if trying to discern the infinite worlds that lay beyond. He jumped back a little and let out a squawk, then he started clapping joyously.

"Bravo, bravo," he exclaimed. "Well done, Eli. A magnificent show." He reached into his pocket and withdrew a piece of paper with a sketch drawn on it, and some writing. "I assume our little problem with… Dolma Nyima has been resolved?"

"Yes," I said, fists clenched by my side. "He's gone."

"I know it's hard, Eli, but sometimes we have to do the hard things for the greater good," Johns said.

"One day," I replied, and strode towards the chapel and my room, "that is going to be you."

He laughed and clapped. "Bravo, Eli. Bravo. Very brave."

I watched from the landing as Johns walked out front, shook my Dad's hand, then got in the white van and drove away.

Not long after Johns had left, my Father knocked on my bedroom door and leant sheepishly next to it. He looked withered somehow, an old man. It hadn't occurred to me up until that point just how old my Father looked. It annoyed me that he didn't have the burden of guilt; his memory was clean of the boy now, though he had seen the boy's name in the Book of Names. I had written "SIX YEARS OLD" in angry cursive underneath his name, then: "Is this what we have become?"

I expected he had come to my room to rebuke me, but he looked concerned.

"What?" I asked bluntly.

"Eli…" He struggled to speak, pulled up a seat, and drew it close to my bed.

"I read what you wrote in the Book of Names, son," he started. "And I know it seems cruel, but you have to understand that the Lord works in ways that might not make sense at first, but given perspective—"

I cut him off with a cruel look.

"Really? Really, Dad?" I said. "Because, how do we know that the people we get rid of are the right people anymore? Who gets to decide anymore? Because it's not us."

He chewed his lip. "Your Grandfather called it the dispensation of heavenly judgement," he said.

"I know. I read his diary. The cycle was broken when Uncle Henry died. He would have been able to see that what we are doing is not right."

He let out a long sigh, his jaw muscles tightening at the mention of his brother. "Don't you think I know that?" he said. "Do you think I don't think about that?"

"It's not right, Dad. Sending little kids to…" I hesitated. "Utter desolation. You've seen it with your own eyes. For the Chinese government as well? Since when did we fucking start answering to them?"

His eyes went wide with shock, and I realised I'd possibly chosen the wrong moment to swear in front of my Dad for the first time.

"Sorry, but I don't like that man and I don't trust him," I said. "Johns or whatever his name is. He's not right. I mean he even *looks* like a bad guy."

He seemed to consider that for a moment, then flung his arms up.

"What should we do, then?" he said and began pacing the room. "What *can* we do? We must avert the end times. It's our edict. Our duty."

"Does it feel like the world is a better place to you?" I snarked.

"We have to do it," he replied, looking into his hands.

It was enough. I started crying uncontrollably and punched my leg in frustration. The words were jammed in my throat and I fought to get them out.

"You know why I did it? Why I took a child through to that place?" I asked.

He didn't say anything, just shook his head.

"Because Johns said he would kill everyone here if I didn't."

His eyes brightened, boldened a little. An idea that held the seeds of the violence that would follow shone in them. "Did he now?"

"Is that the actions of someone who wants to make the world better, someone who works for God?" I said.

He stood in thought for a moment.

"What are we going to do?" I asked.

"For the time being, we will wait and see," he replied, and then left.

▽

It was freezing cold on the other side. The hard earth below my feet was glazed in a thin, icy skin. Webs of glittering white frost traced the barren, scrubby ground. It was just past midnight and the boy was gone. How? I didn't know.

I had waited for three painful hours until everyone was asleep before I chanced rescuing him, but I was too late and he'd wandered off or already gotten killed somehow. I remember how guilty I felt as I cast around in the dark looking for any sign of him. The mud had frozen, so there were no footprints I could follow.

I crossed the field towards the collapsed house. Exposed lintels, broken tiles, brick covered in slippery rime, and an old steel bucket topped off with grue. A fine dusting of snow had fallen and settled in some areas, and in that I saw tiny shoe prints, drag marks from his robe. My relief was almost overwhelming as I followed the tracks, ducked in through the doorway, and saw a pale little face peeking out from under a toppled wooden cabinet.

I crouched and met his gaze. "Hey, over here." I waved to him and the boy slowly, tentatively crawled out. At least he was clever for a six-year-old. His skin was freezing and I rubbed his arms to get some warmth into him, then threw my jacket over him.

I held his hand and we walked across the field together again, and I took him back through. Twenty minutes later and we had crossed once more, this time into the boom box reality. I led him out of the ruined compound and along the road towards town. Above, a familiar moon lit the tops of the trees, the jagged void below darker than the sky itself. The road ahead seemed to swallow the light, and only small patches caught and reflected it. I wondered for a second what passing thought had occurred in the minds of all the players behind the boy's disappearance. Had his temporary re-emergence lit upon their dreaming psyches? Did they wake feeling guilty, anxious, angry? Did Johns surface from a dream, his sleep-addled mind lusting for utter desolation? Then, just as it came, the thought would have fled again, like smoke trailing after a candle. I wondered if another version of me had already done what I was doing. I wondered if he had done it earlier in his timeline, and that was why the compound had fallen to ruin.

It suddenly felt dangerous, and I pulled the boy closer to me. He had a backpack full of food and a note saying who he was and where he was from. I walked him into town to the police station and told him where to go. He was now a doppelgänger for this world to deal with.

On the way back, as the sky began to lighten, I walked by Jess's house. At that point, I had been there only twice before. Normally, it was a two-storey council house in the middle of a terrace. It was pebble-dashed, with most of the pebbles missing, and painted a faded peach colour. Her father had a yellow Capri that had deteriorated beyond any kind of mechanical resurrection. It was propped up on bricks in the drive next to a mouldy brown sofa and an overflowing bin.

In that reality, though, the house was painted a neat white. The drive was gone, replaced by a flowerbed filled with winter flowers, bright sprays of orange dogwood and yellow winter aconite, a small tree in the centre. At the outer borders, bare, brown tangles of roses were waiting for spring to bloom.

I waited nearby until the sun was up, just watching the house, until finally an old man emerged from behind the clean blue door.

"Excuse me," I said. I was suddenly aware it was still early and I looked a mess. The old man started a little.

"What do you want?" he said.

"Sorry to bother," I started. "But a girl used to live here. Her name was Jessica."

"Never heard of her," the man said.

"Oh," I replied, scratching my head. "She used to. Maybe she's moved."

The old man thumbed in the direction of the house. "We've lived here for twenty years. Perhaps she gave you a fake address?"

"Maybe," I said, considering the information.

"Do I know you?" the old man said. He scrunched up his face, visibly trying to make a connection in his brain.

"I… I don't think so," I replied.

"Ah. I know it!" he exclaimed, raising a finger in triumph. "You look just like that boy who lived at that compound. You know the one. The New…" he stammered. "The New Sunset Project or whatever it was they were called, that's the one."

"Never heard of them," I said.

"S'pose not. I read in the paper that they all died when the place burnt down. Heard tell they were killing people and doing sacrifices to the devil and what not, but you know how people are. All talk."

"Oh," I said. I felt my world constricting. I imagined another version of me burning alive. "I've got to go."

"Good luck finding your girlfriend," I heard him say after me, but I had already turned away. Running down the street towards the destroyed compound. A place where I would often go to relax, listen to music. A place where another version of me had died.

My head was pounding. The old reality hopping, centre-of-my-head pain, but it was manageable. The memory of what being chased through five realities felt like still lingered in my mind. It still does now.

$$\triangledown$$

When I arrived home, I fell fully clothed into bed and went straight to sleep. At midday, I was awoken by the sounds of prayer coming up through the floorboards. By then I had decided to skip prayer sessions, unless I was being forced to speak. So I could give voice to those who had been excised from this plane. I was jaded before, but my meeting with Johns had consolidated all of my doubts. I hadn't met my previous government handler, and the lackeys dressed in dark suits who used to bring the offerings rarely said anything. My Father must have spoken to them, but he never had much to say about them.

Behind a fractured sheet of ice over the windowpane, my family moved like shadowy ghosts through the back garden on the way to their quarters.

A few hours later and it was dark again. I couldn't stand the idea of being in the compound. What the old man at Jess's house had said kept playing over and over in my mind, so I slipped out into the freezing night. I needed to see Jess. I remember how clear the sky was then. How alive it was with the most stars I'd ever seen. As I climbed the hill and disappeared under the drooping arms of the trees, I imagined going to Jess's house, climbing up the drain and slipping into her room, then telling her everything. She always wanted to know what really went on at the compound, and I had always wanted to tell her. But I never did, because I didn't think she would believe me, and if she did, she would be disgusted with me, with what I was. But that night, I resolved to tell her. I believed I needed to.

When I finally arrived, I stood outside her house. The bed of flowers was gone, replaced by the usual car, sofa, and overflowing bin. I could see her striding backwards and forwards in her bedroom, raising her hands, throwing things. I could also hear the sound of a vicious argument. A dog in a back garden a few doors down started barking.

I watched helplessly as I saw the dark shape of her father cross the room and start hitting her. She screamed and then everything went quiet for a moment before he finally stood up and left the room. The light went out and the house fell silent. I stood there, hands balled into tight fists. I felt so frustrated and useless. It's not like I could've just gotten rid of him like I did Ronnie. I'd have completely lost her then.

I paced in a circle a couple of times and was about to leave when I heard a window opening. Looking up, I saw Jess climbing out. She carefully dropped a rucksack onto the rotted sofa and then lowered herself down the drainpipe near her room. She was so set on escaping, shoulders back, head down, and eyes fixed, that she didn't even notice me until she nearly bumped into me.

"Jesus, Eli. What the fuck?" she hissed. She grabbed me by my arm and pulled me along the road.

I felt stupid and suddenly very awkward. "I, er, came to see you," I offered weakly.

"Well, it's not a great time right now, actually," she said. "My dad just beat the fucking shit out of me."

Her lip was bleeding and her eye had started to swell up. She grimaced. I caught sight of the thin lines of blood between her teeth. She was on the verge of crying, and I was surprised she wasn't already.

"You should just leave, Jess. Please. You can't stay with him."

She barked a desperate laugh.

"And where am I going to go, genius?"

"What about Paul's?" I offered hesitantly.

She snorted. "He is just as bad. He thought I was cheating on him. I wasn't, obviously, but that didn't stop him."

"What? Why?"

"It's funny, actually. I was telling him about you," she said, and I felt that familiar heat starting to rise on my neck. "Then he got all jealous... and then *he* hit me. Which is not so funny, really. I guess all guys are the same, right?" She sniffed, brushed away a rivulet of tears, and spat.

I felt a flash of red-hot anger. "What the fuck, Jess? When did this happen?"

"A week ago. I guess we kind of broke up. I walked off. Heard he got into a fight with his boss at the arcade and got arrested."

She grabbed a packet of cigarettes from her back pocket and lit up with a match. As it flared, I saw the extent of what her father had done to her face. There was a cut in her forehead left by his ring, her cheek had swollen, and the white of her left eye was heavily bloodshot.

She offered me a cigarette and I took it. My hands were shaking so much with anger that it was hard to light it. I wanted to kill them both. Paul and her father.

"Why did your father just do that?" I asked.

She blew out a plume of smoke. "Sometimes he thinks I'm on drugs. Others, he thinks I'm my mother, or that it's my fault she's dead. Fucking hell, he doesn't even need a reason. Never did. He'll hit me because it's fucking Sunday." She looked me dead in the eye. "You know what it's like."

I did, although somehow it felt as if what my Father had done to me paled in comparison. My Father honestly did believe he was beating the spirits of those who'd been excised out of me. Yes, he hated me because he was envious of me, but his thrashings hadn't ever been random.

I wanted to tell her then. Very nearly blurted it out. What I was. What I did. The words were there, almost out, but I stalled. I couldn't offload that burden onto her. It wouldn't be catharsis—it would be the death of our friendship. It would be the death of any future that I wanted.

We started to wander aimlessly, just needing to get away from her house. As we walked down the street, the blue-grey light of TVs played across the ground. We walked on in silence for a moment. A car went past, two, and she flinched when the headlights spilled over her. A man walking a terrier crossed the street and turned up a side road, dipping in and out of the pools of orange streetlight until the pair of them were finally gone.

"So where are you going to go, then?" I asked, breaking the silence.

"Dunno. Was going to hang around town until the buses started and then go visit a friend in London. Maybe stay there for a few days, until my dad calms down," she said. She spat some loose tobacco from her lip. The filter of her cigarette was dark with blood. She sighed and rolled her neck. "Wanna hang out for a bit?" she asked.

"Yeah," I said, and then after a moment I added, "I'm not like those others, you know. Men, I mean."

"Wicked. I'll try not to cry," she said, and looped her arm through mine. We turned in the direction of town. "And… I know. I just have incredible taste in you lot."

Her knowing felt like an answer to two questions. One of which had never really been asked.

# Five

Have I seen the whole futuristic, shiny chrome version of the universe? Yes, I have. I've been to somewhere that resembles the whole clichéd sci-fi thing. It was breath-taking, with its impossibly tall skyscrapers, crazy technology. Flying cars for fuck's sake. I have been to a place that actually resembled *The Jetsons*.

Why don't I just live there, you ask?

Trust me, I've thought about it, but there are two problems. One: I can only ever seem to get there on my fourth or fifth jump, and that means all that good stuff I told you about before, like bleeding from my eyes. Two: they always seem to be built on the back of horrifying totalitarianism. One that I went to, from what I could tell before shortly puking and blacking out, seemed to have been built during a reigning Chinese empire. There were surveillance drones flying everywhere, masked police wearing elaborate armour patrolling the streets in strange-looking tanks. It really did put a crack in that shiny veneer.

I've been to versions of the world that exist in a state of extreme decline. Water shortages, global heatwaves, terrifying earthquakes every couple of hours, entire cities underwater. A lot of what I have seen is not hopeful. For a long time, that was what kept me doing what I do, and still does, for the most part. But now there are new reasons why I stay doing what I do.

By and large, though, the tattered fabric of all versions of reality seems to be fairly similar, except for the really bad stuff, of course.

Sometimes when I read sci-fi or fantasy stories and see the worlds the authors have written down, I wonder if they have a variation of my gift, like scrying, or seeing through the thinnest parts of this reality and into the next, because they write about places I have actually seen. Maybe they get a brief glimpse through a window into another reality and it inspires them.

When I really think about it, it's that little Dolma kid's fault that I am here right now. That was really the turning point for everything that happened afterwards. When I dropped him off at that police station, I was worried about him, sure, but was hopeful that he would be all right.

He was fine, by the way. In fact, you should see him now. He and his "long lost twin" are regularly on state television all over the world in that reality. He turned out okay. Shame China is in total control of both of them now, though. If only he knew the truth. Should I have stopped him when I had the chance? I wasn't going to kill a kid, so I think I did the right thing.

After that night where we walked from one end of the town to the other until morning, Jess and I spent more and more time together. I was clearly in love with her, and she obviously knew it. She never said she wasn't interested, and I suspected she was just waiting for me to make a move, but I am a dumbass and a coward and she was impatient. Well, I *was* a dumbass, at the time.

I hit the windscreen wipers to full, and it barely clears the curtain of stupid-heavy rain just long enough for me to see about ten feet in front of me. Blood-red rear lights leave bright comet trails behind them. I glance over my shoulder real quick to check on my guest. He's still out, or at least pretending to be. That's what I would do.

My guts hurt from the fight, and it feels a little like a rib might be broken. The place behind my eyes pulses with a headache, and all that leftover adrenaline in my system is making my teeth feel itchy. I also need to shit. This always happens after an altercation.

My exit comes up and I gingerly ease the van onto a long stretch of pitch-black country road. I turn the full beams on and can just about make out the dark fingers of branches, green hands of leaves, waving manically just inside the rough cone of light. The rain sounds like fists banging on the roof.

So, anyway, that night with Jess was an important one. She said to me once that that had been when she finally noticed me. Like, *noticed,* noticed me. All it would cost to seal the deal after that night was a tooth.

Jesus, I remember the conversation like it was yesterday. She was wearing my coat, her hands jammed up under her armpits. I was shivering but telling her I was fine, that I wasn't even cold. In actuality, I felt like I was about to pass out and never wake up, and I had clamped my jaws together to keep my teeth from chattering. We were standing at the bus stop outside Woolworths. Pale-blue sky above, the windows of the office block winking in morning light as a silver disc of sun crested the roof of the cinema and cast our shadows out long across the drab pavement. A bus went by, spewing a stinking, but gloriously warm, blast of exhaust as it passed.

I asked her if she wanted to stay at mine for a couple of days. She jumped at the offer, and so our conversation quickly turned to the logistics, and I found myself warmer, sweating, even. How she would have to hide (in my room, naturally) and what would happen if anyone found us. Guests were of course absolutely forbidden at the compound. Girlfriends, doubly forbidden. I waved off her concerns but then, suddenly, I felt sick at the idea of her seeing my room. Seeing the compound. It was too late, though. So, we walked home to the New Sunrise Project. I casually suggested that it might actually be a bad idea, but she ignored me.

We crawled under the hole in the face and together snuck upstairs to the top of the tower and into my room, no problem. After our nerves cooled off a little, we sat on my bed and she took the piss out of the meagre collection of music I had stashed in the hiding place under the floorboards. It consisted mainly of the albums she had given me copies of.

We slept.

Now, don't get me wrong. I offered to sleep on the floor, but she said no and we slept side by side. I remember that electric feeling of having way too much spit in my mouth as she emerged from the bathroom dressed only in her underwear and a tank top, my toothbrush sticking from her mouth. I remember her sliding into bed first and patting the quilt next to her, my breath steaming the air in the room. Her slowly relaxing into position against me, my arm numb underneath her head. I tried desperately not to prod her buttocks with the fiercest erection I think I've ever had in my life. I kept trying to smell her hair in a way that didn't seem like I was trying to capture her soul and keep it forever. The occasional long deep sigh, like I'd finally arrived at a home I never knew I had. Then, after the euphoria began to fade a little and my eyes adjusted to the dark, I saw the scars on her shoulder. Dark, jagged crescents set between the lean muscles of her back that followed the curve of her ribs.

"Hey," she whispered over her shoulder, "thanks for being my friend."

I still recall the quality of the light falling through the frosty windowpane as she started to gently snore. I had resolved myself to the idea that I was not going to sleep. I would stay up and just savour her proximity, commit as much as I could to memory.

I remember how suddenly angry I felt in that moment. My jealously at the fact that other guys had experienced this moment before me and had squandered it so carelessly. They had the person I most wanted, but had just thrown her away.

Lost in the memory of her skin against mine that first time, I don't see the deer dart out in front of me until it's far too late. I yank the wheel to the right. It doesn't do anything to save the animal, but what it does do is send the van careening off the road, through a huge hedge, and a fence, into a field. It lilts as the wheels turn and smash into the rutted ground of a farmer's field, sending a spray of mud skyward and splattering over the windscreen. Both feet are so hard on the brake and clutch peddles that I am almost standing up. Then the dark blur of the world in front of me goes sideways.

# My Troubled History, Part Five

When I woke, she was up on her elbows staring at me with a long white pillow feather between her fingers. It felt like a bizarre fever dream concocted by my obsessed brain. There was no way Jessica Locke, the feature of most of my waking thoughts and subject of my obsessional desire, was in my bed, tickling my nose with a feather. That was the sort of thing that happened in the magazines we found left by railway sidings, hidden inside conspicuous black bags. She most certainly could not have been in my bed smiling at me.

"Morning," she said. "And oh my god, you snore so fucking loud."

Then it all came back. It was real. It was actually happening. I remembered the quote my Grandfather had scrawled in his journal. We really were in the best of all possible worlds.

"Hey," I groaned. My eyes burned with the lack of sleep, and I was getting hungry.

She sat up, straightened the pillow behind her, and looked at me.

"I thought this place would be… I don't know. Weirder," she said after carefully considering my room again.

"Sorry to disappoint," I replied, following her sight lines.

"So, how come I haven't been here before?"

"If my parents knew you were here…"

"They'd sacrifice me to your Dark Lord."

I laughed, but as I thought about the Great Stone Door in the garden, the noise wilted in my throat. "Something like that. Though I think they would actually also kill *me*."

She got up and crossed the room, collecting her clothes as she went.

"So, like, how many people live here?" she asked.

"About fifteen families," I said. I watched as she slid into her jeans. She caught my eye as she was buttoning them up and I suddenly felt absolutely naked and completely awkward. I mumbled something about the number of houses in the compound, but she cut me off by placing a finger over her lips. Voices had started to drift up through the floorboards. The sounds of prayer and singing from the church below.

"Is that…" she started.

"Prayer," I said. "We do that a lot."

"Oh my god," she said, with a grin. "That is so fucking lame."

She watched me as I climbed out of bed, making a point of ogling me with the same creepy stare I had given her. When I had my own jeans on, she shrugged on her Guns N' Roses T-shirt and started hunting for her socks.

"Yeah," I said, "welcome to my life."

"So, shouldn't you be down there right now? Don't you, like, have to do that too? I always thought that type of shit was mandatory for you... types." She waved a hand at me dismissively. "Ah ha!" she picked up a sock.

"Not for me," I said. I didn't like where the conversation was going, but couldn't see a way to divert it. The sounds below me had never sounded so tuneless. I was embarrassed.

"Oh, how come?"

I shrugged. "I used to all the time."

"So you sung and shit?" she said. "Like *that*?"

"Yeah," I said, my face feeling suddenly very hot. "We all did."

I reached down, plucked her other sock from on top of my music stash, and threw it to her. She sat on the edge of the bed and pulled her socks on, then slipped her feet into battered shoes.

"So, tell me, Eli," she said, crossing her legs dramatically, one over the other, miming a TV interviewer. "Do you believe in God? I mean, what's your whole deal."

I shrugged again. "I dunno. I mean I used to. Maybe not in the whole 'one, single, all-powerful being' type of way. But there is definitely something."

"How can you be so sure? Isn't it just fucking programming or whatever from your parents?"

"I just know it."

She nodded. "Fair enough. My mum believed too. That's what my dad told me once. She had this really nice silver cross. It was her mum's," she said. She looked away, then shook her head. "That asshole tried to pawn it so he could buy vodka, so I keep it hidden."

"Do you?" I asked.

"What, believe in God?" she said and considered the question for all of a second before answering. "No. But if he does exist, fuck him."

An old, mostly suppressed part of me recoiled in horror at the statement.

"Some fucking old white dude with a big beard telling me how I should live my life." She hissed air through her teeth in contempt. "Fuck that. Plus, all the bad shit that happens in the world and he just watches on and does nothing as kids get cancer and die, and people are murdered in wars done in his name. What kind of an asshole does that?" She was on her feet now, fists clenched, knuckles paling. She stopped and took a deep breath. "I'm sorry if that's attacking what you believe. I just—it's just not fair, is it?"

"It's okay," I said. "I don't believe in that. Not really."

I was so close to spilling the words I had rehearsed a hundred times.

"So why do you even live here anymore?" she asked.

I could think of a million reasons why I had to. I had nowhere else to go. I had the government threatening to kill my family if I didn't comply. I hadn't truly considered running away before, not really.

"And why do you live up here? *Here* here I mean, at the top of a fucking church?" she asked before I could answer the previous question. "Seems a bit hypocritical, no?"

"I'm…" I started.

More prayers from downstairs floated up. My Father's deep tenor could be heard.

"Let us give praise," he boomed. I felt a sudden rush of panic. A choir of voices below repeated the words.

"C'mon, let's go," I said, hastily throwing on the rest of my clothes, putting my T-shirt on inside out and then back to front. "Fuck it," I exclaimed, finally getting it right.

"Wait," she said, a sly smirk on her face. "I have to hear this."

"Thank you for the generous bounty that we receive every day," my Father continued.

"No. I want to go. We should—" I said.

"Shh shh shh," she said, and pressed a finger to my lips.

"We give praise for the lives that you permit us to continue. For the best of all possible worlds that we might enjoy the fruit of His divine work."

"I really don't think—" I started, but she shut me up with a look.

"And for Eli, your right hand. The divine Key. The weapon of your choosing, a scythe to be wielded so that this world may continue to flower and blossom."

Jess's eyes went wide. As wide as I have ever seen them. She pointed at me accusingly.

"Are they talking about *you*?" she whispered.

"No," I tried to say, but she was wagging her finger at me now.

"I can't fucking believe it," she straightened in mock pride. "Me, friends with the right hand of God. And here I was, fully under the impression that you were just a normal asshole."

She curtsied low. "Your Scythe-ness," she said in a posh voice, then threw herself on my bed and started laughing hysterically into my pillow.

When she had finally recovered, she sat up.

"What does that even mean?" she asked.

I stammered a couple of non-words as I scrambled for an explanation. Knew that the truth was just there, waiting to be plucked out of the air like a physical thing and given to her. I wanted to, I really did. I could feel the words spilling from my lips, could already see her reaction to it. But somehow, I couldn't do it. So I just shrugged.

"It's a cult. What do you want me to say?" I flung myself into the chair. "My Father wants me to take over after him, so this is how they do it. Tell them that I am a prophet of some kind to be followed after he dies."

"And are you going to?"

"Fuck knows. I don't want to." I imagined Johns sitting in my kitchen, rocking back in the chair and smiling that oily smile. Delivering vanloads of kids for me to dispose of. My lip started quivering. I didn't want to think about it.

She leaned forward and the bedsprings creaked. The prayer ended and a song broke out. I knew it well, "The God In-between Chose a Happy Path." My great-grandfather had written it to the tune of some old folk song.

"So why don't you just leave, then?" Jess asked.

I imagined the violence that would ensue if I did. Johns appeared in my mind again. This time smiling as he casually murdered my family.

"I can't." I said. My eyes flicked to the window, to the three mossy stones sat upon the dais. I thought about the other versions of the compound I had seen in other universes. All the ones that had gone, been burnt down, torn down, empty.

"Maybe we both could," she said. "You know, fuck off down to Brighton for a year or two. Then, go to uni or something."

"What would you study?" I asked, taken by the idea.

"Music, obviously. Maybe art or fashion," she said. "Fuck it, I don't know."

I imagined us escaping, making it to the coast. Spending our days in a little flat in Brighton. Warm light spilling in through a skylight as we lay in bed, her head on my chest. She would study art and throw up these big oil paintings, and we'd show them at trendy galleries. But then, as the sound of the song below us rose, reality surfaced again.

I shook my head. The hope of that idea stung bitterly. It was all that I wanted, but I couldn't take it.

"Stop," I said. It sounded harsher than I intended, because I wanted it to be possible so much.

"All right," she said. "It was just a fucking idea."

"I know," I said, softening my voice. "I want that, believe me. I just can't."

"I get it," she said. "You can't leave your shitty life and I can't leave my shitty life, and so we both have to just fucking deal with it and get on with it."

I wondered why I couldn't just say yes. Why I could only say sorry. She looked hurt as she shouldered past me and went to the door.

"Wait," I said after her, but she wasn't listening. I grabbed her shoulder and she pulled away from me.

"Get the fuck off me," she said and ripped my hand away. She spun and looked me dead in the eye.

I raised my hands in entreaty. "I have to get you out," I explained.

She rolled her eyes, crossed her arms. "Fine." She stepped to one side and I led her down the creaky wooden stairs. The sound of the song reached its apex, a loud refrain of "Thank you Lord, for the path you have set that leads us to paradise."

We went left into the long hallway, past the room my Grandad died in, and continued through the interlocking buildings until we got to the front of the compound. I led her out the front door and across the gravel drive to the tall gate.

"Thanks for letting me stay," she said bitterly, and was gone.

▽

### December 25, 1995

I hadn't seen Jess since that day and had fallen into a depressed funk, deciding to deal with what had happened by listening to the Cure, the Smiths, Tom Waits, and Bruce Springsteen.

You know, the real fucking heartbreak music.

Dancing to music whose creators seemed to know me intimately. Dancing in my underwear to "Boys Don't Cry" by the Cure, crying.

It was clear that I had had my chance with her and fucked it up by saying no, by letting reality intrude on her dream. I was just thinking about this very fact, and how I would try to make it up to her somehow before we started school again in January, when a stone roughly the size of an adult's fist sailed through my window, caught me just above the eye, and split my forehead open. For an instant, just before I let out a high-pitched yelp, my first thought was that I had been shot. Sobbing already, I threw my hands up to my face and blood streamed between my fingers and splashed onto the floorboards.

I ran to the bathroom and inspected the wound. It was only a glancing blow, but a dark-red line cut through my eyebrow where the edge of the stone had hit me. It stung and pulsed with electric pain in time with my heartbeat.

I ran to the broken window, a wad of blood stained tissue pressed hard to the side of my face and I tried to match the trajectory of the rock to its point of origin. It was a good shot, I had to give them that. My attacker must have been able to throw the stone almost the length of the compound to reach the window. That, or they were inside the perimeter. My bed was covered with broken glass.

"Fuckers."

In a sudden fury, I threw on some clothes and ran downstairs, flying past Steven, who had a foot on the bottom step.

"What was that?" he said.

"Nothing," I shouted.

"Are you okay? You're bleeding."

"I'm *fine*, obviously."

I grabbed a broom that was leaning against the front door and ran out into the night, the cold gravel crunching underfoot as I crossed the drive to the gates. I craned my neck to see if I could see anyone, but the road was empty on both sides.

Steven appeared behind me, eyes wide as saucers.

"Eli, you sure you're okay?"

"I'm fine," I called back. "Just some asshole fucking with me," I muttered, and he disappeared back inside.

The freezing-cold gate scraped and squealed as I yanked it open and stepped out onto the thin strip of pavement beyond. The frigid night air carried the sighing hiss of the wind through the trees. A bat looped in an erratic circle around the melting lozenge of orange light from a streetlight and chattered. Blood continued to run down the side of my face and slowly pattered onto the road.

My attacker had fled or had hidden somewhere and I was suddenly afraid that a second rock would coming arcing out of the dark and hit me in the face. So I spun on my heels and went to head back inside. As I did, I saw leaning against the compound's fence a small box, neatly wrapped in red-and-white Christmas paper and tied with green string. Stuck to it with a thin square of sellotape was a card. I picked it up and turned the card over in my hand. Written in big looping handwriting that I recognised instantly was my name.

Of course it was her. She had a knack for being brutal and then suddenly nice. Why change for Christmas? I realised she had been trying to get my attention with the rock and had misjudged the throw somewhat.

I looked up and down the street for her, a big smile on my bleeding face, but she was nowhere to be seen. I went back inside, closed the door, and climbed the stairs back to my room, which was already noticeably colder. I threw myself down into my chair and tore into the wrapping paper.

Inside the box was her red Walkman and a cassette. She had made me a mixtape. On the case, she had drawn a skull surrounded by flames. I pulled the card out and rubbed my thumb gently over the indented pen marks, felt the soft edges of the flames. On the inside she'd written the track listing and at the top "Eli's Mix."

I was smiling like an idiot as I slipped the headphones over my ears, slotted the tape in, and hit go. The opening guitars of "Love Will Tear Us Apart" came in and I felt a wave of goosebumps prickle the flesh up my arms and neck. I must have listened to the whole ninety-minute tape three times that night.

I slipped a finger under the edge of the envelope and carefully tore the card open. On the front was a fat Father Christmas riding behind an exhausted set of reindeer. Inside, she'd written:

*My Dearest Eli,*

*Happy Xmas, you massive bellend.*

*I'm sorry about last time.*

*We are playing a gig at the arcade on New Year's, wanna come?*

*Hail Satan.*

*J*

*X*

I held the card up to my nose and sniffed, hoping to catch some scent of her, but it just smelt of dry paper and faintly of ink. Still, just imagining her writing it made me happy.

I cleaned the glass off my bed as Iron Maiden's "Fear of the Dark" bounced and snarled in my ears, shutting out the rest of the world. As I brushed the last remnants of the glittering dust into my bin and shook my covers out, I plotted my escape from the compound on New Year's.

▽

**New Year's Eve 1995**

The streets were full of people dancing and singing. Huge crowds had gathered outside both of the town's pubs and people stood in the cold holding pints, smoking cigarettes, and shouting at each other. The atmosphere seemed somehow incredibly positive, like a brief wave of something hopeful had lit upon everyone. It had been a shit year, and people everywhere seemed to be eager to see '96 in.

My family normally stayed up for the countdown and then we all went into the church for a midnight prayer. I had managed to skip it by pretending to be ill for most of the day before and then going to bed early. I waited until just after nine, and then snuck out.

Fireworks hissed and screamed in bleeding white arcs, then cracked and burst, blooming in burning flowers in the clear sky above the arcade. Crowds of teenagers oohed and ahhed—well, the ones who didn't think they were too cool to did, anyway. The cold night smelt of gunpowder and alcohol. That sense of hope and intangible feeling of good had caught me, too. A buzz I hadn't felt before or since permeated the general mood. Maybe it was me, geed up and full of nerves at the idea of finally seeing Jess's band play for the first time. She would spot me in the crowd and dedicate a song to me. Afterwards, she would come out into the mass of sweaty people and tell me how much she missed me. How all the songs on the mixtape she had made me meant all the things that I thought they did. Then, just as midnight struck, we would kiss. She would finally see me as I wanted her to and realise that I was who she had wanted all along.

When I first played that fantasy in my head it seemed ridiculous, but by the time I'd arrived at the arcade, I was almost convinced it was going to happen.

I shouldered my way through the busy throng hanging about outside—punk kids, a few metalheads with black- and red-dyed long hair wearing Pantera T-shirts and full-length leather jackets, the geeky kids, and some normals, as we called them. I recognised a couple of them as friends of Jess, others were strangers, stragglers who had found their way there because of the fireworks show or just wanted something different. I stood outside for a moment, watching the movement of everyone coming and going, laughing and swearing. A lot of them were drinking. You have to

understand, England in the mid-'90s, man—
everyone under eighteen was getting hammered on
Mad Dog 20/20 or Thunderbird and passing out in
parks with their friends. A small group of kids,
clearly a couple of years younger than me, was
clustered around a spotty-faced boy cradling a bottle
of Jack Daniels in a paper bag. He took a swig, his
entire body shivered, he had a coughing fit, and
then he passed the bottle to one of the other boys,
and he did the same.

An old man with a stroller stood at the bus
stop nearby and flicked a cigarette butt into the road
as a few cars drove by slowly, their passengers' faces
pressed flat against the glass as they craned to look
up at the light show.

My heart was beating far too fast and my
hands were far too sweaty as I pushed past a couple
at the *Time Crisis* machine and stood back from the
stage that had been built at the far end of the room.

She was talking to the drummer and laughing,
throwing her head back and gesturing animatedly.
The guitarist was noisily tuning up, and then, as if
unplanned, a wave of feedback broke over the
sound of murmuring and general human noise. She
pounded at the strings with her palm, making waves
of distortion ring throughout the room. The bassist
looked over at the guitarist, who gave a nod, and a
heavy rumbling bass line started. It cut across the
distorted guitar rhythm and a few seconds later it
stopped completely as the drums exploded with
noise.

Jess turned, raised the mic up, and started
shouting.

The crowd loved it. Some of them seemed to
know the song already and started shouting along.

More people filed in from outside, and the arcade got very warm very quickly.

I wanted to dance, to feel the songs running through me, but I was transfixed by her—a demon version of her that I barely recognised. She raised her fist confidently as she delivered the chorus in a throaty roar, "I am not one of you," over and over.

For the next forty minutes the band ripped through their set, not stopping for anything, aside from one small break where Jess screamed, "We are the Rotten Ones, and we are coming for your kids." Then they burst into "Doll Smasher."

I tried to get her to see me, raising my arms up, but she never did. Or at least she gave no indication that she had.

The set ended with a crescendo of distortion and feedback that made me wince, hands over my ears. It felt like I'd slipped three realities away and my brain was turning inside out.

"Fuck you and goodnight," she said just before she dropped the mic, a final burst of feedback ringing out, making everyone cover their ears until the sound engineer shut it down.

The venue burst into applause and cheers.

I watched her as people came up as the band was packing up their kit, patting her on the back, kissing her on the cheek, hugging her. Little sparks of jealousy flared and died. It felt surreal to see her in that context, like she was a different person entirely.

When she was done she jumped down from the riser and wove through the crowd, which was still milling about, waiting on '96.

I waved as she walked near, and when she finally spotted me, her eyes went wide and she waved back, a smile creasing her features. I smiled back sheepishly. All my thoughts and all those practised greetings fled in the few seconds it took for her to wander over.

"Hey there, stranger," she shouted at me, then pulled me into a tight and sweaty hug.

"Hey," I stammered, my face turning briefly red. "This place is rammed."

"I know, it's crazy. This is like the biggest gig we've played so far. What did you think?"

"Amazing. You were amazing." My eyes went wide. "All of you guys, I mean. So fucking cool."

"Thank you. I'm so glad you liked it," she said, and puffed up her cheeks. "It was so fun Jesus Christ, I'm sweating my fucking tits off."

I tried not to stare.

She cocked her head and looked at the scab on the side of my face. "What the fuck, Eli," she exclaimed. "What happened?" She touched it tenderly with a finger.

I winced. "Um, that was you actually."

"What?" she said. Then it clicked into place. "The stone?" Her hands fled to her mouth, eyes crinkled in anticipation of the answer.

I nodded. "Hit me straight here," I said pointing to the wound. "Blood everywhere."

"Oh shit! Oh my god. I am *so* sorry," she cried.

"I thought I'd been shot," I said. "Thought I was being assassinated."

She doubled over laughing. After about a minute or so of watching her shoulders bob up and down, only occasionally stopping to look up at my face before going back to it, she regained her composure. Eyes streaming and her makeup running, she said, "I'm really so sorry. Oh my god, my stomach hurts. You ruined my makeup, you cunt."

"It's okay, I can see you are really cut up about the whole thing," I said, and she was away laughing her ass off again.

When she finally stopped, she straightened up and swiped her sleeve at her eyes.

"Honestly, though, it's fine. I mean, I got a Walkman out of it," I said. "Thank you, by the way. It's a wicked gift."

"Really?" She swiped a finger under her eye.

"I love it. Even if I did nearly get blinded."

"Stop it," she said. "Don't make me laugh again. I'm so sorry," she repeated, but a smirk crept onto her features and she began to chuckle again.

"What did you think of the tape?"

"Hmmm, questionable," I said, stroking my chin with exaggerated movements. "I mean, it's okay, but not worth nearly dying for."

"You motherfucker! That mixtape is *gold*," she shouted.

"'Livin' on a Prayer?'" I said. I couldn't tell her that it had just become one of my top ten favourite songs. The other nine also being the songs on the tape.

She punched me playfully in the arm. "I love that song," she said. "It. Has. A. Classic. Chorus." She hit me in time with the words.

"I really loved it though, thank you," I said, and she stopped hitting me.

"That's better," she replied. We caught each other's gaze just then, and it felt like the arcade had begun to melt away. It was just me and her, surrounded by a sea of blur and noise.

"I didn't get you anything," I said sheepishly. "But, I will. I promise."

"You asshole," she joked. "You wanna play for a bit, till the countdown?" She pointed in the direction of the *Tekken* machine. Two kids had just finished and were wandering towards the *Sega Rally* machine.

"Hell yeah," I said.

It was after about twenty minutes of getting my ass handed to me on *Tekken* that I heard his voice. Her ex, Paul. His rough North London accent cutting above the noise of the machines and the music.

"Oi oi, fucking oi. Look who it is," he said.

We both turned to face him. He was standing there in a powder-blue puffer jacket and a pair of big black boots that he had tucked his jeans into, his greasy brown hair slicked back. He was with a bunch of similarly dressed idiots, each one wearing the same dumb expression. One, a rotund manbaby with a rash of spots across his cheeks and a wispy goatee, laughed. His pint sloshed in his hand, dripped through his pudgy fingers onto the sticky floor, as the other two headed for the bar.

"Paul," Jess said.

He sidled up to her, altogether too close, and she pressed her back into the arcade machine as far as it would go. I glared at him, and acne manbaby pushed a fat finger into the place where my shoulder met my chest.

"Better leave the lovers to it, eh?" he said, threateningly.

I stayed where I was, eyes fixed on him.

"I was wondering where the fuck you been. Your dad said he didn't know where the fuck you'd gone."

"I've been around. Busy gigging and shit, you know how it is," Jess said. Her voice quavered, breath caught high in her throat.

"Too busy for me?" Paul exclaimed. He clutched his chest in faux pain. "Your *boyfriend*," he hissed through gritted teeth, forcing a smile that implied only imminent violence. He pressed in even closer to her, pushing the groin of his jeans into hers. He ran a hand through her hair.

"Paul," she said, trying but failing to extricate herself from his grip. "We broke up."

He caught her wrist, squeezed it, and she drew in a sharp breath. I moved, but a hand pushed me back.

"Don't get any fucking ideas," acne manbaby said. Beer sloshed at our feet.

Not far from where we were was a doorway. Where it led, I didn't know, but I had half a mind to see if I could take the scarred mess of a man in front of me through.

"But I miss you," Paul said to Jess. With his free hand, he squeezed her cheeks together, bunching her lips up, and he went in for a kiss. Her eyes went wide and she looked in my direction. "You've gotta forgive me, yeah?"

I looked at her, at Paul, at the tub of shit in front of me, and at the two other idiots walking back with drinks in their hands. I could have walked away. The last time I did this for her, I got the shit kicked out of me and I didn't actually help. She would have gotten over it eventually. She might even have understood that the odds weren't fair. I tried to rationalise my inaction to myself, but I couldn't bring myself to believe it.

"Ah, fuck it," I whispered. Who could say—I might be useful this time.

"Whatchoo say?" The manbaby leered and brought his face close to mine.

I said nothing, and then head-butted him square in the nose as hard as I could. A bright white flash of pain erupted across my vision. Blood flew in a crimson arc as his head snapped back and he tottered into an arcade machine. He threw his hands up to his face, dropping his drink. It splashed everywhere. Paul looked down at the floor, at his friend, and then at me. His face contorted into a sneer. He was about to snarl something at me, but Jess kneed him as hard as she could in the balls and he folded in half, all the air leaving him with a wheeze.

She pushed him away and he gave a moan, falling sideways into the spilt beer.

"Run!" she shouted, and we started fighting through the crowds of people.

Paul's other friends were back from the counter now, and they stared wide eyed at the two men, one with a broken nose bleeding all over the place and the other on his side being sick next to the *Tekken* machine, giddy noises from the cabinet thrilling the air with digitised fighting sounds, jingling coins, and mechanical arms moving inside glass cubes.

The manbaby with the broken nose pointed a pudgy finger at me and I watched as the other two scanned the room until they spotted me staring. I turned and ran in the direction Jess had gone. Slipping on spilt lager, I fell sideways into a machine, regained my footing, and then bounced into someone's shoulder. My feet crumpled underneath me, and I hit the floor. A few seconds later, I was dragged up by the two men. They were clearly at least five years older than me. One had the beginnings of a beard. The other, a fistful of gold rings. I remember that, because he punched me across the jaw as the other held me, the blow whipping my head from left to right and turning the world a phosphorous white. I felt a tooth loosen a little on one side as my mouth started to fill with the iron tang of blood.

I tried to wriggle free as the world spun around me, but with little result. He hit me again, this time in the stomach, sending all the air out of me.

He wound up to hit me again, a cruel grin on his face as he did. I flung my head back and head-butted the man holding me, catching him under the chin and cracking his jaws together in a crunch. Just as I did, Jess appeared with a fire extinguisher in her hand. She swung it with both hands into the knee of the man who was doing all the punching. It gave a sickening thud, and he collapsed screaming, clutching at his leg.

"Fucking, come on," she screamed.

I wriggled free of the hands holding me just as Jess pulled the pin on the extinguisher and the arcade started to fill with thick white smoke. The place erupted in chaos and she grabbed my hand and dragged me through the crowd of panicked people. Outside in the winter air, people were coughing and gagging. Fireworks popped and fizzed high above. A white flash followed by a huge boom lit the street. The world lilted as I fought to breathe, fought to stay on my feet. My tongue already worrying at the loose tooth.

People streamed out of the arcade behind us as we ran, me looking back to see if Paul and his cronies were following. We ran past Blockbuster and all the other closed shops, along the strip of dark street, and down a hill towards the neat rows of houses and a vague constellation of lit windows. A cab passed by, and slowed. We flinched, expecting Paul to come barrelling out of the dark vehicle, but after a moment, it accelerated past and disappeared down the street.

My legs were burning, my mouth was tacky with blood and stinging, my stomach felt like glass, it hurt to take in a lungful of air.

"Stop. Stop," I wheezed, trying to get air into me and finding that it only burnt all the more from sucking in the cold.

Jess stopped, put her hands on her hips and blew hard, her breath pluming upwards. Nearby a house party was raging, and the sound of bass drum thudded out into the night like an erratic heartbeat.

"He's such a cunt," she said. She stalked back and forth in front of me as she said the words.

"Well, you do pick 'em, don't you?" I said, then spat out a mouthful of blood.

"Oh, ha ha," she said sarcastically. "Are you okay?"

I looked at her for a moment. "No. Not really."

She smirked at the recent memory, then her smile got a little wider. "I can't believe you head-butted David right in the nose. That was fucking amazing. You know he's a boxer?"

"No shit?!" I said. "It hurt like fuck. I can't believe you kneed a man so hard in the nuts he threw up. It reminds of when you…" I paused. She hadn't done it in this reality. "A friend of mine kicked this other guy in the balls one time and…" I trailed off, but she didn't notice.

"Oh my god. I'm surprised I managed to find his tiny fucking balls to be honest." She looked at me, dolefully, then came over and gave me a hug. She smelt of booze, sweat, and deodorant.

"That was truly amazing, Eli," she said. "No one's ever stood up for me like that. We need to find you a nice girl who'd appreciate a knight in shining armour. What about Alice?"

I scrunched up my face. "Nah. I'm not into her."

She rolled her eyes at me. "Jesus, Eli. You are so picky. You should just, you know, experiment or something."

"I don't really want to. It's not my thing."

"What, sex isn't your thing? Having fun isn't your thing? Eli, you do realise you don't have to marry the first person you fuck, right. I mean, it's not in that religion thing you do, is it?"

"Of course it's not. I just don't want those other girls." I tried to stop it, but the words were already forming. "Jesus fucking Christ, are you really that blind? Do I actually have to say it? All I want is you. I thought that might have been obvious, but apparently not."

There it was. That awful space between us had been filled with the words that were going to bury me or save me.

She looked away and my stomach dropped out.

"No, you don't," she said. "You think you do, but you really don't."

"That's bullshit," I said. "You are the only person I've ever wanted, and sometimes I think you want that too, but then you go off with all those other guys, and it kills me. It fucking kills me. Because they all treat you like shit. They treat you like your dad does."

"Shut the fuck up, Eli. You don't know what you're talking about."

"I know you deserve something better."

"No," she said. "*You* do. I've been trying. You think I don't notice your fucking puppy dog eyes? You think I want to string you along? I want you to be happy, I really do. But I can't give you that. I'm broken. I'm so fucking broken."

"And you think I'm not. There are things, Jess—things that I haven't told you about. You think *you're* broken? I'm a Million. Fucking. People. Jammed inside my fucking brain." I punched the side of my head in time with the words. She took a step forward.

"Stop it!" she yelled. "You're not. You're my Eli. The sweet boy who's just put his heart in the wrong place."

"That's not true, Jess. I want you so fucking much. It's all I think about. You are all I think about."

She came in close, her face level with mine. We were both crying. "You don't know me. You just project all these fucking things you think I am on to me. I'm not that person," she whispered, shaking her head. "I'm not a good person."

Somewhere a countdown had started. Then we heard it from the house party behind us, from the houses all around us, through all the streets. It was the New Year coming in, but it felt like a countdown for me to tell her some magical combination of words that would make her change her mind. Make her want me. I closed my eyes and waited for the moment to pass. It was too late to change anything now, and I let out a breath. A cheer went up followed by clapping and whoops, and a drunken, slurred version of "Auld Lang Syne" started in the house nearest us.

I was defeated, crushed by the weight of my hopeless desires.

As the countdown finished I felt her lips on mine.

If it's possible to sigh with your whole body, I did it, because that is what it felt like as her shaking fingers found my lumpy, painful cheeks, then got lost in my hair, and finally clasped the back of my head tightly as she pulled me in.

The sour taste of blood in both our mouths now.

# Six

I asked her later on if she had the chance to get rid of Paul, erase him from the timeline altogether, would she do it, and she said yes. He'd hurt her more than once over the course of their relationship. We sat at the back of the top deck of the bus and she told me that, when they'd broken up, he punched her in the stomach so hard she passed out. He ran off because he thought she might have died somehow, and he was carrying drugs.

She called me sweet when I got so angry that I felt the sting of tears on my cheeks, paced back and forth, fists clenched until they were pale at the knuckles. I wanted to take that back, I wanted to protect her from that ever happening in the first place, but I realised in that same moment that I wasn't going to. My own desire for her overrode my willingness—and my actual ability—to make her happier, to disappear Paul and her wounds at the same time. It was a dark moment for me, and I tried to justify it. I had finally gotten what I wanted for once, and there was no way I was going to jeopardise that. I had already given up a version of her once before and I wasn't going to do that again, even if it meant she suffered for it.

I asked her why she had gone out with Paul, and she just shrugged and said he seemed different, just like all the rest of them *before*, just like me.

I got mad that she lumped me in with all her other bad choices, when actually she was right. With my history and what I could do, I would only ever be bad for her. In comics, the romantic interest of the superhero always suffers. I wanted what the sacrifices clung to so desperately as I ushered them from this reality into the next.

Love.

What did I learn about myself from that conversation on the bus, as we followed the circuitous route through town and looped back, heading finally towards the garage? The world outside seen through the foggy lens of the condensation over the windows, a dreamlike ghost town lit by the sickly yellow of shop windows, the intermittent glow of TVs illuminating takeaways. What dark knowledge lit inside of me, knowing that I would put my happiness over hers? That it felt like such a mundane evil. That maybe I was selfish enough to believe that the prize for her suffering would be me, the man who could fix her. Jesus, I was so fucking stupid. Did I even stop to consider what an idiot I was, or was it just another passing thought, like a cloud drifting in front of the sun on a summer's day, making me momentarily cold and then becoming almost instantly forgotten?

▽

I hack and cough as the world slowly resolves itself. My vision swims in and out of focus. My head is filled with a throbbing pain, like a pounding heartbeat in my ears, and it takes me a fuzzy second to realise where I am. A van. Somehow parked in the middle of a field. Mud sprayed all up the cracked windscreen, all over the windows. We've rolled over a couple of times, my guest and I.

My guest.

I steal a painful look over my shoulder. One of the back doors has come off, the other is hanging open, showing the ripped-up earth and trail of destruction behind us. He is hanging upside down from the passenger rail like Batman, both feet planted on either side of it and pulling at it with all his bodyweight, a low grunt escapes his blood-stained mouth as he strains.

"Fuck," I say, understatement in times of crisis being my best skill.

The passenger rail pops off with a metallic ping and I hear the air being smacked out of my passenger as he lands on his back. I turn and fumble my door handle and it comes away in my hand.

"Shit it."

I elbow the window, once, twice, and then it shatters. I try to climb out the window, but I'm stuck. My seatbelt is still on.

"Fuck and shit it."

I unclip it, land awkwardly on the windscreen, and push myself out the window, hitting the soft, wet earth below. My head is swimming. I get to my feet thinking about internal bleeding, broken ribs poking soft lungs, blood clots. I hurt, but everything moves for the moment. A warm line of blood drips from just above my eye. I put a hand on it and my fingers come away dark.

My target is out of the van now and hobbling across the field towards the road.

# My Troubled History, Part Six

**January 28, 1996**

I was in my room, listening to Pearl Jam, when my Father knocked on the door. He didn't know I had a girlfriend yet, but he would soon. His brown hair had turned grey. It hadn't taken long to transition into an old man. Since our last conversation about the little Tibetan boy, Dolma, we had been getting along okay. He hadn't hit me for years, but whenever he came into my room, I still felt anger in my stomach at the memory of it.

He stepped in and scowled at me. He had seen the Walkman before and had accepted that it was a gift, but he hated it as much as the music I listened to.

Shortly after Jess introduced me to grunge and alternative music, I had bought a copy of *Kerrang!* magazine and made the rather ballsy mistake of putting a foldout poster of Kurt Cobain up on my wall. My Dad freaked when he saw it. He screamed that I was desecrating this holy place with that filthy music and tore it down. I was tempted to put up a poster of Marilyn Manson next, but I couldn't do it for fear of actually being murdered. But I was still heavily into him for a while—although anything not produced by Trent Reznor feels like a wasted opportunity in my opinion.

I pulled my headphones off, the faint sound of Eddie Vedder singing on "Black" filling the awkward space between us. I knew he wanted to admonish me for the Walkman, but saw him swallow it instead.

"That man from the government, Johns, is here. He wants to talk to you."

I rolled my eyes and huffed. "Fuck's sake," I exclaimed, and my Dad winced. "I don't want to talk to that wanker."

"Listen," he said as he perched on the end of my bed. "I know you hate him. Your mother and I have been talking about it. Things are different now. You were right—this world isn't getting better. It's getting sicker, and somehow our great work has become perverted." He shook his head. "This, Johns," he spat the name. "He's got the devil in him. I have a plan, but you have to buy us some time so we can prepare."

I knew where this all was going—I didn't need to be a Seer to predict the outcome. I had seen my Father and a few of the others toiling away, extending the basement under the main house. The big pile of earth outside the back fence of the compound. I'd seen the shotguns and hunting rifles lining the mud walls, lit by naked bulbs that hung from hooks in the raw, packed earth. I knew where we were heading. Full Waco. I thought about the abandoned compounds I'd seen, what all the other versions of me may or may not have done to stop it from happening. It was paralyzing.

"You don't have to keep doing this," he said gravely, his voice hoarse. "Your Mother and I want you to tell him no more, it's over. I tried to tell him, but he won't listen to me. We'll find another way to do our God-given task. Go back to the old way somehow. Maybe we should just stop doing it altogether until you have a son and our family has a Seer again, so we can be sure we are doing His great work. Make sure we are doing it right." He looked down at his trembling hands.

"Dad. I never killed them," I said, expecting him to explode again. Expecting him to act as he always did. But instead he nodded, his features brightening a little.

"Good," he said, placing a hand on my shoulder. "Then we may be able to fix things yet."

I smiled weakly, relieved. My mind went back to wondering what might happen after I said no to Johns. Other versions of me had most likely said no before I did, and I'd seen the results.

Johns was sitting in the kitchen, drinking tea as he had last time, wearing the same suit, too. It could have been a continuation of our last conversation. The only difference was that he seemed slightly less well groomed. He also had a thick shadow of stubble on his cheeks. Seemed to be the fashion for assholes at the time.

"Well, well, Eli," he said, raising the teacup in a salute. He swept his free hand across the table and gestured at the empty chair opposite. "Take a seat, my boy."

I sat down and met his curious gaze with my own angry glare. He just smiled.

"Your Father," he said, then paused to sip some tea, "informed me that he is no longer happy with our arrangement. I tried to impress upon him the importance of your work to the government, to the ongoing objectives of the House of August. Our long history of cooperation to make the world a better place." I gave a loud snort but he ignored it and carried on. "I tried to appeal to his pride. I commiserated with him about the great burden that you have to bear. But he was still quite adamant."

He placed his cup delicately back in the saucer and leant forward. "I take it that I can trust you to convey to him what little choice you have in this matter, and the potentially... lethal consequences of discontinuing our relationship?"

I shook my head and sneered, channelling my best Johnny Rotten.

"No. He's right—I. Ain't. Doing. It. No. More." I tapped the table with my finger to punctuate it.

Johns laughed, and for a moment I was taken aback, my punk mask slipping a little, and I almost faltered.

"I can't live with it," I said. "It's too much."

Johns himself sneered then. He leant further forward across the table until he wasn't far from my face and bared his teeth. "Well that's just tough shit. The world is a cold, horrible, and hungry place, but we have do our best to save it, don't we? We all have to do our part to improve it."

"And you think asking me, a teenager, to kill people for the government, to wipe people's histories away so they never existed, is *doing my part*?" I said, then jabbed a finger at him. "You're fucking insane, mate."

His mask of calm friendliness slipped back on and he smiled again, an easy smile, one that was somehow laced with the threat of violence. I'd been scared of what he could get *other* people to do, but up until that moment, I wasn't actually scared of *him*. His smile was a rictus grin, and the reflection of the kitchen light shone orange in his dark pupils.

"Do you know what happens when a machine breaks down, Eli?"

I shook my head.

"In my experience, you have two options. Either you take it apart, show it some love, see how it ticks, how each part works. Then you put it all back together in the hope that it'll function once more, maybe even better than it did before."

"And the other option?" I asked.

His slimy smile stayed fixed. "You throw it all away, shoot the ungrateful fuckers that made it, and start again."

I swallowed, hard, then leant forward and growled.

"I'm not doing it anymore. So get the fuck out of my house before I erase *you*."

"Suit yourself," Johns said, standing up and throwing his expensive-looking coat over his shoulders. He'd lost weight. I saw it then. It wasn't just the stubble that made him look different—he was gaunt, withered. The coat he had filled out before now hung loose on him.

I wanted to hurt him and before I could consider whether it was a good idea or not, I said, "You know I might just bring them all back?"

He stopped, his glare suddenly drilling into me.

"That would be extremely unwise," he said. Was it fear I remember seeing in that face, or anger?

"Then leave me the fuck alone, or I will do it," I said.

He stood there for a few uncomfortable seconds, and I could see him struggling with the urge to say something further to me. Instead, he walked to the door, me trailing lazily behind.

"See you again soon, Eli."

He placed his overlarge hat on his head.

"See you later, House of Night," I said.

His face twitched for a fraction of a second, and then that awful smile slid back into place. "Until next time then," he said, and left.

My Father emerged from the doorway, his face white, his eyes livid.

"I heard every word," he said.

▽

Soon after that meeting, they froze our bank account, but that was fine. My Dad had been siphoning off money since my first meeting with Johns. We had enough cash to live off for the next decade and a half. He did, however, become increasingly paranoid. Our weekly trips into town were cancelled, and instead he went once every two weeks, and only on his own. Leaving the compound was forbidden.

The atmosphere within the walls of the New Sunrise Project changed to one of impending doom. It felt like we had finally somehow tapped into the zeitgeist of fear that was terrorising society outside our bubble. We spoke about emergency evacuation plans. It was decided that if anything happened like Waco, where the police stormed the place with tanks and started shooting everything up, we'd all gather in the basement and I would take us to another reality. There was a door down there. I had seen it the first time I saw the cold rows of guns. I was worried that it wouldn't take us far enough away, like the time I had run into those boys. That we would just bump into identical versions of ourselves shivering in the dark.

My Dad posted lookouts at night. The men now slept in shifts. They became pale shades of their former happy-go-lucky religious selves. Gaunt, like Johns, they rose as the sun fell, took up their shotguns and watched the perimeter in the dark. Once my Dad had explained to the rest of the adults what Johns had threatened us with, it didn't take much to convince them to soldier up. And why would it? They'd seen miracles, they knew they were on the right side. As if there even is such a thing. We still had sermons and prayer, but they changed, too. They became about atonement, about the new direction we had taken as a family, about protecting ourselves from the devil that was the British government, from the evil that was Johns.

My Mother had adopted a look of permanent worry. She had wanted to continue working with Johns, no doubt understood more astutely than my Father and I the threat that he posed. She wanted to negotiate, instead of fight, our way out. It wasn't about the money, she had said one night, it was about all of our lives. I didn't have the heart to tell her what I'd seen on my journeys through the divergent landscapes of reality. The ten, twenty, thirty versions where the compound was abandoned, burnt, left to rot with fading police tape pulled across the doorways and windows. My Father took everything that had happened as a test of faith from the God In-between, a way to find our way back to Him.

The first few months of '96 felt truly like the end of days. Then, as April set in and the world started to come to life, we eased off. Routines slackened a little. My Father still acted like everything was going to come crashing down at any minute, but I caught him smiling once or twice. As his trust in the government, and the Atropos Project, bottomed out, his faith redoubled, and the mood of his sermons slowly shifted again. We started talking as if we might just be left alone. The lookouts reduced their shifts and their pallor abated. For a brief moment in time, I thought we had won.

Naturally, in those months it had become harder to see Jess. I had to wait until it was pitch dark, creep past my Grandfather's grave, move a flat piece of hardboard leant against the fence at the back of the compound, and wriggle out through the gap at the bottom. Jess started calling me her dirty boy.

We spent most of our time together walking along the high street holding hands and talking. We snuck into the cinema and watched *Se7en*. Then *From Dusk till Dawn*. I will always love that film. I was too frightened to make the first move when it came making out, until she berated me at a bus stop for being frigid, then it became easier. She also schooled me on various kissing techniques. I was fresh to the whole thing, so that first kiss as the New Year countdown rang may have been incredible for me, but for her it was just a sloppy tongue fest.

"You need to build a rhythm, man. Try a *little* first, then more, you know? You have to work with me, not attack me. It isn't a race down each other's throat."

I blushed from head to toe, tried to change the subject, ended up apologising. She just laughed and then we kissed. Lots of practice. It felt good to finally have her to myself. Everything with us was good. Of course, I would try my best to ruin it with my paranoia, but she was too cool for that. She was always good at calling me out on my shit.

She would spend her free time not with me playing gigs in London or getting wasted at parties in her friends' flat in Brighton. She'd started working in the town's one and only local bookshop, and now had money to afford the partying and the clubbing, as gigging of course payed hardly anything. Usually they got just enough to cover the drink tab the band rang up. It was frustrating—my family was rich, and yet I couldn't ask for a penny. My Dad would literally have tried to murder me if he found out I had a girlfriend and that I had been sneaking her into the compound as often as I could.

We argued a few times. Then made up. She promised she wasn't cheating on me and I apologised for being a moron. One night, we went back to her house after an argument and snuck up to her room. I remember her dad was asleep on the couch in front of a television playing only static. The flickering light played behind his tilted head, like a head full of empty dreams.

We watched *The Crow* for the fifteenth time, and afterwards we listened to the soundtrack and kissed. She moved my hands up to her chest and it felt like my heart was going to beat out of my chest and smash her in the face. I froze, then her dad woke up, and I had to jump out the window onto the battered sofa.

Like life at the compound, our routine became slack with time. We grew lazy. We had gotten away with it long enough to think we wouldn't get caught.

Until, of course, we did.

She was staying over at mine, like she had a few times before. I would sneak her inside the house just after midnight, when most of the family had gone to bed, and we would creep upstairs to my room. I still wasn't allowed a TV, so we would sit on my bed, listen to music, and laugh silently at each other's jokes, pushing our faces into the pillows and crying until we couldn't breathe. We'd talk and talk and fall deeper and deeper in love.

When we were in that room, or in her room, the rest of the world just fell away. It was just us, only us. Everything else would contract to the point of meaningless. Our worries, the government, the entire fucking world and all its problems just shrank to nothing.

The night my Father found out was the first time Jess and I had sex. Thinking about it now, I was lame and she was generous. At the time, though, my life was absolutely changed and she valued that. Afterwards, we laid there, her head on my chest, a single finger absently tracing gentles circles on my skin. My brain felt like it might have been on fire.

There was a sense memory inside me. A subtle knowledge of what sex was like. The adults I had taken to Purgatory had a keen sense of what it was, and so when I finally did it, I felt the ghost feeling of déjà vu.

"Wow," I repeated for the fifth time.

She smiled up at me.

"Yeah, it was pretty good," she said. She rested her arm gently around the back of my neck, tickled my ear.

"Did you?" I asked, too shy to say "come."

She laughed. "No, sorry," she said. She turned to look at me. "It's fine, I didn't expect to. It wasn't about that. Although, next time you better make sure I do, or I'm going to break up with you."

I hadn't even considered a next time, or a time after that. The idea of years of having sex with her suddenly blossomed in my mind's eye and I looked forward to it. I wanted to share my secret with her. I was *going to* share my secret with her. We had just shared something amazing, and I needed to, *had to*, tell her. The words danced on my tongue, nearly danced straight out of my mouth. We were joined intrinsically by a simple convergence then, just like all the realities that surrounded us. Telling her my big secret was the magical thing that would keep us together forever.

At school we were told that we were all special and that each of us had one thing we could be great at if we tried. It was all bullshit, except for me. I *am* special. There's literally only one person in this version of reality that can do what I do. One Key who can cross the boundaries of our observed existence and enter divergent timelines. And that's me! But it's not the sort of thing you are supposed to say at school. But I hoped it would cement mine and Jess's relationship.

"I'm hungry," I said. "I need some cereal." I was going to eat that, then tell her.

I was bare-ass naked, bent over, and extricating my underwear from our pile of clothes when my Dad came in. He apologised out of instinct when my head whipped around, and I saw his eyes flick from my naked body to my bed. Jess, eyes wide with shock, waved a little wave and pulled the covers up to her nose.

He looked at me, his face white with fury.

"Get her out," he growled. I knew he was never far away. "Now."

He stormed out and slammed the door, then I heard his heavy boots stomping down the stairs.

"Well," Jess said as she clambered out of bed and started searching for her clothes. "That went well."

"Surprisingly, he didn't kill us both," I replied. "So I guess that's a plus."

"Yay me."

"Although he does have a basement full of guns," I added. "He could just be getting a shotgun."

We both got dressed and I led her down the stairs and into the main living quarters toward the front gate. A few family members stood in the common area. We snuck past them into the interconnecting hallway that led to the front of the compound. I caught Steven's eye as he spotted us, and he give me a nod and a sly grin.

My Father opened the door and we both slipped through into the cool night beyond. Frankly, it was a relief to be away from the gaze of my family. I walked her to the gate and pulled it open.

"Well, that was fucking humiliating," she said looking back at the house. My Father was watching us from a window.

"Jess," I started. "I'm sorry. My Dad is a total dick."

She smiled. It was a weak smile, and I could tell she was hurt and annoyed at having been marched through the house.

"It's okay."

"It's really not," I said. I had to tell her something, something that would change things. I still wanted to tell her the big thing, but now it didn't feel like the right time.

"Let's run away," I whispered to her instead. I had already started to formulate our escape plan in my mind.

I walked with her a little way up the street, towards town.

I grabbed her arm. "I said, let's run away."

She stopped and turned to me. An owl hooted and somewhere not far off the sound of an articulated lorry cut through the night.

"Where to?" she said.

"London," I replied, then, "Anywhere you want. We can fuck off to a different country if you want."

"I've always fancied America," she said. "Drive down from San Francisco to Big Sur." She floated a hand in front of her, feeling some mythical wind that would carry us there. "We could go and hang out in Oakland or go see the Deftones in Sacramento."

"Let's just fucking do it then," I said. "Seriously, Jess. You've always talked about fucking off somewhere else, anywhere else. Let's just go."

She looked at me for a moment, maybe wondering if I was full of shit or maybe figuring out the logistics of our new mission.

"Okay," she said. "Let's fucking do it."

▽

# A Brief Interlude

I need to preface this by saying that what happened next was inevitable. I had seen it coming for a long time. It was the end of the New Sunrise Project. I had seen the results of that day played out in thirty different ways, but that day was *our* day. Our crack at the whip.

It was a shitty fucking day.

▽

**October 3, 1996**

The day that Jess and I had planned to leave.

It was a cold day and an even colder evening. The sun had slunk just behind the horizon, painting the sky in vivid layers of red, pink, and gold that all bled into each other, over each other. I watched the slow, beautiful unveiling of the night, until the colours faded into pale blue, indigo, black.

My breath smoked and I hugged my arms, hopping from foot to foot trying to stay warm as I waited on the corner, just outside the Blockbuster Video for Jess to arrive. Standing inside the square of sickly yellow light on the pavement outside the store, I watched people slowly roaming the new releases section, scanning for something to watch. I saw an old lady hunch over and pluck *The Bridges of Madison County* from the bottom row. I hate that fucking film. Still do. Jess loved it. I don't understand why. I knew VHS was going to die out, by the way. I had seen DVDs about ten years before they were invented in this reality. I kind of prefer VHS though. There's something so novel about handling the chunky square of black plastic, the thick cases as wide and sturdy as *War and Peace*. At this one house party I was at, along one entire wall was a library of VHS cassettes. I'd gotten drunk and told a random stranger that the guy who owned them was going to be pissed when they became obsolete. He didn't understand what I was saying.

Jess loomed out of the half dark, preceded by the glow of her cigarette. She had a backpack over her shoulders.

"That's it?" I asked. "That's all you're bringing?"

She nodded, took a drag of her cigarette, and then stamped it out.

"Yep," she said through the coils of smoke drifting from between her teeth. "It's all I need."

It made me profoundly sad that all of her essential belongings could easily fit into an old school bag covered in band patches and held together by safety pins.

I took the pack off her and slung it over my own shoulders.

"Oh, well, aren't you a gentleman," she said, and kissed me on the cheek. She smelt of cigarettes and Lucozade. She said smoking dried her throat out, and so always had a quarter-full bottle of two-day-old Lucozade stuffed inside her coat pocket.

"My lady," I said, leading the way with a flourish of the hand, and we turned in the direction of the compound.

"What have you got in here?" I asked, as irregular-shaped objects jabbed me in the spine. I slipped one arm out from the loop and carried it over one shoulder instead.

"Just my collection of knives and sex stuff."

"Oh, cool," I exclaimed. "Can I play with the knives?"

"Absolutely. Just don't touch my sex stuff," she joked. "Also, I brought food."

"Why?" I asked.

"Just in case."

"Okay, fair enough."

We were both nervous, and the energy between us felt jittery, a little strange, but mostly exciting. A part of me wanted to talk her out of it; another part of me hoped she would try to talk me out of it. I cycled through waves of electric nausea, excitement, fear, apprehension, and hope.

Maybe we *could* get away and start again.

It felt like a distant fantasy and yet somehow we seemed to be moving towards realising it. We held hands, and I felt her slender fingers opening and closing between mine nervously.

Our plan was a relatively simple one.

She would stay with me that night. I was going to steal a large sum of money from the lockbox in the basement. Then we would wait until four in the morning and sneak out through the hole in the fence. Jess had booked us on the first train to Brighton and a hotel for us for a week. After that, we were going to look for our own place and see what would happen.

I may have had parts of geniuses living inside my brain, but I was still seventeen.

Getting in was a simple affair. We snuck back after evening prayers, when the adults were in the social area of the compound. The kids were in bed, and the only rogue factor was Steven, Sally, and Jenny. They were often up, playing board games or chatting in the communal areas. But I had the feeling if they caught us, we'd probably be okay.

We crept upstairs, chased by the angry murmuring of my Mother and Father arguing as we passed their bedroom towards the chapel. Inside my room, I grabbed my rucksack and started packing. Jess offered to help, but I declined. I'd been thinking about what to bring all day. When I grabbed my Grandfather's diary from beneath the floorboards, Jess looked at me with a single raised eyebrow.

"What is that, a secret diary?" she said, propping herself on her elbows, resting her head in her hands, and fluttering her eyelids. "Ooh ooh, can I read it?"

"One day," I replied. "It's actually my Grandfather's diary." I still hadn't told her. It seemed just another thing that needed to be done, but not at that moment. Not when it meant explaining all of it, and all of the things I had done. I imagined the little bald Tibetan child crying in a broken-down house. The way he shivered in the freezing cold.

"Why'd you hide it?" she asked.

"My Dad doesn't want me to have it," I answered. "It's got stuff about him in it. Stuff about our family, too... Bad stuff."

"I always knew you guys were into freaky devil worshipping shit. To be fair, it's the only reason I am going out with you."

I pushed the book deep into my bag and then covered it with some clothes. I grabbed a picture of my family from the shelf by my bed. I looked at the smiling, happy faces. My Nan and Grandad, my Father even. They all looked so young, and happy. I was there, too. A chubby, red-faced child in my Mother's arms. I slipped the picture from the scuffed wooden frame, gently pressed it between the pages of my copy of Stephen King's *It*, and put that in my bag, too. I packed my toothbrush and toothpaste, and that was it, leaving room enough for the money. I was shocked how I could pare everything essential down to one bag.

"You should bring this," Jess said, holding up the very first mixtape she had made me. I always kept it on the side of my bed next to my Walkman. "We could reminisce about old times."

"I was going to!" I said, my voice lifting an octave. I leant over and kissed her, plucked the tape from between her fingers. I turned the case over in my hands and read the back.

"'Love Will Tear Us Apart,' 'Fear of the Dark,' 'Love Cats,' 'Livin' on a Prayer,' 'Take My Scars.' Tell me, Jess, were you trying to tell me something?" I asked.

She held a hand out and quickly opened and closed her outstretched fingers, making a gentle patting sound.

"Gimme," she said, and I handed it over.

"'Love Will Tear Us Apart' is me basically saying that I fancied you. 'Fear of the Dark' is what you have, which is why we always sleep with a fucking light on. I was basically saying I know you. 'Livin' on a Prayer' is you… because you are the creepy cult kid."

She listed the rest of the songs one at a time and connected them to me, to her, to us and the relationship we had built.

"See, I think about the real stuff. It's the key to a good mixtape."

"Did I ever tell you that you are awesome?" I said.

"Hmm," she considered, screwing her face up into a cute ball. "Now that you say it, I don't think so."

She smiled, all white teeth and happy eyes. Before we started going out, she rarely seemed to do that. But I noticed she had begun to smile often. I slipped the cassette tape and my Walkman into the bag, too. I could make it all fit.

"Right," I said clapping my hands together and wringing them nervously. "Showtime. I'll go get the money," I said, my voice sounding more nervous than I had expected.

She swung her legs off the bed and stood to face me. With an intensity that stirred something that felt warm and primal in the pit of my stomach, she stared into my eyes.

"You got this, kid. I believe in you," she said, then pointed to my wardrobe. "Now, I'm going to hide in there until you come back."

She kissed me on the cheek and gently brushed the hair from my face.

"For luck," she said, and handed me my rucksack.

"I love you," I replied.

"I know," she said, then made a whooshing noise and pretended to be frozen in carbonite.

Strange memories of that final night at the compound. I'm not sure if it's just misremembering or what, but it seemed unnaturally quiet in the building. My skin prickled with fear as the stairs creaked and groaned under my weight. At how loud my footfalls seemed as I made my way through the church and into the adjoining buildings. There was a click and a pool of light bled from the space under a bedroom door. I froze, my heart pounding in my chest, a bad lie already on my trembling lips. The loud clock in the hallway ticktocked loud enough to wake the dead. It counted the seconds as I watched a shadow break the line of light as the person behind the door moved around the room. The wind sighed and moaned through the cracked hallway window, rustling a curtain and making it flap gently. An age later, the light clicked off, and I let out a long slow breath I didn't realise I was holding in.

The entrance to the weapons basement was near the front of the compound and I walked as slowly and as surely as I could. I heard voices as I passed my parents' room. They were still arguing. The violent slithering of hushed threats and stifled crying. I was glad to be away. I could live with being just another wound in my Father's heart.

I carefully pulled the rug away from the entrance, lifted the trapdoor, and climbed down, gently replacing the door as I went down. I flicked the light on and the row of naked bulbs lit the narrow passageway to a wide antechamber. It was cold in the basement, felt otherworldly, haunted somehow. At the end of the room, directly underneath our kitchen, was the money. Piles of it that my Father had put into a plastic tub and covered with a rough blanket. I slid the bag from my shoulders and filled it with bundles of fifty-pound notes. I wasn't sure how much I was taking. I only felt my heartbeat hammering harder and harder. as I filled the rest of the space with notes, until it was all I could hear.

When the bag was close to full, I made my way back towards the trapdoor. The plan was going to work. I just needed to get back to my room and then escape. It was going to work. I made the mistake of hoping.

Even from underground, I heard the sound of a shotgun going off. My heart seemed to stop as I froze halfway up the ladder, my hand pressed to the trapdoor. I quickly calculated the family's reactions, what they would do. I knew the plan. Knew where they'd come. Time seemed to stretch out, until another shot came, then another. The sound of gunshots quarrelling in the dark.

We had gone full Waco.

Of All Possibilities | 221

I sprung out of the trapdoor and my aunt, who'd come out to see what was happening, spun on her heels and screamed. I held out my hands and told her to get in. More family members began filling the corridors as I raced past. Somewhere someone shouted. It could have been my Father, might have been an uncle. I ran the length of the adjoining corridor towards the church. One of my uncles stood in the kitchen. He had a bolt-action rifle pointed out of the smashed-out kitchen window.

"They're here," he screamed and fired a shot out into the dark.

"Who?" I cried.

Someone fired back and his head exploded in a shower of gore that covered the kitchen table, including my Mother's fat, blue recipe book. He staggered back, his hands up. The rifle clattered to the floor and he followed with a wet thump. More shots now, and then return fire from around the compound. Bullets smashed through the windows, thudding into the old wood and exploding into the ancient bricks.

I turned, pulse racing loudly in my ears, saw my Father standing at one end of the corridor, along with some of my family. The kids were disappearing around the corner first, and the rehearsed escape plan came flying back into my mind. They were climbing down into the basement, faces alive with fear and panic. They were waiting there for me, but all I could think of was Jess, upstairs, scared. Something smashed through the hallway window between my Father and I. It popped and then acrid smoke began to fill the space, licking and curling up the walls, burning my eyes, my throat.

"Eli," he screamed.

I was stuck again, caught between my past and my future, and I wondered what all the versions of me in all the other versions of reality did in this moment.

He called my name again as I turned my back on him and ran towards the church, towards Jess. Bullets cut the air around me to ribbons and shattered glass. I threw myself to the floor and quickly scuttled beneath the rows of windows, hands raw and cut from the broken glass, lungs still burning, eyes blurry and stinging.

"Eli," I heard Jess call. She had run down the burning stairs and was standing next to the altar. Her face was pale with fear and she was shaking.

"What the fuck is happening?" she cried.

"I don't know," I said, even though I had a fair idea.

"What do we do?"

The door behind her burst apart. Splinters flew and the windows smashed into glittering shards. I grabbed her arm and we ran towards the far door that led out to the back garden. I turned to see a man dressed head to toe in tactical gear. A mask covered his face and I saw clearly a pair of icy-blue eyes.

In slow motion, he raised his gun at me and I just stood there waiting for the pain, and death. Then he flew backwards out of the door he had entered from, a fine mist of blood and fabric left in his wake. My Father limped into the chapel. He had been shot in the stomach and a dark stain was spreading through his jumper and down his trousers. His eyes darted wildly from me to Jess and gave a cough that left his lips a bright red as he propped himself up with a battered chair. One that had been sat on during dinners. One that I had once rocked back too far on and fell backwards. My Father had caught me that day, and I wondered why in this madness that thought had returned as he left smeary red handprints on the top rail of the chair.

"Eli," he said. He coughed again and bared his blood-stained teeth. "You have to get them out."

I didn't say anything.

"Eli, please. Son." He placed the shotgun on a low table and closed his eyes.

Other areas of the compound were burning too, and waves of heat and smoke drifted in. Out of a window, I saw a team of similarly armed and armoured men kicking in the doors on the northern end of the compound. On the grass, Steven lay face down, his arm twisted behind him, lifeless eyes staring skyward. Fallen from his lookout position.

Jess looked at me, my Father looked at me, and, once again, I wondered what a different version of me had done.

"Fuck it," I said, as a plan formed quickly in my mind. "I'll be back. I promise."

My Father sighed a long sigh, and the thought occurred to me that he may have just died. But then he coughed, jerked his eyes open again.

"Go to the basement, I'll be there soon, okay?" I shook him by the shoulders, an inverted gesture of the kind he'd given to me a thousand times. "Okay?" I screamed.

He shook his head, nodding, and stumbled out of the room. It was the last time I saw him.

My plan, short as it was, was to first take Jess through the nearest doorway, into Purgatory, then come back and save the rest of my family if I could.

I grabbed both her shoulders. "Look at me. We are going to be all right, but some crazy shit is going to happen first. What we are going to do is run directly at that big square doorway in the centre of the garden," I said, as calmly as I possibly could.

"What? That's fucking madness, Eli. We'll be killed," she hissed. She was kind of hopping, bouncing low with fear and energy. Fight or flight dialled up to eleven.

"Trust me. Please. You have to trust me," I said. "You can't let go of me either. Promise me."

"Eli, you're making no fucking sense."

"Fuck. Please, Jess. You just need to do this. I promise I can get us out."

*So this is how my big secret comes out*, I thought.

She nodded, and I kissed her.

"We'll be okay," I said. "We'll be okay."

I kicked the door wide open and we started to run. Outside, I glimpsed two armed men on their way into the church and we tore past them, the cold air freezing our already burning lungs. I ignored them as they opened fire, their bullets ripping into the dirt all around us. We hit the stone path, half slid, half fell, and recovered as we crossed the halfway point. I could see the static rolling off the doorway in waves just ahead of us. I had never been happier to see it, to smell the petrichor and burning metal that leaked through from the place in-between.

One of the lanterns exploded as we passed it and shards of orange glass cut deep into my shin. "Fuck," I screamed. Jess pulled ahead and started dragging me. Her fingers slipped from my wet palms and for a second we were cut apart. "No no no," I whispered. Ten feet from the doorway.

"No," I screamed, my fingers clawing empty air. The other world was drawing up now, the bending light of the doorway distorting the air, the static deafeningly loud. It boiled up to envelop me.

Then her fingers found mine again and we pressed forward to the dais, the Great Stone Door looming.

Chips of ancient stone exploded around us and white dust puffed into the air. I was vaguely aware I had been cut along my cheek.

"Eli," Jess screamed. A man stepped from behind of one of the Great Stone Doorway's massive plinths. He held an assault rifle on his shoulder, pointed it down at my face. Jess tried to hit the brakes, her feet slipping on the wet stone, but I pushed her as hard as I could towards him.

We burst through the door and into the nexus of all realities, a place where no bullet could punch through. We were safe.

▽

Fear.

Fear, and pain, and love, and shock, and sadness in limitless measure.

I hadn't thought about what it might be like to travel with Jess's consciousness. It was almost too much to stand. As wrong as it felt all the times before, that time felt like a betrayal. She thought she was dying as we chased a single point of light dotted among the infinite shifting planes. Our consciousnesses stretching and overlapping, parts of me and parts of her, impossible to share or express in any other way, intermingled. We fell apart and came together like waves lapping at a shore. I drowned in her sadness, the memories of her father, far worse than she'd made out. Then I surfaced, lightened with her love, her happiness. She was happy with me. I guiltily saw and felt her feelings for me blossom and bloom from the seeds of our relationship. She had always been curious, and I saw through her eyes that I had been aloof, difficult, and secretive.

Formless, we sang along brilliant tethers of light towards the door on the other side, towards that broken world where we would emerge whole.

She had loved Paul, too, and I watched all of their intimate love together, the first time she sank into his arms and sighed. It was so easy with him when he wasn't drunk. The way he talked to her when he wasn't with his friends. He was tender, experienced. I shrank at his image. Was embarrassed at my own childish expressions of love. I saw as they drank, and smoked, and laughed. Saw them partying in a drunken haze. Felt his hands on us. Then I watched as the whole thing soured. The time we said we didn't really want to have sex and he just did it anyway. The night he hit us for the first time and apologised, crying about how we had made him feel. For a few weeks after, he was attentive and loving. Then the days and nights that followed, even when he did it again, and this time didn't say sorry, didn't seem to feel bad either.

I felt sick, and angry, and selfish hurt that she could be truly happy, even temporarily, with someone else.

Then a flicker book of other lovers, boyfriends, and suitors all the way back until she was fourteen, and I felt even worse.

I felt the hunger for love and acceptance that crept under the veneer of her standoffish personality, just like it did for everyone else. I was the same, too. The one thing I know about absolutely everyone is that, when we are broken down to pure consciousness, we crave only those two things.

I saw inside her heart to her childhood. She hated seeming a cliché, but there that memory sat in the centre of her being, like a pile of ashes. I felt her flinch as it came into focus between us. The day she was born. The day her mother died.

The other side was coming fast now, and I felt a twinge of pain as the light filled everything. Filled us both. I felt the separation as her mind came apart from mine, and then the pain was gone and we were standing on the grass in a dead world, impossibly far, yet only inches away, from the place we had come from.

Above us, the shattered dial of the moon glimmered and glowered at us, sickly yellow and spectral green.

# Seven

My target collapses in the road not far from the wreckage of the van. His trousers are ripped and there's a big gash in his left shin. Black-looking blood oozes from the wound in dark pulsing sheets. His breathing is heavy, raking in gasping breaths and spitting ragged, grey clouds into the night. He tries to stand on the leg, but it won't take his weight properly and he goes down to a knee.

"Well, well, well. Look who's fucked," I say. My lungs hurt, my face hurts. I might as well be referring to myself.

He tries to stand.

"Don't do this," he says, his bare hand splayed wide in the road. I notice the wedding ring. "Please."

"Does she know?" I ask. He doesn't respond. "Does she know what you do? What you *are*?"

He laughs bitterly and shakes his head. "No," he grunts. Beads of rain drip from his chin, hair, nose. White teeth bared, half grin, half grimace. His eyes are filled with a primordial desire to survive the next few moments.

"What happened?" I shout over the rain.

I bend down to help him up and a savage, but poorly aimed, punch catches me just under the chin, snapping my mouth shut and smashing my teeth together with a crunch. Light blooms in a starry explosion across my vision and I stagger back. My feet slip away beneath me and the world rolls over again.

He's going to get away, and then that'll be it. My head hurts, my body hurts. It's funny how you don't notice how well put together you are until a bunch of your parts are hurting.

I groan and try to lift my head. I've a feeling that I've lost a tooth at the back. I've definitely bitten off a sliver of tongue. He will run down the road now, disappear into the slick night. A fist falls like a hammer into the side of my face and I roll over. I feel like I am falling through empty, painful space as my head snaps to the side. A foot follows up, catching me in the ribs. I hear a crack and the air leaves me in a burning plume.

So, he's decided to press the advantage. It's what I would have done.

I roll over and away as a boot stamps down where my face just was. I reach out and grab his raised leg and half stand, half slip, my rib a burning poker, hissing as it stabs at something inside that I hope is not vital. Sapping my strength. If you've ever been in a real fight, you'll know it's nothing like the movies where the good guy and the bad guy fight for ten minutes, flip all over the place, and do all these crazy moves. A real fight is dirty, lasts about thirty seconds, and is won by the person who can land the hits and keep landing them until the other person stops moving. I've been in my fair share. Lost a few, won more, but always walked away with a new pain somewhere. One guy had me down, about to pound my head in, when he tripped over and hit his head on the side of a table, and that was that. Most of the time, it's a little skill and a little luck.

I twist his foot and he gasps as his ankle cracks. I hear his knee give a sharp pop too, and he screams, falls back, and now I am the one standing, leering over him, bloody spit looping from my puffed up lips. He doesn't quite see the punch coming, and he turns at the last second. The blow hits him square on, taking his jaw out of its socket and breaking one of my knuckles. The pain is sharp like an electric bolt of agony glancing up my forearm. He flops back, arms reflexively pulled up to his chest like he's riding a tiny horse, his tongue lolling from the side of his mouth.

# My Troubled History, Part Seven

**Purgatory**

We both lay on the hard earth, the frost quilting the exposed mud, the wilted flowers, dead grass. I was propped up by my backpack at an awkward angle.

"Holy fucking shit," I shouted up at the sky. The sweetest feeling of relief washed over me and I laughed. "We made it. We fucking made it."

I rolled over onto my side to kiss her, to maybe start to try and explain what I was.

She was dead. Her eyes were rolled up just about to the edge of her pupils. Her blood was slowly soaking into the frozen earth.

"No no no no" is the only thing I remember saying in the hours that followed.

I was full of her. I could feel the parts of her personality, her memories, her feelings spreading out to join the rest, even as she lay dead in my arms. I felt her love for me and it destroyed me absolutely. I cried until an all-encompassing numbness fell over me. I shivered and my teeth chattered even though I felt nothing. I wrapped my arms around her and kissed her cheek, smelt her hair. I tried to capture all these details before they would be gone forever. Steam rose from the gunshot wound in her head and then finally stopped. I don't know how long I was there for, but morning came in threads of scarlet that wove the pale dawn together under a watery sun. The frost disappeared in increments as weak sunlight crept across the ground, a phantom evaporating in the day. Jessica had paled now, still beads of water clinging to her skin. Her once beautiful eyes had become milky.

I prised my fingers from hers and slowly extricated myself from under her arm, my cramping limbs cracking painfully. Air escaped from her in a sigh as her body flopped back. I remember so clearly looking down at her, propped up by her rucksack, her face staring out from beneath the shredded hood, her features slack. Some feral agony loosed from the very pit of my heart. I howled and screamed and tried to split the air with my grief, break the earth with my pain. I died and died again, wanted to only feel darkness, but instead felt that tiny part of her inside me recoil in horror at the thought. Then, when my throat was hoarse and constricted, my voice blown and my head pounding, I stopped. I felt that piece of her inside me, her resilience, and, as much as I tried to tune it out, to instead let my grief destroy me, I listened to her voice in my head that was telling me what to do to survive. I crawled to a spot not far from her and began digging. First, my hands hurt as they bit into the cold ground. I winced as I turned out stone and chunks of glass. Then they went numb and just worked and worked. After an hour or so, my hands were cut and raw; they felt like bloody stumps. I'd somehow ripped out most of the nail from my little finger and hadn't even noticed. I also hadn't made much progress at all, so I got to my feet and staggered to the broken-down house.

I found some wooden boards in fairly decent shape and the rusted end of a spade among the ruins of the garden. I took them back and started digging. It was night again when I was done. My arms and shoulders burned with pain and my back felt welded into position. It clicked loudly as I straightened up. The usual headache flicked bright sparks of pain along my temples and behind my eyes. I was delirious. Drunk on psychic agony and no sleep. Was she dead to history, too? Had anyone that might have mourned her forgotten her, or had she been dead before she went through and they would instead think she was missing? I tried to remember the chain of events, but nothing came. It was still too soon.

Standing over her body, I imagined my Grandfather's corpse back splayed across his bed. Then I thought of my family back in my reality, and panic rolled over me in a bright wave. It was too late to do anything now. It was too late when I had decided to leave. It was too late when I had turned Johns down for a final time and had set the course of action. I tried to push the thought away. Hoped that they were okay, because not knowing allowed for hope, even though I was certain they were dead. But I just carried on.

I buried her under that broken moon. I stopped when I had covered most of her body, and just her head remained uncovered. I stood there with a handful of dirt just looking at her, unable to move. Something glimmered in the muck—her silver cross. I knelt down beside her and gently removed it. Then, I covered her face until I could no longer see her.

With a stone I scratched her name on one of the boards I'd used to dig her grave, and I drove it into the dirt above her head. Then I picked up her rucksack, my rucksack, and walked to the house. The frost had crept back and I hadn't even noticed it.

▽

I couldn't go back home, that was certain. I expected that if I did, Johns and his murderous underlings would be waiting for me. I'd pop back in and receive two bullets to the back of the head. It was all so painfully clear then. They obviously couldn't let me live. I was an asset, a very important and unique asset, with some very serious dirt on the country. They couldn't have me shooting my mouth off to the press or to other, less friendly countries. They couldn't have me working for another government's agenda.

I went through our backpacks and took out the piles of money. It couldn't do me any good in a dead world, and I felt stupid even having it. So, I wrapped it up in a couple of plastic bags and hid it in the house. I took out Jess's clothes, folded them, and left them in the drawer of a mouldy wardrobe. It felt wrong to just throw them away. I kept one of her T-shirts, a Nirvana smiley face one that she usually slept in. I found a weapon in one of the side compartments of her bag, a butterfly knife that I slid into my pocket. I put her makeup bag in with her clothes, except for her nearly empty bottle of Eternity perfume. I sprayed some, closed my eyes and inhaled deeply, then I slipped it back into her rucksack. I took the food she had packed, though, a few cans of soup, some crisps, and a bunch of chocolate bars. I made sure I still had the Walkman and the mixtape.

I waited, watching the clear skies wheel silently through a dark punctuated by brilliant points of light. Whether the light came from the scattered, disparate fragments of the moon or distant stars, I couldn't tell. It was beautiful though, in a strange way at least. The night was filled with the sound of creatures, the skittering and trilling of insects. The buzz of flies and the odd mosquito dressed in ghostly white. Maybe not such a dead world after all. The wind rushed through the grass and nearby trees like a whisper and shallow water burbling over rocks. The dilapidated building creaked and sagged and groaned, fighting a losing battle with time.

The headache hung dead in the centre of my skull like a poisoned weight. I tried to think of anything else, but it was maddening. I was exhausted. I'd been up for nearly two days, but I couldn't sleep. I knew what would come when I finally did, and I couldn't bring myself to allow my unconscious mind to live Jess's life. The thought of it made me feel sick with sadness. It was as inevitable as death, but I couldn't bear to face it. To lose her again. I bit my lip until it bled, the pain of it enlivening me momentarily.

The unmistakable edges of roofs and towers caught the moonlight and shone in the distance. It wasn't far to town. I had made the journey hundreds of times in all the dozens of realities I'd been through. So, to stave off my growing exhaustion, I set off towards it. Before I left, I stopped at Jess's grave, buried in a place so far from her own home, and I told her I was sorry.

The road leading away from the compound was still there, albeit considerably narrower and much more rutted. Great divots had been carved here and there, and in the dark I fell, painfully turning my ankle. I took it easier, slowly and carefully picking my way through the night, until I arrived where the town should be. Blockbuster and Woolworths had been replaced by sloping plains of wild grasses, cut through by a cobbled road. The town seemed to start a few dozen streets over. Rows of blocky buildings with their doors and windows shuttered, glass smashed and glittering in the broken streets. One of them had partially collapsed from the rear, a flood of bricks, timbers, and furniture spilling into the gardens. Further down, in the place where the Baskins-Robbins had opened a few months earlier, was a pub. The sign, rusted to its hinge, still bore an image of a cartoon-looking devil. The faded and mossy sign read *Old Scratch's Tavern*. I cupped my hands to the grimy window but couldn't make out anything in the darkness beyond.

The cinema was there though. A squat, square of cement pillars and red bricks. It was half Parthenon knockoff and half utilitarian brick structure. The leering grotesques that adorned the cinema I was familiar with weren't there, just plain black guttering. The sign above the door, rendered in peeling paint and spotted with mould, simply read *THEATRE* in big, bold capitals.

I half remembered a trip to the local history museum and seeing a sepia photo of the town taken over a hundred years before, printed onto a sheet of thick cardboard. The town looked exactly like a rundown version of that photo. Though it was mainly farmland, Scratch Hill had been an affluent area both before and after the First World War, so its culture was a strange mix of agriculture-based simplicity and burgeoning modernity. It was also one of the first towns outside London to be hooked up to the national grid.

I walked towards the arcade, but that was gone, too. Even the suburban sprawl of houses that ran in parallel lines nearby had disappeared, replaced by sparse clusters of homes dotted about the sloping hills.

As I stood there, enveloped in the dark and looking for somewhere to go, I tried to figure out how far I might be able to walk. Then I saw something orange and shivering out of the corner of my eye. In one of the houses cut into a hill I saw the flash of a fire as a door quickly opened and closed.

My heart was suddenly in my mouth. My mind raced. I had never thought that this place could foster human life of any kind. It was supposed to be empty, an inescapable prison for all the people I had brought here, a place where God's eye did not fall. Utter desolation.

Then it dawned on me that maybe the people I brought here hadn't died. I'd never seen a body, after all. A cold feeling of dread washed over me.

▽

Vladimir Petrikov was bony thin, had a long beard and wild hair. Even though he appeared as a shadow of the man I remembered, somehow I knew it was him. I watched from a bush as he stopped at the doorway of the house and looked out. When his glassy, bulging eyes passed over my hiding place, my heartbeat hammered painfully in my ears and my stifled breathing took on the volume of a gale.

"*Privet*," he said cautiously. His voice was croaky and hoarse. He coughed, cleared his throat, and followed with the English version. "Hello. Is anybody there?"

He waited a few more moments, warily staring out into the dark, then shrugged and disappeared back inside the house. I crouched motionless, catching my breath and waiting for my heart to slow down. I had no idea what I would say to him. "Sorry?" He'd been trapped on a desolate earth for the last eleven years. If he tried only to kill me, I'd be lucky. But I was determined to speak to him nevertheless. In those fevered minutes and hours after Jess's death that spun out like years, I'd decided I would try and put right some of the wrongs I had committed. If possible, I was going to start by making amends with Vladimir Petrikov. If he decided to kill me, I probably would have counted that as a blessing as well.

Slowly, I approached the house. Even in the evening gloom, I could tell that he had spent a good deal of time fixing it up and making it liveable. He had mended the roof and row upon row of mismatched tiles that resembled bad teeth slanted down on either side. The windows on both floors had been wiped clean and a set of curtains Frankensteined together from scraps were pulled closed on the second-floor windows. The garden had been carefully maintained, and two rows of turned dirt lined either side of the garden path. Under a thin layer of glistening hoarfrost, the earth was waiting for spring to be seeded.

I could hear the fire inside crackling and popping inside its brick hearth. I watched Vladimir as he settled into a beaten-up chair, pulled several blankets up to his chin, and started singing gently to himself.

I was unsure of what else to do, so I walked up to the front door and just knocked.

"Hello," I called, wanting to run back into the dark and forget the whole stupid idea. I worried that he might have gone insane from loneliness. I was also vaguely concerned that he might instantly pounce on me and kill me. My hand instinctively felt for the handle of Jess's knife stuck in my trousers.

Vladimir cautiously opened the door a crack and I met his gaze. A large part of me hoped he wouldn't recognise me, maybe take me for another poor soul brought here by that evil cabal of government lackeys parading as a cult and take me in, make me a cup of tea.

His eyes narrowed as his brain cycled through his memories and then blew wide and white as boiled eggs. "You!" he cried. My cover was blown.

"Wait, wait," I cried back. "I can explain. Please, just let me explain."

He disappeared for a second, then flung the door open and stood framed in the firelight, wielding a chunk of firewood over his head like a club. He looked comical almost, a skeleton wrapped in rags holding a club that probably weighed more than him.

"Why?" he said. He sagged and let the club drop from his bony hands and it clattered on the stone floor. "You tell me why did you did this to me."

Here it was, the emotional reckoning I had worried about all my life. That horrible guilt coming home to roost.

"Can I come in?" I asked. "I'll explain, I promise."

"I should kill you," he screamed, and took a few steps towards me.

"I know, you're right," I said, one hand raised up to him in weak defence. "You're right. Please, just let me talk. You can smash my head in afterwards if you want."

He considered it for long moment, then stood to one side. I walked in, my hand still gripping the handle of the knife, just out of sight.

The room was cosy enough. He'd had just over a decade to make it so, and I winced at the thought of what it might have been like at the start. The walls had been replastered and painted a sandy-yellow colour. It looked faintly like a place in the Mediterranean. He'd hung some paintings up that he'd found. The sofa was patchwork, but as I eased myself into it, I found it was incredibly comfortable.

"How did you do all this?" I asked, after he had pulled the door shut and swung a wooden bar down, locking it.

"Time, mainly," he replied. "I spend my days fixing this house against nature and wandering the streets, scavenging what I can. The seasons are cruel in this place." He sat down on a wooden chair that looked as if it had been made by someone who wasn't very good at DIY. "This season in particular."

"The crops out front?" I asked.

"Half of last year's yield, a quarter of the year before. I have several patches around the town."

I stared at my hands, hoping a heartfelt apology would suddenly appear in my palms.

"Look," I started. My throat felt constricted, burning with the regret of all those years doing this dirty work. "I'm sorry. Sorry about what happened. Sorry for what I did to you."

He squirmed in his chair, with an expression that suggested he regretted dropping the club. I saw the muscles in the side of his jaw clenching and unclenching. He wrung his hands.

"I have a child. I do not know what has become of her, or my wife. I have lived in this hell for god knows how long, barely able to keep living, if it can even be called that, and you think sorry is going to help?" Spittle rattled from his mouth as he loosed the words at me.

"I know," I said, hiding the lie from him that she, his daughter, didn't exist anymore.

"You know, do you?" He stood to his full height and loomed over me. "You know what it's like to live in a dead place with no hope, you know what it's like to have to smash your own teeth out with a damn rock because there's no one to help remove them when they get infected? You know what it's like to slowly starve to death, or to spend every evening standing on a chair with a noose around your neck, just waiting for the strength to let go. Do you know these things?" He was shaking with fury.

I shook my head. "I know *you*, though. Do you remember when I brought you here?"

He nodded. "It felt like the very fabric of reality had imploded."

"When I bring people through…" I started, not sure exactly how to articulate the next part. "They leave a piece of themselves behind. I can feel them inside me. This happened with you. I could feel your feelings. I know you. Know your family."

"And what do you know of me?"

"I know you miss your family very much. I know that you loved your country. I know that you thought you were doing the right thing. I know you are a good man."

Tears brimmed in his eyes.

"I want to bring you back to them. To your daughter. To Olga."

A dangerous look lit upon his features, one of savage hope. He almost smiled. "You do?" he croaked.

"I do," I replied. I hefted my rucksack onto my lap and rooted through it. "I need your help first, though."

"Oh?" He stiffened again.

I unslung the bag from my shoulders and grabbed one of the Mars Bars. I handed it to him and he looked at me as if I might be the Lord Himself before feverishly unwrapping the chocolate bar and inhaling it.

"I need you to help me find the rest of the people I brought here," I said. "I'm taking everybody back."

# Eight

The van's engine coughs, splutters, dies. I turn the ignition again and it does it again. It's not going to start, but I dumbly try it again, the bones in my fingers vibrating with pain.

"For fuck's sake," I say.

My target slumps next to me in the passenger seat. Apart from some minor cuts and bruises and a steady stream of blood running dark from a clearly broken nose, he's okay. He's still out, and I've recuffed him to the passenger rail.

I try the engine again, and it turns over and starts to idle. Fat rain plops onto the dirty glass. I try the wipers and all that does is smear mud across the windscreen. I pull away, bouncing across the torn-up field, the van sounding far less healthy than when I first rented it.

I only need it to last a little longer.

I bump back out onto the road and carry on.

"Why?" the man next to me burbles as he is jostled awake. He blows a scarlet bubble from his lips, tries to wipe it away by rubbing his mouth on his shoulder.

"Do I even need to dignify that with a response?" I say. "I'm pretty sure you know why I'm here."

The man laughs a little. A sad, resigned laugh. "Yeah, I guess." He spits a fresh wad of blood between his feet. "No point bargaining?"

"Nope."

I reach over and click the dial on the radio. It still works despite the acute bend in the aerial. The last half of "Livin' on a Prayer" crackles into being and I tap along.

Ha laughs, slowly, painfully. "This is one of my favourite songs," he mumbles.

I chuckle. "Hey, me too!" I say, and start tapping at the wheel along with the beat.

# Jess's Troubled History

I managed to stay awake for one more day before I gave in. Vlad insisted that I sleep in his bed, and even as my eyes drew closed with unimaginable weight, I struggled against it, knowing what dreams would come. I repeated over and over in my head like a delirious madman, *I will remember. I will remember.* I retrieved the Walkman from the bag, slipped in the mixtape, the first one she had ever made me, put the earphones on, and fell into it.

It began as it always did: incomprehensible darkness so deep and black that all ideas of direction or navigation are rendered meaningless. Then, the pulse of a heart in newly formed ears. The muted cadence of talking, or maybe the dull, sweet melody of a song, until finally light breaks upon me like the brightest dawn. Then with new eyes, we watch the doctors pulling apart her mother's abdomen, blue hands and arms slick with blood up to the elbow. Then the cold silence before we start screaming and crying.

Long moments pass as I stare up at ceilings with faces looking down on me. It's mostly her father—now our father, as each moment has been stolen by me, the experience now co-owned. Sometimes he's crying so hard that snot hangs out of his nose in long, grey tangles. He balls his fists and shouts at us when we cry, so we cry harder. Throws things at the wall, breaks a knuckle on the door. These moments come and go, emotional topography like some rugged terrain. Other days he looks upon us with love, because it's definitely there under all that resentment, under all that pain, and we see that it hurts him to face it.

We mark the time in steps soon after, faltering, falling ones, then confident strides until we are looking up at him, and he is sobbing with happiness this time.

The first time he really hits us is when we are five and we accidently drop the photograph of our mother and break the glass. A chunk of it cuts a neat line through her face. We look around and see him rushing at us, an undefeatable colossus. He lifts us up by one pudgy arm, pulling it out of its socket, and smacks us so hard that it leaves our ears ringing.

He screams when we won't stop crying, and then when he sees the dark bloom of colour and swelling around the joint, he cries as he drives us to hospital. He lies to the doctor's face and says we fell over. Our arm is put in a sling and when we get home, he gives us ice cream and puts us to bed, and says that he loves us.

This is a pattern that he will repeat over and over again. Except the trips to the hospital become infrequent and the causes of his outbursts become less predictable. We feel the threat of inexplicable violence rolling off him at all times like a sickness. It's worse when he drinks, and he does it a lot. We learn to cook when we are young. We learn to move quietly so as not to wake him. To not stand out in a room. To steal insignificant amounts of money from our father's wallet so we can buy takeout. To steel ourselves for when we know what is coming, because he can't stop escalating until he gets what he wants and explodes.

We are in his car on the way home from school. He is happy, the radio is on. It's the summer, near the long break that we dread so much. He is telling us about this new woman that he is seeing. Her name is Simone, and, wow, he can't wait for us to meet her. We are thirteen, belligerent. Angry even. So we say that we don't want to meet her. How could he? Mum is only dead thirteen years. And at the traffic lights he punches us in the face so hard that for a second it feels as if the world has exploded. We don't cry that time because crying doesn't work anymore. We learned that a long time ago. So we store it, drop it into that pit where a cold anger waits for its moment. He throws a tissue at us and pulls away, singing to Paul Simon's "You Can Call Me Al."

Six months later, he puts us in hospital.

He is drunk, reeling back and forth, wobbling as if the house were a fairground funhouse. He's waving a half-empty bottle of vodka at us, another lays empty at his feet. We've made the mistake of cooking late, and the smell of scrambling eggs partially covers up the alcoholic fug that follows him around. Old sweat marking tide lines in his stinking T-shirt. He staggers forward a step and knocks the pan off the heat. We reach for it and all of a sudden he is grabbing our wrists and screaming. So we push, and somehow the pan comes up and hits him in the face. Clusters of sticky egg streak across the tacky fat-stained wall. The half-empty bottle of vodka is in our hand now as he shows us a bloody snarl. We think we might die, but that cold thing that lives inside us tells us to break the bottle across his head. The glass doesn't break and the hit just sounds heavy. Sounds like a wooden steak hammer on meat. His face turns away, eyes close, so we do it again. This time it shatters and we are now holding a jagged glass knife.

The cold voice says to stab him in the neck. Whispers it so sweetly that it could never be wrong to do what it asks.

He screams and falls back, clutching at us as he goes. We fall backwards too, and underneath us the empty bottle breaks and we feel the shattered glass slip into our skin and then muscle. Feel the ping and pop of tendons separating under the million fine blades.

We can feel the blood leaving us in dark sheets, and we search ourselves for some consolation from that cold voice we keep deep inside, but it's gone as if it were never there.

We dial an ambulance and sit outside until it arrives. They ask where our parents are and we lie and tell them that we don't know, because we started the fight and we would get in trouble.

One hundred and twenty two stitches and a blood transfusion later, and our father shuffles into the hospital. He has dried blood in his hair, in his beard. He stands in the antiseptic light of the hallway like some shambolic ghoul, and when our eyes meet for a second, we turn away.

For the next year, we fall into an unsteady and unspoken alliance. He doesn't drink as much, and we stay out of each other's way. It works for a year until his mother dies and he starts drinking again. In the meantime we meet me, Eli me.

School was never anything we gave a shit about. Apart from the occasional bullying, and pervasive air of poorly covered up racism, we were left mostly alone. Then, one day, we see me walking up to us and pretending like we are friends. We'd heard of Eli, but never spoken to him. Never had reason to, and to be honest, couldn't care less.

We start a band with Rachel from our art and history classes, who can play guitar, and Phil, who can play the drums. It feels weird singing in front of people. Writing things down. Writing pain down and speaking it out, screaming it out. First rehearsal, we face away from the other two and scream at an invisible crowd. After six months, we recruit Rachel's friend Julia to play bass. She's not great and constantly talks about the circle of fifths, and we have no idea what she is on about. We call ourselves the Rotten Ones.

Eli is persistent in a way that is only mostly irritating. He has this eagerness, or innocence, about him, which seems like a mask. We know he's damaged. And when we start talking to him, it feels like we've met him before.

We start hanging out with older boys, spending more time outside the house than in. We get drunk for the first time at fourteen. A house party where all the boys look the same. Bright shirts tucked into jeans, black shoes. Hair gelled or in curtains hanging down over acne-scarred faces. We drink vodka and Cokes, and a boy called Matt who we recognise from school shouts at us as the bassline to the Prodigy's "No Good" rattles the windows in their frames. He tries to kiss us and we push him away. Pursed lips, closed eyes, a cluster of angry spots just by his nostril. We stagger out into the night air. The back garden. A group of boys smoking weed leer out from under the angled roof of a shed. We fall up the steps and back into the house. The air seems cloying. Thick with cigarette smoke and the sweetness of spilt alcohol and mixers. Queasy, we go upstairs to the toilet and there are two girls there, one is crying and the other is hugging her. They tell us to fuck off, and we turn around. Matt is there again, blocking the door. The music seems too loud and we can't hear what he is saying, but the smile he smiles is false, and when he reaches a hand out, we push him and he falls backwards and rolls down the stairs. People point at him and laugh and before he can get up, we stomp past and leave the house. The music slowly fades to a distant heartbeat of bass. We throw up on the way home, the lamp posts swaying, dragging bright trails of orange light like lit matches. "It's okay," we say to our reflection in the shop window.

Matt apologises when we see each other next. He says he was drunk and acted like a dickhead. We agree, and then, at Sophie's house party, he tries it on again. Standing in the packed hallway, we kiss. Lips wet, stinking of Jack and Coke, our own breath smelling vaguely of cigarettes and vodka. That was our first proper kiss. He grabs our waist and slowly grinds into us. The pressure is uncomfortable, so we push him away a little, but he persists. We stop the kiss and smile. "You're so fit," he says. "I just can't help myself." He comes in again and we kiss him, because we are drunk and no one has ever said we were pretty and meant it, and fuck it, why not. His hands slowly snake upwards. We have our eyes closed but can hear people cheering him on.

His hand cups one of our tits and we unlock, push him away.

"What the fuck, man. What's your problem?" he says. "You fucking frigid or something?"

Someone barges us and we pull away. He grabs at the sleeve of our top and it rips. A girl laughs obnoxiously, so we turn to her and punch her across the mouth. Matt's eyes are wide as we flip him off and disappear out the front door and down the street.

The Rotten Ones plays their first gig. It's a small pub in Archway and only about five people turn up. The regulars idly watch as we play for twenty-five minutes, hammering through each song at double the speed we normally play them at. It feels amazing to sing in front of other people and we don't forget the words.

Afterwards, we throw up.

We get invited to a house party by a guy at the arcade. He looks pretty cool. Leather jacket, long, dyed-black hair, and a Cure T-shirt. We ask him where, who is going, and he just says, "It'll be cool."

Drunk again. Staring down into the vomit floating on the surface of the shitty water. The acid smell of it, burning our nostrils. Someone pounding on the door in time with the music, shouting through the wood at us.

On our fifteenth birthday we have sex with a nineteen-year-old. We tell him it's our seventeenth birthday and he wants to give us a birthday present. Outside the arcade he smokes a joint and passes it to us. A warm, dizzy haze follows, stuck images like still frames slowly move and spin until they resolve themselves into the image of a bedroom. He is fucking us from behind, long pale fingers holding the curve of our ribs, the other hand pulling our hips into him. It doesn't hurt and we wonder if this is what an approximation of love might be like.

When he is done, we lay in a tangle of damp sheets. We are both naked, his warm hand resting lightly on our stomach, and it feels good. We sigh. Outside, it's raining, great sheets of it. The blurry numbers on a digital clock say 3:37, cast red light on our bare legs.

The next morning, he wakes us up with a shake. Tells us we have to go, he's got work. Our head feels like it's been stuffed with cotton wool, and as we slowly get dressed, we realise he isn't as attractive as we first thought. His teeth are crooked, yellow from smoking and drinking. He has a bunch of scars cut into his slender forearms. Neat rows of them up to his elbow, counting off something. He doesn't resemble the man dressed in midnight light. Bathed in the orange of streetlight and red LED. He seems diminished, as if maybe what we did was a mistake. That we were inadequate to fill the hole he sought to fill. That made us want him all the more. As we gathered up our clothes, we felt an urgent need to be enough. If not to him, to someone else. We kiss awkwardly as we leave, rushing out the door with a weak smile.

Slouched on a hard plastic bench in the café just opposite the flower shop in town, we drink bitter-tasting tea and try to piece together the evening. Our insides cramping a little from the sex.

We see him again, and he is angry. Someone has told him that we are fifteen and he thinks we are going to tell the police. He's shaking. His long, bony fingers balled up. We remember the feeling of them inside us. The sharp edge of a fingernail scratching us as he moved them in and out. It seems strange in that moment to remember such a detail when he is hissing at us. We laugh him off. He seems less concerned three hours later when we are back at his, sucking his dick. A little way into it, we throw up because he is being too rough, and he tells us that it's okay, and we end up having sex again. This time is much shorter than the first, and when we finish, he asks us to go. He seems sad, but we are too angry and upset to try and talk. The whole way home, we feel the wet slug of cum soaking through our knickers.

We don't see him again, and we are told that he killed himself six months later. We feel the weight of it and wonder, only in passing, if it had anything to do with us, but we are too far past caring to really examine it.

We drink with our new friends down by the arcade and after gigs. It starts as evenings, then it's also after school. The gigs pick up and we play a bunch of pubs on the periphery of Camden Town, like we are slowly circling our prize. We support bands like the Bloody Dubliners, Mary Celeste, Gorerot, and Hammerdark. Most of the metal crowds don't really like us, but we start to become a bit more popular.

Eli tags along when we meet friends sometimes. We are not sure about him. He seems too young. Too eager. Too broken. We feel like we need to fix ourselves before we take on another burden.

*Burden.*

The word sits there between our shared consciousness and I feel myself momentarily extricated from her in the dream. I try not to look, but there we are, him and me, looking at her with hangdog obsession. I know that he lost her once and thinks he is clever, hitting the right buttons in the right order, but we can *feel* that somehow, Jess and I. Some form of psychic turbulence. We like him because he is easy to be around, and he is interesting. A fucking cult. But it's frustrating when he won't share the details. Just waves us off, deflects. He's also funny though, so we let him stick around.

We watch the friendship blossom, and even haunted by the phantom of another timeline, we adhere to one another. Our thoughts stray to him often in moments of distress, and we find ourselves looking forward to seeing him.

We travel to London, and a year passes in a flicker book of hook-ups, drinking, drugs, and gigging. Phil leaves the Rotten Ones and is replaced on drums by a guy who will only let us call him Bug, even though his real name is David. He's a great drummer though, and so we all just give in and address him by his preferred nomenclature.

We play the Roundhouse supporting the Junkie Punks, and *Kerrang!* writes about it a week later, gets our name wrong. Drunk after the gig, we are sick in Camden Lock, then fall in, the icy-cold water stealing our breath before a punk boy with a bright-orange mohawk throws us his jacket as a lifeline and pulls us back in. The bleary lights outside the Stables Market playing off the murky water. A houseboat bangs against the concrete canal edge. In the piss-slick bathroom of the Electric Ballroom, a girl with her lip pierced three times offers us a line of coke and we laugh together and talk manically like we've always been friends. Then she disappears into the swell of sweating bodies and we don't see her again. We approach a skinny black boy with his top off and end up making out in the corner of the sweltering room as Bauhaus plays at jet-engine volume and steals our words. He writes down his phone number on a receipt and presses it into our sweaty palms. This place feels like home, and every week for six hours, we feel like we belong. We aren't judged for being black or for being weird. We are among our peers in a period of life marked by a sense of movement. Whatever we are doing feels like an act of rebellion somehow, and by simply enjoying ourselves, we are doing something good. Then, on a bus back to town, we realise we lost the boy's number. We wonder idly if maybe we will see him again and hope we do.

Eli is waiting for us at the arcade and we talk and smoke and laugh, and we don't feel the ache between our legs of a night of coked-up sex. He feels like a slow medicine somehow. A comedown after a heavy night.

Then we meet Paul. He's been dragged to the night club by some girl he fancies, and we think that it's cool that he seems so confident, even out of place at a goth club. He laughs as he tries head banging and asks us how to do it. He does a poor facsimile and waves it off, then offers to buy us a drink.

Outside, in the smoking area, he is charming and funny, and even though he is everything we don't really like in a guy—an Essex wide boy dressed like a chav out on a bender with his loud mates, trying to pick up alternative women—somehow it kind of makes us want him more. He kisses us, one hand gripping the back of our neck and the other holding a lit cigarette out behind him. The girl he came with, forgotten. We end up at his, a small shared flat in the next town over with a fan of black mould creeping up the bathroom tiles, a huge punctured bean bag in the middle of the front room, and a sun-faded poster of a topless Pamela Anderson on the back of his bedroom door.

We talk and drink and fuck and talk some more before we fall asleep listening to "Love Will Tear Us Apart" on his stereo system that has only one working speaker. He tells us that it works just fine as long as we don't want to listen to the Beatles.

The next day as we are digging through piles of discarded clothes looking for our own, we catch him staring at us. He is cut in half by a slice of light and we can see all the blonde hairs along his muscular arms. He says, "You're fit," then adds, "I've never fucked one of you lot before."

Jesus Christ that makes us angry, and when he sees it, he tries to play it off as a joke. He tells us that he means a goth girl, but that is bullshit, and so we storm out, heart pounding, on the verge of tears. He stands at the threshold of his flat wearing only a pair of grubby pants, calling our name.

Eli again. We don't tell him what's going on. Instead we head down to the park and talk for a couple of hours. It's in moments like this that he seems so fucking young and we feel like he's from some distant, other world. We are sat on a bench and he seems sullen. Tells me it's been a hard weekend for him. We talk about how we hate our parents, and we realise we haven't even seen our father in a week. Imagine him lying on the sofa decomposing, an army of maggots around him, dripping from his open mouth like rotten, squirming teeth.

"You should come to the Ballroom," we say. "I know the bouncers, I could probably get you in for free."

"I really want to," he says. "It sounds wicked."

"So many cool people there," we say. "Sexy ladies, too."

He looks away, then back, his face a little blotchy red from embarrassment.

"Nice," he says weakly, and we laugh.

"Jesus Christ, Eli. You need to fucking relax, man. You'll never get anyone pulling that face every time you talk about women."

"I don't really want to get... laid. I want a relationship. I want..." He catches himself staring at us. We can feel what he wants so acutely that it almost hurts. We want him to say the words that are clearly there and, for the first time, we realise that a part of us might smile and say okay. Because he would never say the sort of thing that Paul did, or even think it. He's one of the good ones, and we think that maybe we don't deserve that. That we were cursed at birth, or maybe that we've outgrown him somehow.

"Ahh nothing," he says. "Fuck it. *Tekken*?"

"Eli, do you ever think you might be cursed?"

His eyes goes wide. "Yeah," he stammers. "All the fucking time."

"Me too." The distant headlights of a car trace the dark fencing as we walk out of the park. "I think it's this fucking town, man."

Not long after Eli leaves us, Paul turns up wearing a sad face and holding a bouquet of roses. He fumbles over his words, and when we step outside for a cigarette, he tells us that he really did mean a goth girl and not a black girl. We get in his car and he drives us around. Just outside town we pass Eli's compound and slow to a stop.

"I heard they fucking murdered a bunch of people here in the '70's," Paul says.

"Stop," we say. "But, they definitely worship Satan."

"Fucking, freaks. Should burn the place to the ground and hang the lot of 'em."

He laughs. We don't correct it, or tell him that we know Eli. We feel sick that we didn't say anything, but rationalise it because it was just a joke. But that feeling persists.

Paul pulls away, nearly hitting a white van coming the other way.

Two or so miles out of town, we park up in a lay-by at the top of a hill. It's cold and he throws his puffer jacket over our shoulders. Behind us are the dark carved lines of the hilly countryside. On the top of one far slope is a farmhouse, orange lights in the windows, grey curls of smoke rising upwards. In front of us, the town spreads out in a beautiful sea of lambent lights. We sit on the bonnet of his car and smoke and talk about what we want in life. He wants nothing more than enough money to have fun every weekend. To buy a Cosworth and a nice place of his own. We say that we want to play music for a living, or paint, maybe write a book. He doesn't understand art, doesn't understand a desire to create something just for the joy of doing it. "It isn't really my thing," he says, and flicks the butt of the cigarette down the hillside. Just then, we wonder what we saw in him. Wonder if maybe we should leave, but then he leans over and we feel the warmth of his mouth on ours, his fingers creeping inside the lent jacket, and we think that this is why. Someone safe. Confident. Someone who wants us and knows how to make it easy. So we pull him closer and lose ourselves in the moment. The cold stars and streetlights shiver in the night air, above and below.

It doesn't take long for things to go south. In six months he goes from effusive and fun to questioning our every move, demanding to know where we are at all times. He accuses us of cheating on him at gigs. Then he asks us to move in, and when we say no, he screams at us. Driving around one Friday night, he asks again, and we say no again, so he stops and opens the car door and screams and screams at us until we get out. When we get home, the sky is tinted with morning light, and our feet are blistered and bleeding. We try and break it off, but he says no. Then another fight at the arcade happens and he is given the sack. What was exciting and dangerous quickly devolves into just dangerous. Hopped up on adrenaline and probably coke, he accuses us again of cheating. Of leading other men on. He calls us a slut, and when we push a finger into his chest and tell him to fuck himself, he smacks us across the face.

There's blood on his knuckles, smeared up past his wrists, and we think about his hands pressed against the small of our back, the rising goosebumps as those now bloody fingers delicately traced invisible lines on our back as we mumbled in half sleep.

His eyes widen when he realises what has happened. Recognition of a line crossed that cannot be taken back, and he tries to say sorry, but we cut him off with a look.

Just about holding it together, we growl, "We're fucking done," and he looks out past the bright, blinking, merry lights of the arcade and just nods dumbly.

Heartbroken we return home and settle into the familiar pattern of arguing with our father, and for a split second, we consider killing ourselves. We think about it, not in an emotional way, but in a flat, objective way. As if it might be the natural solution to a problem that keeps presenting itself in different ways. We think about the first boy we slept with, and we think about how it must have been for him. Hung himself, or OD'd. People didn't seem to care too much about him. We headline a gig at the Dublin Castle, the sweaty pub filled with jostling bodies bouncing against each other, moving to our songs. We play our asses off, and we sing as if it might be the only thing that saves our life. We feel like a god when we see people screaming the lyrics to our songs, and it's hard not to break the veneer of cool, of uncaring. This love feels somehow unconditional.

Then Eli happens. We don't plan for it, or even want it really, but that's the way it always seems to happen. He makes us so angry sometimes with how earnest he can be, but after New Year's and the fight with Paul, we see something there. Some edge glinting under the surface and we think, yeah, *maybe*.

We kiss. It's all eager tongue on his part. Lessons learned from movies maybe, or a loose idea of what kissing should be, and we think that it might be a mistake.

I try to pull these moments apart to lengthen them, but holes appear, and I start to feel a rising, floating feeling in my consciousness, I'm starting to wake up, and I don't want to wake up. Now that I'm in it, I want to feel everything, to intrude upon her every thought. To know her, to force a piece of her into me like some poisonous fragment, but the images become increasingly fleeting. I watch now through her eyes as we argue after being caught together. Feel her guilt as she compares me unfavourably to Paul. His experience and ease at everything. How thoughts of him slipped into her mind's eye as she closed her eyes and moved against me.

Then the long moments afterwards where we realise that Eli isn't easy at all. We spiral towards our last moments, me slowly falling out of sync with her consciousness. We see a present wrapped and a stone thrown. Kissing. The feeling of a love that isn't just about trying to meet someone's expectations or trying to fill an emptiness. It feels more of a peace, and a worry that it might end. Then the escape plan, and as we tumble towards Jess's death, we try harder to cling to it, but our consciousnesses slip apart and we separate. Only echoes of her thoughts and feelings break through the static.

It ends with fear and noise and smoke, then, finally, a gunshot.

Vladimir shaking us awake.

"You were screaming," he said afterwards, as I sat in the chair sobbing in front of the embers of a dying fire.

I tried to keep the dream of her life in my head. Turning each scene over and over, trying with all my bitter frustration and grief to hold the images together. But with each cycle, a sliver of detail slipped away here, and a stray thought fell away there, like leaves in an autumn wind, until just the feeling remained: her hunger for love and acceptance. A thing that should have been so easily given by those in a position to give it. The rawness of that desire felt alive somehow. Rabid, ravenous, unquenchable.

Did I love her more in that moment?

Before, she was sort of mythical to me. A woman whose hunger I was desirous of. But, yes, I loved her before I lived through those moments. I loved her from before I erased the original version of her. But after I dreamt her life, all the versions of my love became replaced with something all-encompassing. My grief and my desire became a singularity from which I knew I could never escape.

The batteries had died in the Walkman.

# My Troubled History, Part Eight

It was a week before we struck out for London. The supplies from my reality had pretty much run out, and Vladimir and I had salvaged what we could from the town to repair two ridiculous-looking bicycles we found in the back of a supply shop. It had taken most of the rest of the week to get them into some kind of working order.

"And you're sure they're going to be there?" I asked.

Vladimir made a face. "That's where they *said* they were going. How am I to know?"

I learned that since I had left him stranded a decade before, Vladimir had been acting as the gatekeeper for anyone else I brought through. The apocalypse being the great leveller and all, it appeared that anyone who came through the doorway, despot and dissident alike, were washed of their sins and sent on their way. I guess having an existential blowout might change a man. Neither of us had a good idea of how many people I had sent through, but it was somewhere in the region of two hundred and fifty. Enough to start a small town maybe—and that's what they had done. Vladimir had been left there on his own while everyone else started their own community.

"Why London? Why not stay here?" I asked.

"For a start, lots of shelter and salvage. Probably stockpiles of dried food and wine and supplies are still okay," he said, waving his hand in a motion that said maybe, maybe not. "The latest we could age this town was 1809." He had his bike upside down to work on it. He cranked the pedal with his hand, and the huge back wheel clanked and grinded, spinning cleanly, if unimpressively. He smiled for a moment, then remembered what he was talking about.

"Whatever happened to this place, must have happened then."

"What about all the people?" I asked.

He shrugged, curled his lip. "No one," he said. "Seems they go—" He did the universal sign for something going *poof*. "It's, how you say, ironic. Back home, I predicted something like this would happen, and then I end up here."

"Really?" I said, and gave my own wheel a spin. It wobbled a little, and Vladimir stepped over and tightened the nut with a rusty wrench until the wheel began to run more smoothly.

"Da. I predicted that the climate was changing for the worse—catastrophic even— because of fossil fuels. So, I took it to the government." He looked around shaking his head. "Big mistake. I should have known, but I was younger. *Ya byl idiotom*. More stupid."

The wind yowled through the house like a wounded cat stuck in the walls.

"Why not just kill me?" he asked.

I couldn't bring myself to tell him that he had been erased. That his daughter no longer existed, and that no one was looking for him because he was one of hundreds of forgotten people in the Book of Names.

"I should have come sooner," I said, apologising for what was only the third time that day.

He stopped the wheel from turning and looked at me.

"Why *did* you stop?" He nodded in the direction of the door. "Bringing them through there."

"I realised some things were wrong. We were supposed to be doing God's work or some shit, but I think our handlers—some suits with the British government—were just lying to us." I told him what had happened, why I couldn't go back. "And then I met someone…" I wanted to carry on, to say her name, but couldn't. My throat closed up and I could feel tears not far behind. I coughed, cleared it, and changed the subject. "Anyway, what do you think happened to the fucking moon?"

He shook his head, upturned his lips into a grimace. "That, I am not sure. Maybe a collision with a celestial object. It is fascinating. It is a sad shame that your—" he fumbled for the word, "—ability, was not used for science. But, as all things, it was instead manipulated by the government."

I told him about Johns, about the lie that we had been told.

"At first, I honestly thought we were doing good," I said. "My Grandfather helped changed the outcome of the Second World War."

"I am sure he did. But, was it the right outcome?"

"Let the Germans win?" I scoffed.

"No no no," he said, waving his hands at me. "Not everything is about winning and losing. Maybe that outcome was won at the wrong cost to ensure the benefit to the right people."

"My Grandfather was a hero," I protested. "I have his diary—the things he did. The places he went."

"And what about your Father, could he do what you do, too?"

I didn't want to talk about him. I kept remembering him, slumped forward on the kitchen table, shot and desperate. I kept waking to his voice ringing in my ears, begging me to save the family, and me just abandoning them all in the end.

I shook my head. "This—my ability—it skips a generation apparently. Lucky me, I guess."

Vladimir took a sip of twice-boiled water from one of the big green-glass bottles on the table. He wiped his mouth and offered it to me.

"Interesting. So, genetic then. How did your Father take it?" he asked.

"What?" I saw his bloody stomach, tried to shake the image away.

"Not having the ability."

"He hates me for it. Feels like it's wasted on me. At least, that's what he thought when I was six."

"That must have been hard."

I laughed bitterly. "Not quite as hard as living here for the past decade."

Vladimir nodded. "Da, that is the truth."

We turned our bikes right way up and started loading our makeshift backpacks with what little we had left. Enough to last a week Vladimir had said. When I proposed the plan, I had told him that I could just travel to other realities and get us what we needed, but I had soon come to realise, with a sense of creeping dread, that there were no other doors in this place. Purgatory was a sort of end of the line. I couldn't just dart out of it if I needed to. It was an unsettlingly claustrophobic feeling, being trapped and vulnerable like that.

After we were done on our final checks, Vladimir led me out to the front garden. He locked the door behind us, checked his hopeless crop one final time, and then we were gone.

Dappled in watery daylight, the tawny shades of the English countryside slowly rolled past. Wide expanses of heathland, hills, and hillocks dressed in patches of bruise-coloured gorse. Trees, shaped and twisted by the wind, stood lonely among the sharp brush and olive-coloured ferns. We rode out to where the motorway should be, but found only more unchecked landscape. Old fields marked by stone walls. Scarred with ancient desire lines and holloways instead of macadam and lamp posts.

Bleached white fields of wheat gone feral wavered in the wind.

We bounced and juddered on our oversized bicycles past jagged wrecks of farmhouses and through empty, forlorn towns, the slippery cobbles painfully shaking our bones as we clattered over them on our ancient contraptions.

"What sort of fucking surface do you think these bikes were made for riding on?" I shouted over the horrible noise.

"I'm starting to suspect," Vlad said, every word a forced staccato laced with discomfort, "these aren't for people."

Flies zipped and darted around us, chasing unknown paths. Birds twittered unseen from trees and occasionally lit upon the lilting and ivy-strangled walls and moss-covered gateposts. It was beyond eerie. We were two ghosts haunting a history we had never known. We watched as curtains of freezing rain swept across the distant, smudgy hills. As it reached us, we pulled up our hoods and carried on, but that didn't stop our hands from freezing. Each bullet-hard pellet of water stinging and pinging off the bike frames like stones.

We stopped and sheltered under the shade of a big oak tree, the deluge barely making it through the lattice of twisted branches above us. Our heads ached and hands vibrated with pain from the ride. We waited for the weather to pass as distant shafts of light poked through the rotten clouds, searchlights scouring the knotted hills. It was oddly beautiful, despite the rattling and drumming of the rain making me need to piss. The air smelt heavily of damp earth and dying flowers.

"Eli," Vladimir said. Our eyes met briefly, and then he looked away. "You want to know why I didn't kill you that night you arrived on my doorstep?" He turned to face me, and in that second, I saw the damage I had wrought upon his face. He looked like an old man. A forgotten prisoner found skulking and mad in the corner of some abandoned asylum. I tried to recall the man I had brought through to that place, but only the eyes seemed familiar to me.

"It was the child," he said.

"Child?" I replied, and then the memory registered. Dolma Nyima, the one I took back through. "Oh, him."

"I was walking in the night and I heard the child crying. Saw you there, in that house, looking for him. At first I thought I must be dreaming. Then I recognised you. All those years that I had spent trapped in this place came up like poison. I *was* going to kill you then. I swore it, but I was a different man then. Da, a desperate man." He waved the idea away and tried to smile, but under that massive beard, it just looked more threatening. "I watched from the bushes as you took the child back through, and I think to myself, maybe you come back for the others one day. Maybe you come back for me." He pointed at me. "And here you are. Several years too late, maybe, but here all the same."

"And now we are riding these gentlemen's bicycles around the fucking countryside like a right couple of plums."

"Maybe you should have come sooner."

"I wanted to, believe me. It was always my plan. As soon as I realised what was actually going on."

"Despite that, did you ever think that it is right to do this? To judge men and women in this way?"

"It wasn't like that," I said. "I grew up in this. I don't know if you remember, but I was just a little kid doing what I was told, and thinking it was the right thing to do because everyone said it was."

"And your Grandfather?"

"Him too."

I looked out at the shards of jaundiced light breaking through the murky clouds, shifting across the desolate fields. It had gotten colder now and a wind wrestled with the branches above, shaking and pulling at the tree.

"It cost me, too," I said. "All those people—you as well—left something inside me. A part of themselves. You must have felt it too."

"I do," he replied and tapped his chest. "I remember parts of you. Memories stuck like splinters in my mind. I dreamt your life, I know that much. But it all faded."

"Every time I did it. Every time I *do* it, a piece of me is cut away, replaced by a part of the person who came with me. I hardly know myself anymore."

"You are like broom."

"What?" I barked a sad laugh.

"Broom. You are like the story about the man who replaced every part of broom, but still considered it the same broom. Your parts have been replaced, and you worry if you are still you."

"Oh," I said. "Yes, something like that."

▽

Hayes was somewhere I had visited in my own reality. It was a busy town, and I knew roughly how to navigate it from one side to the other. The version I saw as we rode through towards London was nothing like the one I had experienced. I didn't even recognise it until I found the sign, and even then, I had trouble believing it was the same place. I was used to row upon row of shops lining busy streets. We came into the town following a low slate wall surrounded on both sides by squares of empty fields. It was still raining, and deep puddles had turned the track into a slippery bog. Dark clay squidged out from beneath our ridiculously thin wheels, and I nearly fell off twice as we slipped and skidded down a short hill. It was hard enough to maintain a walking pace, let alone a decent riding one, so we hopped off and rolled the bikes through town.

Dilapidated two-storey terraces lined either side of the cobbled streets. Most had fallen apart completely and mossy bricks lay strewn across the road, only small shards of their dull red peeking through. Some down to just two walls and a square space in the centre filled with rubble and vegetation. Fat roof beams and gables lay among rotted, ivy-strangled tables and chairs. A tree curving out from a fireplace, its branches twisted sunward, curling like arthritic fingers over a window ledge.

"This place gives me the creeps," Vladimir said. He pulled the collar of his coat up around his ears.

"It's fucking spooky, that's for sure," I replied.

Deeper into the town we found shops and pubs. In their clusters, they were mostly intact, as if the erosion had started at the outskirts and had not made it to the town's centre yet. Even the signage here was in much better condition. The rain picked up again, so Vladimir kicked in the door to a pub in the town square and we hid inside, watching the weather lash at what was left of the place.

We listened to the cold static hiss of the rainstorm on the ancient roads, its pitch changing a little with the intensity of the wind. Some errant downfall came over the stone threshold and wetted the thirsty dust covering the floor. A slow orchestra of rhythmic drips began to build as the water worked its way through the guts of the pub.

"What is she like?" Vladimir asked, breaking the silence between us.

"Who?" I asked, even though I knew who he was talking about.

"The girl. The one you met after you stopped bringing people here."

He let out a groan as he stood up, his knees clicking as his legs straightened. He walked behind the bar and started rooting through drawers and pulling cupboards open.

The place smelt of damp—damp wood, damp walls, damp rotten fabric, and damp leather covered with a white patina of mould. Under a lopsided table, a clutch of pale mushrooms bloomed. In the murky half-light, I made out webs of black mould creeping across the bloated plaster. I thought about Jess, her body buried not far from that of my Grandfather, only a reality away.

The thought brought her name to my lips. "Jess," I said, and it seemed to echo. "We were going to run away together."

Vladimir placed two dark objects on the countertop, two pipes side by side. I squinted: a pair of pistols.

"You ran away to here to escape marriage, I suppose?" he said, his eyes gleaming. What light could be found in that place glinted on his teeth, revealed by a wry smile.

"She's dead."

"Oh."

"I buried her here."

He walked back around the bar and came close.

"Tell me," he said, and I did.

The whole mess. The years of it that had weighed so heavily on me. I hadn't truly realised how much I was carrying until I unloaded it. I told him about the sacrifices. The beatings. About Johns, about Jess, and then, finally, about the raid on the compound and my family dying while I lay there next to her body, unwilling to move as they were most certainly murdered. He just listened, shaking his head. After it was done, I got up, walked to door, and looked out at the broken world. Because if I looked at him, I was pretty sure I would start crying and not be able to stop. Why he cared at all after what I had done to him was a mystery, but I was glad he did.

He stood up, the old chair he had been sitting on scraping across the dirty floor, leaving four dark lines on the wooden floor. He clapped me on the shoulder with a bony hand.

"I found something back there that might help," he said, and grabbed a dusty bottle from a shelf.

He brought it over and waved it in front of me.

"We can commiserate just like we do at home," he said, and unscrewed the cap. He wiped the neck with a sleeve and took a swig, shuddered, then wafted the bottle in front of my nose. It was that familiar acrid smell of vodka. Jess loved the stuff, had it in everything. I had drunk it only once before that day, and it had ended up with me lying face down in a park bush, vomiting up a bag of chips. He caught my arm before I could drink any.

"We toast," he said. "To lost family. May we find our way back to them some day."

I took a swig, the glass tasting just as foul as the liquid inside. Then I coughed and hacked as the liquor made a burning trail down my throat. It took everything I had to keep it down, but down it stayed.

We finished off the bottle, ended up drunk. I sang songs as Vladimir, whom I'd taken to calling Vlad, managed to get a fire going in the brick hearth as night began to fall. Long banks of smudgy black and grey clouds coalesced around a weak sunset, the last silvery light waning into a murky, cold dark. Wind pulled at the shutters outside, and they banged over the grimy windows. The building was alive with creaks and moans, dripping water, rain drumming on the shingled roof.

Vlad pushed some cut-up strips of bedding onto the kindling fire and, after a tense moment, it caught, black smoke rolling and curling up to the ceiling. He covered his mouth and coughed, then gave a small cheer of success. We sat by the crackling and popping fire, the shifting orange glow throwing our shadows monstrous across the old walls.

"Do you think we'll find anyone alive?" I asked.

He pursed his lips and rocked his head sideways, considering it. "Maybe, maybe not. Who can tell?"

"It's a waste of time, isn't it?"

He repeated the motion, but said nothing.

"Great," I said. I held my hands out to the flames. My skin had turned ruddy from being so close, could feel the tightening of my forehead.

"You know, in the siege of Leningrad during the Second World War, many millions of people ran out of food. Many people died. You know what the hungry people did? They started eating the dead people. Lots of them around."

"Holy shit," I said.

"Some decided: Why eat only the old dead? So they murdered their neighbours and ate them. And then they realised they liked it," he said. Fingers of flame reflected in his dark eyes. "That is the real reason why I live on my own. Why I did not go with the others to London." He paused, saw the horror in my eyes. "But, it is worth trying to find them," he said, finally.

"And they told you where they would be?"

"Like I said, they told me where they planned to go, not where they would be staying."

"Better than nothing, I guess."

"Da. That is, if the rain ever lets us leave this godforsaken town." He threw another few shreds of bedsheet onto the fire and poked them with a blackened and lightly smoking stick. "Tell me, Eli," he said and leaned back on one elbow. "Will you go see her again?"

For a long time I didn't answer. I couldn't. The idea that I could see her in another reality hadn't even crossed my mind. I was still grief addled.

"No," I said finally. "She wouldn't be the same."

Vlad nodded thoughtfully. "That would only be a bad thing. Sometimes when we lose something, we must let it go."

I had told Vlad I wouldn't, but the idea of trying to find Jess lingered, and the thought hung there for a moment. "I know," I said finally.

I lay on back, my pack propping my head up, and watched the flickering shadows dance across the ceiling as I pretended to sleep.

▽

I woke up cold and aching and hungover. My spine felt like it had been fused and my stomach was coils of fizzing acid. My mouth tasted foul and my tongue had grown fuzzy. A woodlouse was scurrying across my chest and I flicked it away with a dirty finger. Under a row of stools, I spied a small semicircle of pale mouse bones. The fire was just ashes now, and no heat came from it at all. My skin, clothes, hair, all felt damp. From the corner of the room, I heard Vlad cough, spit, and then an urgent, spattering stream of piss.

"Finally!" he exclaimed. "This damn rain has finally stopped."

I eased myself up onto both elbows and got to the hard work of sitting upright. The sunlight streaming through the mottled window was bright. Offensively so. I slowly, uneasily, got to my feet. I pulled away the chair we had used to keep the door shut and opened the room to the outside world. The vast columns of storm clouds were gone, and in their place was an azure sky and only a few small white tufts hanging just above the horizon. The ground was still slick, but at least it wasn't raining anymore. I thought I caught sight of a bird, but it was only some dangling ivy moving in the breeze.

"It is a sign, no?" Vlad said, coming up behind me and looking over my shoulder.

It did seem hopeful.

"Yeah. So, what's for breakfast?" I asked.

"Ha ha ha, good one." He laughed, clapped me on the shoulder, and laughed again. "You are funny. No food until later."

"I feel fucking awful," I said. "Why did you make me drink?"

"The best cure for heartbreak is vodka," he said. "Now you do not think about her, just your aching head."

"That is, like, the worst fucking cure ever."

We wheeled our bikes out of the derelict pub and down the rutted road. As we crossed to the opposite side of town, I swung my leg over the bike's strange bucket-like seat and we were away again. Painfully bumping towards London once more.

Half a day of hard riding across the reclaimed landscape and we had arrived. It was a subtle shift from farmers' fields to more densely built-up villages, loose collections of buildings constructed on the outskirts of the city, linked by broken and pitted roads. There were a few ivy-covered wooden guideposts that pointed the way in miles. Not long after that, the buildings were taller, more ornate, and less utilitarian. Outside Wembley, we rode past cramped terraces, black- and red-brick houses. The roads were more intact, but grass and weeds had still pulled down and destroyed most of them. After

Vladimir flew head first over the handlebars of his bike, crashing down onto his back, we were forced to walk again.

We followed alongside a slow stream that wended its way through the outskirts of Stonebridge towards Harlesden. The water curved and sped down a broad weir, where it foamed and churned, eventually smoothing out again into a caramel-coloured sheet. A nebulous grey swarm of midges hovered above its surface. The cluttered streets were lined with sagging trees whose roots had burst through the surface of the road and woven together, so that the ground seemed folded over and over on itself, compressed and layered it in a way that made it almost impossible to ride on with the unstable bicycles and their comically oversized wheels.

On the eastern outskirts of the town, we crossed a set of ancient train lines. The rails were rusted and brown but perfectly marked the route towards inner London. Pale grey and lilac flowers bloomed in the spaces between the sleepers.

"Hmm," Vlad said. "This is strange."

"What?" I said, seeking out whatever he was looking at. "They're just train tracks."

"This world must have been more advanced than ours was at the same time in history. Tracks like these, they didn't exist for another one hundred years in our world."

"Dude, how do you even know that?" I asked.

"I like trains," he replied, sheepishly. "But it's not the only thing I've noticed that seems strange—out of place for technology at this time in history."

"Perhaps you just got the date wrong? Maybe whatever happened to this place wasn't really that long ago, not even close to 1809."

"I do not think so," he said, first waggling a finger at me, then pointing to our bikes. "In our world, these horrible bone-shaking machines had been replaced by much more modern bicycle models by the time we were laying train tracks."

We rode alongside the tracks on the grassy berm rising to one side of them. It was tough going pushing through the weeds, but less painful that bouncing along the sleepers.

As the city grew around us, I couldn't shake the feeling of being watched. All those empty buildings, so many with mottled and murky glass still set in their stone window frames. I wondered then if ghosts might be real, whether the fragile barrier between this world and the tenebrous murk that lay beyond had somehow dissolved, and the two had become overlaid. I couldn't help but imagine that legions of the dead, somehow quickened to life once more, stared out at us, their pale fingers pressed to the windowpanes, watching these two interlopers with some kind of malicious envy.

I shivered at the thought, my scalp tingling with the uncomfortable sensation of being tracked. "Have you ever been to London?" I asked.

"Not this terrible version," Vlad replied. "I did once before, though. Beautiful city."

"This place is giving me the fucking creeps," I said. "What happened to all the people?"

"That is a good question. I've asked myself that many, many times, Eli."

We clattered down the abandoned streets.

"It's St. Paul's we're heading for, right?" I said.

"Da."

"Shall we stop and eat first?" I asked, worried that we might have to share our food with anyone we came across.

"Da."

We found a tall, swanky-looking brick hotel near Pall Mall. It was a huge square building with a row of vacant flagpoles jutting from above the wide entrance. I recognised it from pictures I'd seen somewhere. We set about breaking in. The heavy wooden double doors didn't budge at our first attempts to kick them in, and we nearly gave up and went elsewhere.

But Vlad held up his hand. "At the same time?" he said, then counted off three, two, one on his fingers. We threw ourselves shoulder first into them, and they gave. We flew through the wood, the lock flying inwards and the two of us falling with a loud thud onto the dusty marble floor.

"Ow," I grumbled as we disentangled ourselves. He gave a throaty chuckle and picked himself up, went back outside, and brought our rucksacks in, closing the door behind him.

It was bright inside the hotel. Pale-green shafts of daylight streamed into the foyer through the tall moss-covered windows, giving the black-and-white marble floor a sickly cast. High above the centre of the foyer and the long reception desk was an elaborate chandelier hanging from a thick chain, a grey-green patina dappling the surface of the metal. The light flared from the rows of gently moving cut-crystal pendeloques that dripped from the ornate gold arms. Spiderwebs hung from the ceiling in low lazy arcs that shivered and broke apart in the breeze that had followed us in.

The whole place had been extremely well preserved. There was a whiff of something stale on the air, but other than that, it was only the husks of flies, spiders, and other assorted insects littered across every available, dust-covered surface that made the place seem abandoned.

I clapped, and the sound echoed around the great room. In one corner sat a giant black piano, an empty stool angled away from it invitingly. Vlad sat down, lifted the lid on the keys, and played a few ghostly sounding notes on the horribly out-of-tune instrument. There were large plant pots everywhere, sad-looking terracotta half filled with crumbly dirt, the plants that had once lived there long since rotted away.

"Nice place," I said, and whistled. Vlad stood straight, cricked his back with a long sigh, and made for the giant marble fireplace. Two leather chairs and an ottoman sat in front of the blackened hearth.

"Finally," Vlad exclaimed, moving to a set of upturned wooden chairs near the centre of the room. "Some dry wood." He set about breaking them down and building a fire to warm our lunch.

"While you do that I am going to have a little look around," I said, and left him to it.

"Be careful," he called after me. "Might not be safe."

Now, I know I had a sheltered life, but after I met Jess, she introduced me to a slew of things—drinking, music, films. Basically, everything that I ended up loving for the rest of my life came from her. Among all the things that Jess introduced me to that I now love, the one exception was horror films. We'd sit curled up in her bed, blankets pulled up to my face, and watch movies like *The Evil Dead*, *The Texas Chainsaw Massacre*, *The Driller Killer*, and *Dawn of the Dead*. All I could ever think about was how her drunken father might kick down the door at any moment and try and recreate any number of the ghastly scenes that Jess subjected me to. In those moments—the ones where someone splits off from the group and gets themselves murdered, or when the masked killer is bearing down on the good-looking protagonists—I felt real, tangible fear. Real monsters lurked in Jess's house. One that she knew, and one that she had no idea about.

One particular film surfaced in my mind as I walked away from Vladimir and climbed the split marble staircase that wrapped around the reception desk, my footsteps becoming muffled at the top of the stairs, the sound deadened by expensive carpets, as I quietly walked the vacant corridors. *The Shining*. I couldn't get it out of my head, and I nearly ran full tilt back to the foyer. I became hyperaware of the sounds around me. Ghostly thumps from upstairs, my shallow—on the verge of hyperventilating—breathing. My all-too-loud heartbeat that wanted to give me away to any feral, bloodthirsty creature that might be hiding behind the gallery of locked doors that lay ahead.

"Don't be a fucking idiot," I hissed to myself through gritted teeth. Blowing out a short, controlled breath, I steeled myself and pushed further on.

It was considerably darker in the guts of the building, but a stream of sickly mossy light still streamed in through a long window at the far end of the corridor. More webs stretched from the upturned gaslights that lined the walls. Ghostly membranes of spider's silk crisscrossed each other, made opaque by the decades of dust they had caught. It looked like a clichéd haunted house. I looked over my shoulder at a wet clicking sound, but there was nothing. When I turned back, I got a mouthful of cobweb.

"Urghh!" I snatched it away from my mouth and spat.

The walls were spotted with mildew and mould but, for some reason, the doors appeared almost spotless. I half-heartedly tried a few, but they were locked. I had a vague idea to go back and get the keys, but I couldn't see the point. The rooms inside were likely empty anyway. At the end of the hall were more sets of stairs on either side, twisting curlicues of dark wood set underneath balustrades running up and around to the floors above. I took the right-hand steps out of habit and went up a floor. Looking down the corridor, I could see that it ended on a balcony overlooking the foyer. I went up another level, to the top floor, and stopped. A prickly coating of sweat had started to spread across my back.

The window at the end of the hall was almost entirely obscured by years of accumulated bird shit and dirt. What caught my eye was a thin sliver of light coming from one of the rooms about halfway down the hall. The door had been left slightly ajar. All I could think of were the two dead little girls.

"Come play with us," they said in unison in my mind. "Forever." Thwack. "And ever." Bloody corpses. Impossible to discern which messy bit belonged to which ripped apart body. "And ever."

I pushed the thought away. Okay, so I was in a different reality. One where every human had somehow vanished and the moon had exploded. Kind of creepy. But I resolved to believe that there was no such thing as ghosts.

The door creaked and a tiny scream popped from my lips like an unstoppable fart.

I laughed, my heart DJ-ing some drum and bass loudly in my chest. The great reserves of adrenaline that my body kept for emergency situations suddenly loosed into my bloodstream. My muscles felt springy, and I needed to run, fight, or shit. Possibly all at the same time.

The door creaked again. It was just a breeze moving through the building.

I let out a huge sigh, then walked through the doorway.

It was bright inside the room. The curtains had been thrown open and dust, stirred up by my footsteps, floated and winked in the stale air. No ghosts. No undead, cackling woman in the bathtub. Nothing. The carpet had mouldered a little, but otherwise the room was fine. I scoured it, but there was nothing there, so I left.

Halfway back towards the staircase, I noticed another door slightly ajar. Behind the thick wood, I heard the familiar static crackle of a doorway to another reality. Excited, I pushed the door open, but instead of a doorway, I was confronted by an explosion of black flies. They burst through the widened gap and sent me staggering backwards against the wall, my arm up to my mouth. When I finally fought my way into the room, I found lying on the bed the mostly decomposed body of a man, a mass of writhing maggots and flies busying themselves on his rotten flesh.

# Nine

Distant thunder percolates under the sound of the radio. It's the news now. Wars in the Middle East. Mass shootings. Weather going utterly batshit and blowing towns away like it's *The Wizard of Oz* hopped up on crack. This reality isn't perfect, but you take what you can get if you are forced to live here.

Things are the same in almost every reality I've visited. It's almost always war, and famine, and rich people doing their best to stay that way at the cost of others. Celebrities on the TV asking poor people for cash for even poorer people. Nature always wanting to maintain the status quo. Everything kind of shitty in all the same ways, but nothing really *apocalyptic*. Maybe things are different eight, nine, ten divergent realities away—but almost every reality is shit in its own way. It's taken years for me to arrive at this conclusion, and maybe I'm wrong, but every time I walk through a new doorway, that little glimmer of hope that I might be arriving in the best of all possible worlds is extinguished almost instantly. It's really just tiring, man.

I can feel my passenger's gaze on me. He's thinking what I would be thinking if it were the other way around. Escape plans being made, weighing up all the options until there are none left. That vague hope that some chance event will miraculously occur and save him.

"I won't tell you," he says finally. He winces, adjusts the cuffs to take the weight off.

I turn to him for a moment and smile. "Look, I don't want to make you feel bad, but your plan to engage with me or whatever is not going to work," I say. I hit the wipers again and the windscreen clears for a second. The automatic sensor appears to be broken, and I have to manually wipe the screen. Up ahead, it's all just silvery rods of rain and savage darkness, crooked trees looming on the periphery of the one operational headlight.

I can feel him staring at me.

"Look, I've been at this game a long fucking time—and you *will* tell me. I promise you that."

# My Troubled History, Part Nine

Vladimir looked into the room for a long moment. He had his T-shirt pulled up over his nose against the smell, but I wasn't sure the air he was breathing under it was any fresher.

"About three weeks, give or take," he said, and pulled the door closed behind him, stepped gingerly around the pool of vomit I'd left soaking into the carpet.

"Oh," I said. "Do you recognise him?"

"Da," said Vlad. "I think so. He arrived one or two years ago. It was a harsh winter. Two of his fingers went bad, fell off. That was him."

"Fuck."

"That, we did not do."

It occurred to me again that I had just as assuredly been sending people to their death when I let them go free instead of murdering them the moment I brought them through like I was supposed to do. That maybe they were ill-equipped to deal with survival out here in this apocalyptic wasteland with no food, clothes, or water. I always thought that in some small way I was doing the right thing, that I was absolved. The thought that I had still been killing them all along, just much, much more slowly, made me feel sicker than the sight of the actual body.

"We should go," Vlad said, and I nodded. "Food will be ready soon."

"Are you really going to be able to eat after seeing... that?" I asked, holding my stomach.

He nodded. "I am hungry."

He'd made a potato soup and, despite the lack of seasoning and any other ingredients at all, it was actually even more disgusting than I could have imagined.

"It's okay?" he asked as I spluttered and coughed hot, starchy potato broth all over myself.

"Jesus. That's fucking awful," I replied.

Vlad took a small mouthful, grimaced, and then said, "It's not *that* bad."

"Wasn't there anything left in the kitchen?" I asked, spooning another mouthful of it into my mouth.

"I hadn't finished looking when I heard your scream. I thought it was the spirit of my babushka come to haunt me."

"Oh, fuck you," I said, and he laughed. "I'm going to go see if there is anything that can help make this edible, some spices or *something*."

The kitchen was expansive. Long rows of wooden tables in neat lines with rows and rows of pans and utensils hanging from hooks above them. On the shelves at the back of the room stood stacks of ceramic jars, but I couldn't read the handwritten labels on them in the gloomy light, cast only through the propped open door I had come through. I found a pot of black pepper and another with salt. Triumphant, I walked back in and put them on the ottoman between us.

Vlad took the salt and liberally sprinkled it on his soup.

It didn't help much, but I put some on my own food anyway and forced myself to eat. Each porridgy mouthful punctuated by the image of the dead man upstairs. The fat, off-white maggots that pulsed in his empty eye sockets. The mephitic stink of it, somehow warm, somehow sweet.

Vlad coughed and flecks of potato dislodged from his beard and splattered on his lap.

He cleared his throat. "You should eat it all."

"I'm not really hungry," I replied. "Not after…" I pointed upstairs.

"No point letting it go to waste," he said. As if to illustrate his point, he lapped at the empty bowl like a cat until it was clean. I nodded. "Feeling bad won't help," he continued. "Getting the ones left behind is the only road to salvation."

"What if they want to kill me?"

He mulled over the question for a moment.

"Maybe you should have thought about that before you stole them away and brought them to this terror planet."

"Great," I said. "Thanks for the advice."

"Try not to worry," he said. "You are the only way for them to leave. They know that." He swallowed with an audible gulp. "When we get back—well, then it may be a problem."

He smiled a smile that didn't help me feel any better.

▽

Inner London along the banks of the Thames had been decimated. It looked as though the buildings had collapsed all together, each bringing others down with it, like dominos. Along the place that had been the Embankment, blocks of buildings had collapsed into the water's edge. Eroded away until they had spilt into the dark waters. A partially constructed London Bridge lay in two halves, each end dipping down into the cold river, ancient pulleys and ropes snapping in the wind.

We pushed forward towards the intact Big Ben, a dark finger raised in silence across the broken skyline.

"Do you think they'll still be there? or will they have moved on from St. Paul's?" I shouted to Vlad, who was lagging behind.

"Who knows?" he replied, his voice juddering as we clattered over the cobblestones. Weeds that had pushed up through the cracks thrashed against the wheels of the velocipedes.

We rounded a corner, taking it wide and skirting around an abandoned apple cart that had been pulled lengthways across the road. I heard the sound of footsteps and turned to see a man running full bore out of the darkness of a shuttered doorway straight for me.

He collided with me and we both sprawled sideways, the bike flying out from under me and into Vlad's path, nearly sending him over the handlebars again.

A great pain lit up my ribs and ankle as the stranger climbed on top of me. He threw a punch and I managed to get my arms up to protect against it, but the fist caught my elbow and made my entire arm go numb. He drew his hand back and yelled, then threw his left. It slipped over my arms and caught me in the forehead, driving the back of my head into the edge of a cobble and sending sparks of white across my eyes.

"Fucker," he screamed at me through gritted teeth, a feral look in his eyes. "Fucker! Kill you. Kill you."

He punched again, this time catching my ear and making it ring loudly.

I tried to hit back, but I had no strength. What was worse was that something sharp was digging into my leg and I could feel it dragging along the skin as I flailed underneath my attacker, hot blood starting to pulse out from the deep gouge.

Out of the corner of my eye I saw Vlad, and then what felt like a year or two later, he pulled my attacker up and off of me. He had one wiry arm locked tightly around his neck and the point of a dirty knife pressed against his throat with the other. The man's eyes went very wide, as if he'd just snapped out of an awful waking nightmare. He raised his hands in submission, bent his neck to try and see the blade.

"Easy there," Vlad said soothingly. "I do not want to hurt you."

"All right, all right. Stop. Just stop," he pleaded, though his eyes were still narrowed at me.

Vlad looked at me and I nodded, so he let the man go. He brushed aside Vlad's outstretched hand and stood there, staring at me, as if contemplating another attack.

When I tried to stand, I realised that the thing stabbing my leg was a jagged shard of metal stuck between two cobbles. It had gone straight through my clothes and torn a chunk of skin away in a crimson flap. I pulled my leg away from it and inspected the damage. It wasn't that deep, but it throbbed and burnt all the same. My head felt tender. Thankfully, I wasn't bleeding, but already a lump was blooming at the back of my skull and the constant headache from being so long out of my reality was about ten degrees worse.

"You okay?" Vlad asked.

I tried not to cry, but failed.

"Oh don't give me that shit," my attacker said, throwing up his arms and pacing back and forth in front of us. "You fucking sent me here to die and you want me to feel bad about hitting you? Fuck yourself."

"Easy," Vlad said, the knife still drawn, kept low by his side. "He's here to take us back."

A mix of emotions fell across the man's heavy brow.

"He's here to what?" he said.

"Why do you think I'm here, you fucking idiot?" I shouted between sobs. I recognised him now. His name was Michael. I had brought him through not long after my thirteenth birthday. He had been crying much the same as I was now. I had seen his wife and child so clearly in his mind's eye. I felt the utter devastation of losing them. "Michael," I whispered. "I'm sorry that I kept you away from your family. But I can take you back to them."

It occurred to me that maybe I deserved far worse than a couple of punches to the head. I climbed up, swiped at the tears with my sleeve, and hobbled away from them. I left Vlad to talk to Michael and walked to the banks of the Thames and sat on the rocky shore. I rubbed at my aching head and watched the dull, grey water running east towards the sea. I wondered if the thing that had happened in this reality was confined to the UK, and a strange daydream came to mind of me crossing an impossibly wide, flat ocean on my own as vast pale creatures circled under the surface. It gave me the shivers, and when Vlad came to join me, the sound of his boots crunching on the stones was enough to make me jump.

"He said that he will gather the others," Vlad said. He let out a long groan as he sat down next to me.

"That's good, right?" I said, and spat some blood into the dirt. "I mean, that's great. How many people, did he say?"

"Eighty, give or take."

"What about the rest?" I asked.

"Gone."

"Gone like gone, or gone like…"

"Dead."

"Yeah, like dead."

"They are dead, Eli."

I bit my lip. "I was worried that's what you meant."

I'd killed easily over a hundred and fifty people. What made it worse was the fact that I couldn't even remember them. I didn't know exactly how many. I didn't know their faces. They lived inside me in the parts that I had stolen, but I would never remember them completely, just feel their pull.

Vlad tried to put a consolatory arm around my shoulder, but I shrugged it away. I got up and started laughing manically.

"It makes total fucking sense now," I said. "Losing Jess, losing my family was my punishment. It's the cost for what I've done. And I don't deserve happiness. I don't even deserve life."

"You're wrong—" Vlad started. But I caught Michael's glare, could feel the unmitigated hatred burning in it.

"Am I? Am I wrong? I fucking murdered those people." Saying it aloud made it hit me again in a fresh wave. I bent over double and gagged.

"No. You were made to do it."

"I could have said no. I *should* have fucking well said no."

"They were going to kill your family."

"They did that anyway, didn't they?"

I felt utterly empty, and I can tell you now that the only thing that stopped me from snatching Vlad's blade and cutting my own neck in that moment was the fact that I could at least fix some of the shit I'd done. My parents had wanted to bring them all back, or at least they'd hinted as much when we finally realised what Johns really was. I figured it was the least I could do.

"Tell them," I shouted to Michael, who was keeping his distance. "Tell them to meet me at the doorway. Just tell them, tell them I'm going to fix it. I'm going to fix all of it."

I turned to Vlad. "How can I look any of those people in the eyes after what I've done? I want to go back to your place now. We should just do that."

"Da," Vladimir said, and got to his feet. He slapped his thighs. "We can do that."

Vlad walked over to Michael and explained the plan. He was to bring everyone that was left to Vlad's shack in five days' time. After they agreed on the details, we turned our bicycles back the way we had come and travelled home.

That night, we took shelter in a squat, decaying cottage on the outskirts of Buckinghamshire. We stepped over the broken gate and made our way across the small patch of what would have been a small field of wild grain. Ivy and moss covered most of the building, and we had to chop it away from the door before we could get in. Inside was cold, dark, and smelt of damp earth. I tried to convince Vlad that we should find somewhere, anywhere else, but the air was bitterly cold, and he had become petulant and refused. We'd both come off our bikes during the ride out, him slipping sideways on the muddy, uneven ground, and me bouncing over a ditch, missing the pedal, and falling painfully on my chest.

He stretched out his arms, taking in the sullen view, and said, "And where is it you think we should stay?"

So we sat wrapped up in our damp clothes and stared at each other in the gloomy living room until night fell. In the dark, we sat listening to the distant hiss and crack of a storm blooming in the east as it grew closer and closer until it finally swept over the house. There was a fireplace in the centre of the room, but Vlad didn't want to take the chance of burning the house down while we slept, although a part of me wished exactly that would happen.

"Do you believe in God, Eli?" His voice came from the darkness, like some ghost from my past. Jess had asked me the same thing once. She was now in a better position to know than I was.

I shrugged, then realised he couldn't see me. "I don't know," I said. "I used to. We used to worship the God In-between, but I didn't know any better."

"The God In-between?"

"Yeah. In-between the spaces of reality, you know?"

"That space between our world and this?" He shuddered. "I try not to think about this."

"Yeah. It's pretty fucked up. I've kind of gotten used to it now. The God that we worshipped—he was supposed to live there. That place was his realm, and we did his work."

"And do you know better, now?" Vlad asked.

"I've never seen him, but if he does exist, he has a lot to answer for. I mean why the fuck does he let people die?"

"When my mother died, I asked my father the same thing. He told me that grief could be just as beautiful as joy."

"Doesn't feel that way."

"He was a drunk, but he has point."

"I don't see it."

▽

It was still raining hard when we finally arrived back at Vlad's place, drenched and miserable. The last stretch of it we cycled in silence, eyes firmly fixed on where we were headed, driven only by a grim determination to get home. I followed Vlad into the house and he disappeared, then reappeared a few minutes later with some clean clothes. Not long after that, the fire was going and we were drinking hot nettle tea from cracked crockery and talking again.

Arriving two days later than expected, the others came after a week in a huddled ragtag mass. Like a procession of degenerate ghosts. A cavalcade of dirty spectres. Refugees from some godforsaken place most people couldn't even comprehend. It was like hell—or some version of my own personal hell, anyway. I had personally wronged all of these people. Tiny flares of recognition lit the dark places of my mind for some of them, but not many. I had dreamt all of these people's lives at some point, and most had become just a blur to me now, an unending carousel of faces and memories, and despair.

Vlad stood by my side and tried to get everything into some kind of order. "Who is sick?" he cried. "Sick people first. Then women. Are there children?"

A man and a woman stepped forward, political dissidents from some burgeoning rebellion somewhere in the Middle East that thanks to their evaporation from the timeline ended up amounting to nothing. In the arms of the sallow-faced man was a baby.

"Okay," Vlad said, ushering them to one side. The man covered the baby's face with a rag to protect it from the rain. "You first."

A young woman came forward after the couple. She was pale, sickly looking with a sheen of sweat plastering her dark hair to her forehead. She didn't speak English, but it became all too apparent what was wrong when she showed the two of us her arm. A long, ragged cut ran the length of her arm from wrist to elbow. The skin around it was mottled and stunk.

"Jesus," I said and drew back, not wanting to see any more of it. Vlad leant forward to take a better look.

"She may not survive this even if we can get help," he whispered to me.

I tried not to meet her sullen gaze. I scanned the crowd. Most were staring directly at me, some with bitter, angry faces. Others just looked desperate to get home.

We walked the short distance to the doorway back to our home reality. It felt strange to return to it with the intention of undoing all that my family and I had done, but it also felt good. We passed by Jess's grave. The freshly turned mound stark among the dead grass. Vlad put his hand on my shoulder and squeezed.

"She would be proud of this, I am sure of it."

Those familiar waves of static rolled from the doorway. It was comforting to know that I was so close to home, even if I would have to face the reality of what I had left behind.

The odour of ozone and burning metal leaked from the place between realities, bringing to mind the raid on the compound. I was afraid of what I might see on the other side, even though I'd already seen so many other versions of it in ruins. This time, it would be my own.

"Wait here," I said to the crowd. There was some murmuring and discontent. I raised my hands. "I'll be right back. Just need to check that the coast is clear." I nodded to Vlad. "Be back in a sec," I said, and he nodded, smiled.

Like an old reflexive action, I slipped between realities, the venous strip of convergence guiding me back to my own version of the world. I felt the tiny remains of the headache float away. I had barely registered the pain after the first three days, but felt its absence keenly.

▽

Stark daylight.

All around me were the charred remains of the compound. The brick buildings mostly still stood, but were scorched, pocked by gunfire, their roofs collapsed inwards. The tower where my room had been was completely gone, reduced to a pile of charred beams. I recalled my Father then, sitting at the table. Dying and talking like it was the end of everything. I felt a fresh pang of loss. And guilt for the ones I had left behind. Choosing to save Jess over my family and failing even at that. So many wrong choices. I remember how urgent my need was to go back and save all those people I had left behind in Purgatory in that moment. I needed to at least partially redeem myself. It was all I could do.

A moment later, I felt a sting in my leg. Looked down to see a dart in my thigh just before the world went sideways and I flopped bonelessly to my knees and then onto my back, a swatch of warm sky filling my vision.

Expressionless faces regarded me as a bag was pulled over my head and everything went black.

My last thought before I slipped into a deep ocean of sleep was that I'd failed Vlad for the second time.

# Ten

The single headlight casts a bright searchlight over the ruins of the New Sunrise Project compound. The van rolls the last fifty feet, crunching on the gravel drive, slowing to a stop just in front of the gate. The engine idles for a moment, then coughs, the wounded machinery under the bonnet crunching and whining. It sputters and finally dies, and I wonder if that is it—kaputski, a write-off.

I pat the dashboard fondly. "You can sleep now."

My guest looks up and smiles weakly at the remains of the buildings, his teeth a grid of red lines. The blackened fingers of joists and walls rise stark against the grey and purple night behind them.

"Last stop," I say.

I climb out gingerly and walk around to the passenger side. When I yank the door open, he kicks wildly at me, trying to push me away and catching my shin.

"Stop it, you fucking moron." I grab his leg and move in close, then punch him a few times in the guts. "Stop it."

The air goes out of him and he sags back into the seat. I uncuff one of his wrists from the passenger rail and then recuff it to the other hand before he can draw it away. Grabbing him by the back of the head and pushing the small of his back, I lead him to the gate and kick it open. The squealing metal sets my teeth on edge as it drags across the cement, a clump of earthy weeds going with it.

The compound is as dead as it has been for the last ten years since I emerged, bleary eyed, back into my own reality and was black-bagged. The whole place is an overgrown ruin, largely untouched since the raid and mostly reclaimed by nature. The government fenced off the land, and aside from a few drunken parties and Halloween dares, it's been left to rot. Blackened beams, now mossy and covered in ivy, litter the courtyard. The front door is still there. Oddly untouched after all these years, except for a patina of gunk and bird shit colouring its pale-blue paint. I wonder idly who made the decision to paint it that colour, why they went a different way.

We walk slowly through the shell of the main building. The ghosts of childhood lurking somewhere in the curled strips of paint and discoloured wallpaper that peek out from under the rot and mould.

We pass through the kitchen, still intact somehow. The place where Johns sat. The place where my Mother had cried at the knowledge of my abuse at my Father's hands. She bore a burden of silence with febrile kindness, and I couldn't bring myself to hate her for it. But now—now there was nothing and all these people were gone to dust and bones.

I right a chair and push him down into it. He looks around with a sort of dismal wonder and then back at me. It's weird looking at my own face. Like watching a memory being played back.

"Why?" he says. It's the most obvious question, and one he knows the answer to. I roll my eyes, and he adds, "I mean, why now?"

I shrug, "Just took me this long to find you. Truth is, I wasn't even really looking. Just sort of stumbled across you."

"Oh," he murmurs.

"You don't sound very surprised."

He smiles, something unpleasant tugging at his features.

"Keep smiling," I say. "We'll see how long that lasts."

In the cupboard above the sink is a bag of equipment I had stashed there before I rented the van and kidnapped myself. I grab pliers, a blowtorch, heavy-gauge clippers, and a length of chain. Brutal and somewhat cliché means of information extraction they may be, but I've learned that they cut straight to the heart of the matter.

I snap another set of handcuffs around the first pair and the chain, then wrap that around the table until his hands are pulled to the centre of the table top. He looks at me with a fucking hangdog expression that I've seen before in others, but these tiny emotions on his version of my face are foreign to me.

They drop away as I place the items of interrogation on the table in front of him, and he just stares at them madly.

# My Troubled History, Part Ten

A white room. Bright fluorescents buzzing like angry insects. It took a minute for my eyes to adjust, for the room to stop lilting, and for the table to stop looking like it was being slowly pulled away. I realised there was someone else in the room. Half expected to see Johns standing there, his face pulled into a skeletal grimace, but it wasn't him. The man standing just inside the door was round faced, older looking that Johns, and with a neat white beard. He was holding two cups of steaming tea that gently shook as he negotiated the path from the door to where I was sat. Gently kicking out the chair opposite me, he sat down and placed one of the cups in front of me.

"I do have to apologise," he said. "We don't have any beds here, so we had to put you in the interview room."

I reached out for the tea and brought it to my lips.

"Be careful," he said. "It's very hot."

"Haven't had a cup of tea in fucking ages," I said, eyeing the old man up and down.

"Yes, we've been waiting for you to return. I've been wanting to have a conversation with you since I heard."

"Is this what you do with all of your guests? Fucking shoot them in the leg with a sleep dart and put a bag over their head?"

"Once again, I do have to apologise for the level of enthusiasm with which you were detained," he said. "I had asked for something somewhat more civil. I must confess that those instructions may have lacked sufficient—erm, detail—as to the hows and so forth."

I leant back on the legs of the chair, crossed one leg over the other, and shot him a look of juvenile defiance.

"And you are?"

"My name is Jeffries. I'm the new head of this department. Well, I say 'new,' but really 'old' is more accurate. I did this job for quite some time, and now, because of this"—he cleared his throat—"unfortunate situation, I have been asked to return to my previous position."

"What happened to Johns?"

Jeffries's eyes moved to the boxy-looking camera mounted on the wall.

"Ah, unfortunately Mr Johns represented a certain rogue element within the government. I'm afraid to say that once his plan became apparent…" He paused. "Well, he took his own life, so as to ensure that we could not reverse any of his work." He sipped his tea and jerked a little from burning his lips on the cup. "So I have once more been given oversight of this department and all its assets. I can assure you that I am not interested in any of the chicanery, obfuscation, and, dare I say, treason, that Mr Johns was involved in."

Dead. Once again, the image of him saying the words "utter desolation" came to mind. He had beaten me, even in death. I doubt Johns even realised what he had taken from me before he killed himself.

"What about my family?" I asked.

The look on Jeffries's face was enough for me to know.

"I can only extend my sympathies, and say that I am sorry," he said. "It was this very stunt that brought into sharp relief Johns's intentions and misconduct. There were certain rumblings going on upstairs, and we were almost on to him. The attack on your family's compound was his attempt to cover up what he was doing. Unfortunately, there were many causalities."

"Survivors?"

"There were some children in the basement hidden inside a makeshift armoury."

The memory of sneaking down there that night and stealing bricks of money entered my mind. Money that I had buried with Jess.

Jess.

Jess who, I had come to realise, no longer existed in this reality because she had died after she was removed from the timeline. Jess who had no one to mourn her except me.

I shook my head. Stared into my drink, waiting for some words to come out, but it felt like my throat had tightened.

I looked at him. "I tried to make it right," I said. "I was bringing them all back, but you took that away from me, too."

"Excuse me?" he said, angling his head.

"All the people," I choked, feeling tears rolling down my dirty face. I corrected myself, then said, "All the people that were left. The ones I had taken through. I was bringing them back. They are waiting there for me now."

His eyebrow arched steeply, then quickly dropped again, his face regaining its composure. "Really?" he said. "Well, their return is something that we might be able to help facilitate."

"What, really?" It was my turn for surprise, I swiped my eyes with a dirty sleeve.

"We shall see. I will need to check with my superiors. There's a chance, of course, that it may be too risky." He pressed a finger thoughtfully to his lips. "Also, there may be some individuals that we legitimately need to isolate for the good of the timeline. We'll need a list of survivors."

"Did you recover the Book of Names?" I asked. "A big, thick, leather-bound book. Filled with names."

Jeffries shrugged. "I will have to check with the recovery team."

"That has a list of all of the names of everyone we ever brought through and what they did or would have done." I stood up. "I need to get back to them now. Before they go away again. Some of them are really sick."

Of All Possibilities | 313

"Eli, if we do this—if we help each other like this—I would like for you to consider formally joining the department. There's some vitally important, world-changing work that we continue to need your help with. Things that we should have been doing all the years that Johns was in charge. Now we must first fix the havoc he has caused, but then our focus returns to our real work.

"Which is?" I asked.

"Well, making the world a better, safer place, my boy."

I laughed bitterly then, but told him I would consider it, because I needed so badly to get those people out of Purgatory. I was desperate to put right at least some of the things I had done.

▽

Jeffries arranged for a containment centre to be set up among the ruins of my home, and they let me travel back to Purgatory.

▽

Luckily, Vlad was there to meet me on the other side, along with some of the group. I told him what had happened and most of them still agreed to come back through. Vlad told me that the young woman with the infected wound had died the night she'd arrived. I asked if anyone knew her name, but no one did. She was just another ghost in this place.

One by one, I took them through, and each time we crossed the threshold between universes, I felt some type of hope—well, hope *and* fear—and the sense of each individual's relief. *It's finally over.* At least they were heading back to where they belonged, even if to uncertainty. I saw in them their memories of Purgatory, each one playing out like a horror movie. Despair, loss, hatred. Some felt these so greatly that I felt like I was breaking. They each hated me equally, and I couldn't blame them.

Vlad was the last to come back. Night had come early in Purgatory, and I found him sitting on the remains of a tumbled-down wall. He had his back to a signpost and he was looking up into the freezing-clear sky. Stars and glittering lunar debris, a spray of icy diamonds upon the black. The slowly turning shards of moon caught the light and glimmered a little. The wind picked up and whispered through the field.

"You ready?" I asked.

"Da," he said, his smile a flash of yellow peeking out from somewhere under a great mess of beard. "I wonder if my wife has moved on."

I didn't know quite what to say, so I sat down next to him and stared upwards. There was an infinite number of universes matching this one, shades of them falling away like mirrors reflecting mirrors. I saw a kind of beauty in the desolation of the world. I pinched the bridge of my nose with thumb and forefinger. Going back and forth had given me a migraine.

"I hope that everything works out," I said. I wanted to thank him. I wanted to tell him that he may have saved me, but instead I said nothing.

"I guess I will find out soon," he said with a shrug.

"I'm sorry," I said, looking around. "For all this."

"Sorry for making me smash my own rotten tooth out?"

"Definitely that," I replied, and he clapped me on the shoulder.

"There will be a reckoning for this, I believe." He grimaced for a moment and then brightened. "You are a strange boy, with an incredible power. You could do so much good with it. Blood is merely circumstance. You do not have to continue your family's work."

I hadn't really thought about it in that way before. My ability had always been just the tool I had to punish people or to get away from danger. My Grandfather had thought he was working towards something greater, but I was just a weapon to be wielded by my Father. By Johns. I wondered if my streak of rebellion had been Vlad's all this time.

"I don't really know how," I said.

We stood before the doorway, bending light rippling around the invisible seam. The warm thrill of static vibrating through me.

"The door is here?" he asked. "You can see it?"

I nodded, feeling slightly nauseous.

"What does it look like?"

"It's see-through, just a kind of heat haze really. It's more the feeling that gives it away. Kinda like static buzzing up and down my neck. I can feel it in my fingers." I held up my hand and they seemed to distort, flickering and flaring like a candle flame caught in a gentle breeze.

"Fascinating," he said, screwing up his eyes as if to try and perceive it.

He took my hand and we stepped through.

▽

Relief again. I felt it crashing against my mind, couldn't stop it from filling me. My own grief rushed out to meet it, but Vlad's sense of joy, impending reunification, and tentative hope overtook everything. His self, now so many years older, slipped against the earlier version of him I had assimilated inside me like beads of mercury. It ran to meet him, and I felt a sliver of this new version of him break apart and lodge itself in me. He was angry, too. An undercurrent of it swelled just beneath everything else. The injustice. He had forgiven me, and I sensed something like a kindling friendship there. Then it was over and we stood among the bullet-pocked stones and my ruined home. A man cradling a submachine gun waved us on, and Vlad stumbled, bleary eyed but laughing now, towards the bright-yellow plastic tent the crew had set up as a temporary holding area. It was mostly empty now. The rest of the people I had brought back had been taken away to wherever they were going. Vlad looked over his shoulder one last time and smiled, and then he was gone.

Jeffries approached me, moving slowly as he crossed the garden, taking it all in as if for the first time. He was wearing a long jacket that seemed too big for him and had a tartan scarf wound several times around his neck. His hands were locked under his armpits, giving the false impression he was a petulant old man.

"Is that everyone?" he asked.

"Everyone who was still there. A couple less than I left yesterday."

"Oh, that's a shame," he said. He looked around at the tent and watched as the men started to disassemble some of the tents on the periphery of the cluster. One of the lights that cast a sharp angle of white light along the scorched lawn went dead, and a soldier began winding the power cord around his hand and elbow.

"Yeah," I said. "It is."

I gritted my teeth and watched as the men, dressed similarly to those who had raided my home, moved around the garden taking things down. I remembered summer nights, my family singing songs in the warm half-light. Then, Steven face down in the mud, arm bent up awkwardly behind him, dead.

"You figure out why Johns did what he did yet?" I asked.

"Eli, we are constantly at war," Jeffries replied with a grimace. "It's a subtle, shifting, insidious thing that doesn't understand borders or geopolitical alliances. It is fought on the battlefield of reality itself. Johns was allied to another faction. Was using our resources to steer the course of fortune and history to favour them."

"The House of Night?" I said, remembering them from my Grandfather's diary.

Jeffries looked surprised.

"Yes, very astute," he said. "I am surprised you've heard that name."

"My Grandfather wrote about them in his diary," I replied.

"I knew your Grandfather quite well."

"Really?"

"Absolutely. I was most saddened to hear of his passing. I do miss him and our lively conversations. Although, it does give me comfort to know that he is likely alive and well in another version of this life."

"Yeah," I said. Images of the destroyed compound as I had seen it so many times came to mind.

"I can assure you, Eli, that we will do our best to correct our mistakes."

I stood there watching that space between the stones—the doorway to oblivion, my salvation, a grave of a world for a person only I remembered. The world reordered, restratified, without her in it. Her absence replaced by someone else, something else. A flower clipped away by accident.

"It doesn't feel like anything has changed," I said. "Shouldn't it be—"

"Different? Oh, it is. Unfortunately, we know that the progress of the timeline halts when someone is removed, and it doesn't just rewind upon their return. It is more as if they have been absent for some very long years. I imagine there are myriad ways in which this version of things has been altered because of Johns. It will take some time for the people you've returned to again have an effect on how this universe is shaped."

I knew the answer, but I had expected cascading waves of change for some reason. I expected it to be better already.

"Eli, consider working with us. We can actually do some tangible good."

"I've been disappearing people for the government most of my life and all it's ever done is brought pain."

"It's not just people, Eli. There are numerous duties that fall into the remit of our department that exist in, shall we say, somewhat strange spectrums." He pulled his coat up further, strangling the flow of his cloudy breath in the air. "There are dark, ravenous things, pressing up against the very fabric of our reality, and they view us with envious eyes. This—what you can do—is not entirely unique. There are others who are gifted like you, and we work to protect this reality. Your Grandfather knew this well."

"What about my Father?"

"Him," he said with an attempted disinterest that couldn't quite hide his obvious contempt for my Father. "Well, he was a man of *quite* a different constitution to your Grandfather. We did not see eye to eye on a number of issues." He paused, took a few tentative steps around the dolmen and stepped through the middle where the air shimmer-shook. "That was actually how Johns ended up being your handler."

"My Dad had no gifts, like my uncle did."

"Yes, he was a Seer. To be the only one lacking must have affected a man of such rigid faith as your Father was. Tell me, the doorway, can you see it now?" he asked.

I stared at the bending air, the shifting sick light that I could almost perceive beyond it. I nodded.

"I would greatly like to see that place one day," he said wistfully. "Still. Your Father's hubris and Johns's allegiances led us to this very crossroads, and here we are."

He touched my shoulder with his gloved hand. "Before you make up your mind, let me at least show you around the place."

# Eleven

Like the broom Vlad compared me to, there is a Greek thought experiment called the Theseus's paradox. It asks: When a part is replaced on a ship, does it remain the same ship as before? And, if so, at what point does it eventually become a different ship, if you keep replacing parts until all are new?

Obviously, this concept applies to me at a fundamental level. Each person I take into other realities leaves a permanent piece of themselves inside me. And it's not like their consciousness just has an influence over me or something like that. It feels more like an actual, distinct replacing of aspects of my personality at a psychological level. All these years, these people, these victims that represent a plank here and there on the ship that bears my name, slowly becoming my only remaining constituent parts until I am me in name and face only.

I am my Father, his envy and anger. I am Vlad, his quiet contemplation and objective, logical thinking. I am Jess, her impulsiveness and need for love. I am a dictator, a child, a dissident, a terrorist. I am a torturer, a soldier, an artist. I am sure that there are pieces of the original me in there somewhere. I have my own tastes in things that I think have stayed constant. The music I love, the food I love, the people I love. But I have assimilated so many people that I feel like a patchwork person, no longer sure of my actual identity. And of my constituent parts, the original parts of me are the lesser. The whole less than the sum. I can almost discern my original parts through the eyes of the other people I am, and I feel only shame.

Maybe I am something entirely new.

The reason I say this is that, no, I don't believe that I am me entirely. I am the accreted wrongs of dangerous and broken people. There's some violent alchemy inside me that I can call upon when the need arises, and while I am clearly not blameless in this, it's those other parts in me that take the wheel when needed.

I'm telling you this because I don't want you to hate me for cutting off the fingers of another version of me.

Is there a real version of me? A pure version? One that has only been influenced by nature, nurture, bad TV, and good friends. One untainted by the hundreds of lives of other people. Undamaged by their struggles. I often wonder what he might be like. What trajectory his life took. Whether he is good or bad. Whether he would be cool with what I am about to do.

Self-reflection is extremely hard for me.

▽

I clip through the ring finger first. The heavy-gauge wire cutters snip neatly through the flesh just below the gold band and cut cleanly through the bone with a chilling snap without facing much resistance. I'm not really interested in a dramatic build up when he already knows where this is going. He gives an animal scream that rides up a few octaves I didn't know I was capable of reaching and strains at the handcuffs. The gold band slips off and clinks on the table, followed by the pattering of dark blood.

I pick up the bloody ring and slide it down the appropriate finger on my hand until it rests just below the knuckle. I look over at his, only a white circle of bone peeking through the gore.

"Fuck. Fuck. Stop. Stop it, please," he says. His cool exterior melting away in a bloody instant.

I pull the clippers up to the tip of his little finger and take it off at the nail. He screams again, then starts to sob. His shoulders bobbing up and down.

"Each little part of you I take is a short step away from me, and the easier this gets. C'mon, man. The difference," I say through gritted teeth. "Tell me."

He starts to laugh. It's a sad contorted thing pitched somewhere between defeat and arrogance. "Isn't it fucking obvious?"

# My Troubled History, Part Eleven

### November 12, 1996

Jeffries walked me through the London offices of H.P. Lewis and Sons Accounting. It's a large brown-brick building just around the corner from St. Paul's. Before it was repurposed, it was once a meeting place for the Freemasons. Affixed above the wide marble entryway was an aggressive-looking stone eagle painted a rather tacky shade of gold. The effect was somewhat further diminished by all the pigeon shit.

I felt a vague sense of déjà vu—the part of my Father that I carried with me that had been here dozens of times—as Jeffries and I walked between the rows of vacant desks and boxy computer screens, a thin layer of grey dust covering everything. The slight smell of the damp, stale air as we walked between the desks and into the back room made goosebumps prickle the back of my neck and creep up my scalp.

It was a pretty shoddy facade if you really looked at it. But no one ever did.

At the back of the room a drab concrete corridor turned right and opened into a kitchen. Just before that was a door. It was innocuous enough, but seemed too heavy to enclose a simple supply cupboard, which was what the little bronze plaque affixed to it said.

"What type of brooms you keep in here?" I asked.

"Expensive ones," the old man said with a wry little smile.

He pushed the door open with effort and we stepped through. I felt a mild headache come and go, as if I had crossed a threshold into another reality I couldn't quite see.

A set of stone stairs led down to a short corridor that ended at a glass-fronted entryway. I felt a little seasick, so gripped the metal rail a little tighter than I normally would have, making it squeak. Through the frosted glass, I could see a few people milling about in the room beyond. A couple of them looked up from their work, eyed me somewhat suspiciously, and then went back to whatever they were doing.

"Welcome," he said, with simmering excitement, "to the House of August."

He pushed the doors wide and we walked into the room. The air seemed deliberately too cold, and I shivered as I shuffled behind Jeffries, my footsteps sounding excessively loud on the stone floor.

"Ladies and gentlemen," Jeffries said with a little showmanship, opening his arms wide to take in the mostly disinterested workforce. "This is, Eli. Some of you may have heard of him. He is the Key."

At that, one or two more faces looked up from their work and craned their heads to get a good look.

I raised my hand. "Hi," I said sheepishly. "Nice to meet you all."

"Now," Jeffries continued. "Eli will be back when he is ready to start working with us, but I thought I would show him round, introduce him to a few people, and give him a rundown on the history of the department. I'd like everyone to introduce themselves to him at some point today or tomorrow, if you please."

"MURDERER," a young woman shouted abruptly. "WHYAMIHERE?RUNAWAYI COULDJUSTRUNAWAY."

Jeffries looked at her, then to me, and cleared his throat. "Ahem. Thank you, Eve. If you could put your glasses back on, please."

She offered a pointed look and slipped a large pair of dark glasses over her eyes and went back to work.

My mouth was slack. She had just spoken my exact thoughts at that moment, and not just the fleeting ones that occupied the conscious part of my brain, but my actual intentions.

"Eli," Jeffries said, and motioned towards an office at the back of the room. I followed behind, continuing to stare at the young woman, who was now clearly glaring at me through her sunglasses.

Looking at him, you'd think Jeffries was the sort of person who was tidy to a fault, but his office was an explosion of paper. Towers of files with no real discernible order to them were piled on almost every flat surface. Most were stamped *Top Secret*. Some lay open and many others filled the overflowing wire bin in the corner. Under a particularly large stack was a table, although only about a quarter of it was actually visible. Jeffries tottered to one side of it and lifted a pile of records from a chair, then pulled it out for me to sit on.

"You'll have to forgive Ms Karasky," he said, then let out a sigh as he fell into his own chair. It was high backed, leather, and protested as it tilted back a little. "She can be a little confrontational. I think you two will likely get on, in time, though. Her past was problematic too."

"How…" I started.

"She read your mind, correct?"

I nodded dumbly.

"It's her gift. Same as you, my boy, same as you. She can't help herself though, that's why she wears the, you know—" He mimed the shape of sunglasses. "They block her ability enough so that she isn't shouting out all the things that pop into people's heads. Got her into an awful lot of trouble as a child."

"She's a psychic?"

"'Telepathic perception' is the technical term for it, but she hates that."

"And she works here, for you?" I asked.

"Yes. They all do, and most of them, like you and Eve, have gifts. Hers is particularly useful."

"Other abilities? Like what?" I asked.

"Well, most of the team have varying degrees of psychic ability. Mostly sensitivity to particular aspects of or certain changes to the timeline." He cleared his throat. "Places where the walls between realities thin, overlap. These are the same places where gateways to other realities occur," he looked around at the drab walls with something approaching reverence. "The House of August, for instance, exists in a place where reality itself is more, well, pliable. Your great-grandfather found it for us, I believe, when he first brought his powers as a Seer to us under the Atropos Project just before the Great War."

Jeffries leant forward in his seat, and placed his spread fingers across the desk.

"Eli, I wasn't lying to you when I said we were at war. And you were right: it's the House of Night we are at war with, and they are most ruthless." He furrowed his brow. Knitted his knobbly hands together and swallowed.

I thought about my Grandfather's diary and the intricate notes he had made.

"And the Nazis were part of it?" I asked.

"My boy, it goes back further than that. This war has been raging, to some degree or another, forever." He sighed, looked out at the team of people poring over files and maps, making notes, trying to hold our universe together. "But you are right, of course. Himmler brought it to the attention of Hitler—by 'it' I mean 'the occult,' of course. The Nazis were part of the Thule Society, which, in turn, was part of the House of Night. They were working towards similar goals as us."

I raised my eyebrow.

"The best of all possible worlds?" I said. I repeated the phrase written down a dozen times in my Grandfather's neat cursive.

"That's right, although what that means is subjective. Himmler wanted what *he* perceived to be the best of all possible worlds—and that would have been some wretched reality, I can tell you that much."

"And what has that got to do with me?" I asked.

"Eli, you can remove objects and people from the field of play. Not just dead or gone—invalid. Unavailable. We can hold or bury or try to destroy an object like the Spear of Longinus, the Antikythera Mechanism, or the Porcelain Kittens, but we cannot remove them from the fight entirely."

"The what?"

He flapped his hands, waving away my question.

"Powerful devices, Eli. Objects of often peculiar power, used to alter the course of our timeline or as weapons. Things that can knit together or pull apart the fabric of other universes and manipulate our version of reality, or simply cause destruction and death."

"What about the people? What about all the people I disappeared?"

"It's the same principle. Seers can foresee that the effect of their work will come to sway the course of this reality. If such people are merely dead, their influence on the timeline can still be felt, psychically or otherwise. But *removing* them—taking them to Purgatory, as your Grandfather called it—means that their influence cannot be felt in our reality at all."

My head was throbbing. I felt a rush of panic. An awful heat prickled the back of my neck. "What the fuck did *I* do to the timeline then?" I asked. I swiped at my eyes with the back of my sleeve. "How badly did I fuck everything up?"

Jeffries looked grave, swept a hand over the files, each one evidently a record of my misdeeds. Dossiers on all the people I had removed from the timeline painstakingly put together by employees of the project who could perceive the changes to the timeline.

"We are still trying to work that out. Hopefully nothing we can't reverse in time. But ultimately we don't know how deep Johns's influence ran." Jeffries coughed, absentmindedly lifted a couple of folders, sorted them so their edges were flush with each other, and then placed them back down. "Just looking at the rough trends of people he brought to you, it seems he was enabling powerful totalitarian regimes in China and the Soviet Union. Makes sense, seeing as we are just out of the Cold War and no one seems to have gained much out of it. Johns may have just been playing a long game, or maybe it was harder than he thought to derail centuries of good work."

*Good work.* The phrase stuck in me, because by contrast I had been doing the opposite. Where had that gotten me? Where had it gotten all the people I loved? My family. Jess.

I needed to go. I was half tempted just to say fuck it and leave all the other freaks to it. I was upset that I had been responsible for taking all those people out of the timeline, but I was furious too.

"How the fuck was Johns allowed to just use me like that? How could he get away with it for so long? Wasn't someone supposed to be watching him? Who holds the fucking leash?" My blood was boiling. "Aren't you government lot supposed to be watching us at all times?"

Jeffries's expression was deflated. He looked tired, exhausted even, and he shrugged.

"Johns was well respected. Liked. A family man who always seemed to put the greater good above everything else. He was an extremely talented liar and assembled a team of other extremely talented liars around him."

I couldn't imagine Johns being liked. Couldn't see him at parties, dancing and getting drunk and telling dirty jokes. Couldn't imagine people smiling and being glad to see him.

"He assembled his own team of people, mainly sleeper agents of the House of Night. Their Prophet kept some very detailed… notes." He sifted through the papers idly, looking for something, then gave up.

"Prophet?" I asked.

"An individual capable of seeing across timelines. Inside the Houses, their work remains unchanged. We have had a Prophet working in our department since its inception. It's how we keep tabs on the work that we do."

"Oh yeah, of course, right," I said sarcastically. It was too much for me. I had thought that my family were the only people with these types of gifts, and the revelation that I was one of a few was at once comforting and frightening. I rubbed my temples and blew out a tense lungful of air, causing a couple of sheets of yellowed papers to lift and fall gently.

"So, Eli—will you join us and help fix this world and elevate this reality to its potential?" Jeffries asked.

I looked around the office. The wall full of sketches of all the people I had hurt, the photos of the ones I would need to hurt. The mountain of case files filled with my mistakes. I looked at the old man, his tired eyes gleaming with hope, and I wondered what Jess would do. Then I remembered that she was gone.

"Haven't I fucked things up enough already?" I said, voice caught in my throat.

"We can fix it with your help, we can make it better." He looked somehow younger, angry. "Up until now, it was just battles. With your help, we can win the war."

"No," I said thinking of what my Father had said about doing it the old way, the *right way*, if there was such a thing. "I can't. I can't do this anymore. It's just too much."

"Oh," was his only reply, and then we were done.

▽

I was given access to all my family's funds, which I shared out among the three members of the New Sunrise Project who survived the attack on the compound. I thought about seeing them, but couldn't face it. Couldn't stand to hear them ask why I didn't save everyone, why I just left them to die. So I never saw any of them again.

I bought a detached house in North London at the end of a tree-lined street and wondered what to do with myself. It felt strange sitting there in an empty kitchen with everything done and finished. No more family and their prayers. No more people I had to erase, part of them stealing a part of me. No more Jess. My whole life had had a sense of desperate momentum and now, without warning, it had abruptly come to a stop. I finally had the freedom that Jess and I had both wanted so badly, but now that it was mine, it felt empty. I kept feeling that vivid need in her to be wanted, mixed with my own need to be with her. My co-dependency and the memory of our love coalescing into some increasingly bright fever the more I thought about it.

I would find myself driving past her house at three in the morning, or parked up outside, staring up at her bedroom window. Other people lived in the house—I had no idea what had happened to Jess's father without her in his life—but every time the light went on in her room, I hoped it was her.

I tried to plug the gap with other things.

Despite what I'd told Vlad about not looking

for her in other realities, that's exactly what I did. I tried to fight the urge for a little while. Told myself it wouldn't really be her, but in the end, I couldn't stop myself. Still felt that rebel part of her inside me, telling me to "fuck it, come get me."

I spent a year doing that before I gave up. I tried to stay only one or two jumps away, but inevitably found myself shaking and broken, bloody nosed and crying, at the remains of her house or by her graveside. It felt like she was destined to die. In some realities, she had walked out in front of a bus. In others, her father had murdered her and he was in prison. There was one where she was the one who had died during her birth instead of her mother—her parents still happily together with a son. Every permutation I encountered felt like a brutal defeat. The universe nixing her like she was meaningless, her life inconsequential.

I crawled into bed one evening in December '97 a bloody mess. My hair dirty and stinking, matted from the blood that had poured in thick, dark streams from my ears. My vision doubling and lilting from the migraine, occasional loops of old songs running through my thoughts until I wanted to throw up.

I slept for two days and woke up on December 17—my nineteenth birthday. The house was empty as always, my bare footsteps creaking on the dark floorboards. Outside, it was snowing. The streets dressed in a thin coat of white. The world beyond the garden was just grey fog, familiar buildings looming ghostlike at the edge of what I could see.

I made a cup of tea and sat at the kitchen counter in the half-light, watching the snow fall silently outside. I remember knowing I would never see her again, and at that moment the part of her that lived inside me fell silent. I could scarcely remember all the things I had done just after returning from Purgatory. It could have been some sort of brain damage, all of it kind of falling into one compressed memory of failure, bitterness, and drunken anger. It's weird thinking about it now, because right then, everything seemed to snap back into focus.

I was done looking for her, done existing in a haze, so I picked up the phone and called Jeffries.

"You still want me?" I asked, dirty feet on the kitchen counter, leaning back on an ornate wooden chair I'd bought impulsively, telephone cord wrapped between my thumb and forefinger and around my elbow.

"Eli! Dear boy. It's so very good to hear from you," Jeffries said, then a muffled cough. "We would certainly be grateful for your skills."

"The same agreement we talked about before?" I asked.

"You vet everyone we remove from the field? Absolutely."

"Okay," I said. "Then there's just one other thing."

"What is it?" The line was quiet apart from quiet intermittent crackling.

"Meet me at the New Sunrise Project," I replied. "I need to be sure."

"Be sure of what?" Jeffries asked. He coughed again, hacked, and then slurped some water. The sound of it made me wince and cringe away from the receiver.

"You."

▽

Snow covered the blackened beams that lay in the back garden. The gables of one of the collapsed buildings poked up from the thick layer of snow like the uncovered rib bones of some long-dead giant. The exposed parts of the main house had fallen in on themselves, leaving only a rough shell, the wood burst and split and creaking in the wind blowing up across the empty field. The fence had fallen at the front, brought down by wind or vandal, and the plastic wrap left behind by the government flapped and whipped in the cold air. Other than that sound, it was eerie quiet.

I arrived before Jeffries and stood by the grave of my Grandfather, the wildflowers trampled and dead under a dusting of glittering snow and frost. Memories transposed over each other like the laying of photographs. I could clearly recall the way everything had looked before. Even from before I was born, observing it from my Father's hopeful eyes. I remembered the day we had buried my Grandfather, and then, in the years that followed, how all his secrets were disinterred. I saw the place as it was now, a mere ghost of all those moments. The inevitable conclusion of decisions made too long ago.

Jeffries pulled up in his car, the headlights sweeping across the ruins. I met him at the dais, the two pillars and lintel of the fallen Great Stones

Door webbed by ice, their jagged seams of cold quartz glistening. The flakes of falling snow distorted and bent as they drifted past the door to Purgatory, the sickly tide of static rolling from the space in-between.

"Eli," he said, warm breath escaping upwards, whipped apart by the biting wind. He had his hands wrapped around himself, rubbing his arms, the collar of his thick coat turned up, half his face hidden. He smiled, and despite the cold, his eyes shone.

I thought back to the moment when we had stood at that place before. Vlad gone into the tent, and Jeffries stood there wondering if he could see the world that existed just outside this one. My own demand playing to his curiosity.

"You ready to do this?" I said.

Jeffries nodded. "But I think I would have been happy to wait until summer. This type of weather cuts right through my old bones."

"Just to double check, you're absolutely sure it won't erase everything you've done from the timeline?"

He smiled and pulled his scarf loose, revealing a chip of stone or metal cut into an arrow shape that hung round his neck.

"This is a fragment of the Spear of Longinus. It's an artefact that allows its bearer to not be bent out of reality."

"How?"

"Honestly, we can't say with any degree of certainty. We have people called Seekers whose gift enables them to detect objects of great power. How they come to be is a mystery, but there are many of them, mostly seemingly mundane objects, and each has a unique property. We hunt them down as we can and store them at the House of August." He wrapped his scarf tight again. "And this one ensures that my actions cannot be erased from the timeline."

"Okay, then. Sure."

"There are so many mysteries in this universe. So much magic that is as yet unaccounted for."

"For so long I thought it was just my family," I said as we walked towards the dolmen. Each stone scarred by bullets, charred with fire. Covered in a thin skin of ice, so that the veins of quartz seemed to coalesce with the mundane, grey rock beside it.

"Don't we all always think it is 'just us,'" he said. "But in a universe of infinite possibilities, everything is, in fact, a little mundane. It's all been done before."

I touched his arm and gently pulled him towards that space between realities. The place where our minds would shred apart and comingle as we sped out. Out into the burning nexus. Out towards Purgatory. An end-stop reality. One of the infinite net results of all our poor choices, or maybe just simple happenstance outside our control. I felt all Jeffries's wonder and fear. The pain that was slowly needling his guts, the worries and anxieties. He saw into me as clearly as I saw into him, felt his own mind wicking away my failure of the last year to find Jess. I felt my own shame and his own reaction to it. The understanding of the loss. I saw the work laid out like a map. The impossible convolutions of the House of August. The plans of the men above him, the complicated design of a possible future. Finally, I felt Jeffries's desire to do some good. For him. His wife. His daughter.

▽

We stood in the field, wind whipping up the loose snow and sending it skyward in curls like sea spray on a beach. Off to the eastern side of the field stood the remains of the building. Only one stone wall was still visible; the rest had fallen in and was buried in snow. Above the black shape of the jagged treeline, portions of the broken moon peeked through the ragged clouds. The largest chunks glimmered in the roiling murk, making dull points of lights in the blanket of grey-green.

"Dear God," Jeffries said. He was fighting to get his collar up higher, but the wind kept pulling at it.

"Yeah, he's really let this place go to pot," I replied, shouting into the screaming air. "Also, this is the only door here that I know of. I travelled all the way down to London and I didn't see any others."

"None?" he cried.

"Nope, nothing," I drew a thumb across my throat. "It's like a biblical apocalypse."

"What about people?"

"Don't know," I said. "Didn't find any. It's as if they all just up and vanished." The image of the dead man lying on the bed came to mind. Then Jess. The woman whose septic arm killed her. I didn't even know her name.

"Like the Rapture."

"Exactly."

"Do you believe in God, Eli?"

"I really don't know," I replied. "Some days I do. This universe feels like a living thing. You know, all these realities bent into some kind of living shape."

"And on the other days?" Jeffries asked.

"God knows."

I crunched across the hard earth to where Jess was buried, the sound of it setting my teeth itching. It was hard for me, the idea of leaving her there at the end of a world, but I couldn't bear the thought of letting someone dig her up. It was hard enough to keep the part of her that lived in me quiet. Somewhere in the dark, it was screaming at me like the wind. I remembered her dead in my arms. Tried to piece her face together, but it was fading already, replaced by a perfect construct devoid of scars, marks, context.

Jeffries stopped next to me.

"I am sorry," he said, and squeezed my shoulder gently.

"I tried to find her," I said, tears suddenly stinging my eyes and blurring my vision. "I tried, but I couldn't."

"I know," he said, though the buried sliver of me must have already been slowly fading from his mind. "I know that this will sound cliché, but you really can't blame yourself for what happened."

"It was my fault though," I said. "If I had carried on just doing what Johns had wanted…"

"Then the world would have been a much darker place already. Who knows where we would be. It might be like here."

"I think…" I said finally through gritted teeth, hoping the wind would carry away the words before the old man could hear them. "I think I could have lived with that if it meant that she was still here."

Jeffries looked away at a wide patch of revealed night sky surrounded by a halo of clouds lit ghostly green. His expression was subdued, curious, and he looked upon the fractured remains of the moon in quiet contemplation.

# Twelve

He's crying again, the other me. Those snotty, rattling wheezes shot through with sobs. Face bruised, hair matted with dried blood, watery eyes puffed up and swelling into a mockery of my own. His hand is missing three fingers now. Cut loose and sticky with blood, they lay on the old worktop like strange sausages. I remember my mum cutting carrots on there, the old scars of stray knife cuts filled with my blood.

There's a point when you realise that the situation you're in is too far gone, and it always happens way too late. Before that moment, you think you can somehow escape the inevitable. That you can live with four fingers, three fingers. That the gun to your head won't actually go off. You can normalise anything in the moment, just as long as you keep breathing and your heart still pumps. It's the moment after that realisation when people show who they really are. When the other person knows it isn't going to get better, that even they can't live with what's coming. I watch with mild interest at how I might react in that situation.

"I finally accepted his offer, and I've been working with Jeffries ever since," I say. I take up the knife and start carving neat lines in the countertop. "It took ten years. Ten. Fucking. Years. But you should see the place now, man. It's a veritable fucking paradise."

"If you let me go, I could just go there," he says. "I won't come back. I mean, I can't go back to her now. Not like this."

"You could, I guess. But how can I trust you? I'd be forever watching my back. No, it's probably for the best that I kill you."

"Unless I tell you?" he asks, hope snuffed out at the wick.

"I think you know it's too far gone for that," I say. "Now, it's all about how fast you go."

He laughs then, a sad thing, with pink-stained teeth.

"The question is: You wanna go fast?" I gesture to the gun. "Or you wanna go slow?" I hold up the knife and gently twist the blade so that the cold light from the hook lamp moves along the metal.

"I don't even know the thing that you want."

I huff, move the blade to start in on the index finger. "You know what I'm after," I say.

"No. I mean, *seriously*, I don't know it. I never found out what she did that was different." I must look confused, because he continues, "You don't really think I was the first of us to do this, do you? Fuck, I'm not even the third or fourth. I'm just another of the endless procession of us desperately clinging to a ghost."

"No," I growl.

"Yes. You're just slower and more inept than the rest of us," he says, and spits onto the scarred wood. "You know, she's thinking of leaving us? She told me that she feels like she doesn't even know us anymore."

"I can fix that," I say.

"I thought the same way too," he says.

"How long?" I ask.

"Two years. I left Jeffries's programme shortly after that stuff in Japan."

I cluck my tongue at the memory of it, try to suppress the smile at the shared familiarity. I had stayed on.

"I asked the one before me the same question. He didn't know. Didn't have time to ask the one before him. Just shot him and stole his life."

"I see," I say, stiffening. The next few moments begin coalescing in my mind. Steeling myself as I envision dark thoughts turning to actions. Letting those slivers of me capable of doing black deeds take the wheel a little.

"It's endless," he says, his face blank now, staring at the place next to the sink where we had both clutched onto our mothers, a mirror image in time for that moment. "I look through our photos in a home that I didn't choose and I see memories that aren't mine. I look at our things and I wonder which of us chose them." He laughs sadly. "It's not what you think. It's just an empty lie."

He's wrong. He's me, but he doesn't know, can't know the depths of my feelings or understand the desperation. "But it's better than the truth," I say, my hand tightening around the grip of the knife, knuckles turning pale. My heart is pounding in my chest, mouth full of hot spit. I see myself sat in front of me, struggling against the inevitable moment that is rushing at us.

"I know," he says. Sad resignation now, eyes still fixed to that spot. "But there will be a reckoning."

When he says Vlad's words, I almost falter, because what if he's telling the truth? What if he does understand? He looks away, I imagine into the past at some point when all his choices still lay before him. His jaw muscles are working as the moment spins out. Is this being played out anywhere else?

His eyes turn back to meet mine, and he says, "Just don't—"

I bury the knife up to the handle in the side of his neck. His eyes bulge, go wide, looking as they're almost going to pop out as he wheezes and gasps. He coughs a spout of blood, spattering it all over the table, tries desperately to pull his hands up to stem the bleeding, but can't, so he leans over the table, his tongue dangling out of his mouth as he gags.

It takes a few moments, but eventually he dies, giving one final rattling wheeze. Then he goes limp, eyes rolling up in his head as he slumps flat on the table.

"There always is," I whisper.

It feels strange seeing my own dead body there, like an out-of-body experience. I could be his malevolent ghost. I uncuff him and he falls sideways, lands with a thump on the stone floor, the stumps of his missing fingers leaving three neat red lines across the old wood of the table. I pick up the loose fingers and jam them into his pocket, then I drag him outside to where the Great Stone Door has cracked and fallen apart, the stones laying on their mossy sides. Sick waves of static roll over and around them. My head feels like it's going to fucking burst as I finally heave him up again, and pull us both through the gateway. The pain suddenly gets worse.

Way worse.

The jump from two realities to three stamping all over my corneas and filling my brain with rusty nails.

I've never jumped with a corpse before, or even another version of myself, and a fleeting thought makes me wonder if there is a chance we could switch places somehow and I'll just blink out of existence on the other side. Not that I'd totally snuff out. There are things that lurk in the in-between space that I know about, have seen. There are beings and life that exists outside our sphere of comprehension. I've seen evidence of it in the crossing of timelines, in their sewing together.

# My Troubled History, Part Twelve

**Two days ago, Crouch End**

I have no idea why I went through the doorway that day. No reason to. I wasn't on a job, wasn't even really that curious. Wasn't looking, but isn't that just how true love works?

As I passed the doorway to her reality, I felt some needle-thread pull in my guts that made me stop. It was something cold and certain and gave me pause. Eve, my girlfriend, came up sharp, almost tripping as her arm in mine suddenly wrenched her to a stop.

"What is it?" she asked. "Doorway?" She was used to this.

I narrowed my eyes at the space and nodded. It was just another door, but that ghostly pulling sensation was there, growing even stronger with my scrutiny towards it. A quixotic impulse pulling all the hairs on the back of my arms and neck to attention.

"Yeah," I said, taking a small step closer, feeling the air hissing around me, that familiar smell of ozone and burning metal filling my nose.

"Just leave it—our reservations are for half eight. We'll be late if we fuck around jumping about the place."

I shrugged and we carried on, but as we sat opposite each other, making small talk and laughing, eating expensive food and listening to the tinkly music in a ridiculously overpriced restaurant, I couldn't help but think of it.

"Are you okay?" Eve asked, staring at me through the dark lenses of her glasses. "You seem... distracted."

"I'm fine," I said, spearing the last bite of a chocolate orange cake and shoving it into my mouth.

She eyed me with vague suspicion, a thin smile spreading across her face. "Don't make me take these off and shout the place down."

She always had me with that.

I waved her off. "It's fine, honestly. I just keep thinking about that door I saw earlier. I had such a weird feeling from it, you know."

She huffed, angled her head. "Seriously, Eli. You're not even working today!"

"I can't help it, I'm just a naturally curious person."

We went home and followed our usual routine, flopping lazily on the couch and turning the TV on to watch some mindless bullshit. Eve sat in the corner, her glasses on, reading a novel, legs stretched out and feet resting on a stool. Then bed. Brushing teeth and laying in the dark staring up into the darkness until my eyes adjusted and I could make out the shape of objects in the room. The wardrobe, the alarm clock, the pale curve of her shoulders facing away from me.

"I love you," I said, and I did mean it. She would only have to turn and look at me to know for sure, but I hoped she wouldn't.

"I know," she said, her voice thick with sleep. For some reason, a memory surfaced. It was the moment that Jess had said those same words to me. It might have been the last happy thing we shared before it all went to shit. "I love you too," she added.

Eve drifted into sleep, releasing a noisy mixture of mumbling and snoring, and I slipped out of bed. By the thin moonlight that caught the edges of things, I grabbed some clothes and left. I manually pushed the car back from the drive until I was in the road, then jumped in and started it.

All the while, as I drove, I felt guilty. Thought to myself that this wasn't something that I was actually going to do, now was it. Then I was standing there in front of it, just waiting for the moment where I would turn around and go back to my home, slip into bed, and try to forget about it. But it was too late, and I let my legs carry me through.

▽

The doorway dropped me off outside the same house in the same quiet suburban street. It was still dark, but I could see a person inside moving from room to room switching the lights on and off, my heart thumping so hard at the idea that had begun to form that it felt like it would leap out of my mouth. No, it was just ghosts surfacing from the depths. That cold certainty asserted itself again as I tracked the shape of the person as they went downstairs into the kitchen, which was level with

the street. I saw a glimpse of a face—a woman—
but I couldn't be sure it wasn't just my imagination
firing off, because what I thought I might be seeing
couldn't be true.

A car passed nearby, the broken exhaust
causing a racket and making her turn and look up
and out of the window.

Jess.

Time slowed to a crawl.

She caught sight of me, squinted, but I was
already turning my back, walking up the hill away
from the house, trying my best to fight the urge to
look back over my shoulder, my aching heart
beating hard in my chest, tears forming. My mind
spinning, already planning, planning, planning. That
was when I saw me, the other version of me,
coming the other way, and I knew.

Some van rental places in London open at six
in the morning, did you know that? I didn't, until
that morning. But I guess if you're moving home,
you need as much time as you can get.

# Thirteen

I'm back at that house now, the place where she is. Where we live. Can feel the pull of my old life not far behind me.

I love Eve, and I feel so terribly guilty about leaving. She will know that I've gone by now. Fled just like all the other men in her life. I will be the villain in her story, and that's okay. There has to be one sometimes, I guess. I've tried my whole life to be good, but it's just never worked out. I hope she might understand.

The wind picks up and soughs through the trees, shaking the branches, and I think of all the promises broken and all the lives I've taken that have led me to here. The simple acts of divergence and convergence that have brought me back to her. Is it destiny, fate? Is that what all the other versions of me thought, too?

A light shines behind the front door, and I can see the outline of her, hear her talking on the phone. Maybe to her dad, maybe to some friend. Her laugh is deeper, rougher from all the years that have passed, but it's still the same. It takes me back to when love was such an easy thing in a life filled with complications. Time is like snow: each second, each week, each month, each year unique, but uniquely similar. Slowly piling, one tiny flake after another. Piling and piling, until it's crushing you and now you know it's too late. All those opportunities buried in the past, and all of your life squandered.

Parts of me hum with manic excitement. Expectation. Parts of me that can barely contain themselves. I feel other, bloodier remnants slip into something that feels like slumber, sated, perhaps, because this might be some kind of ending for them. I feel her there too, desperately aching to be whole again.

The rational parts of me try to tamp down this feeling within the wilder parts of me, because I know I might fail at this subterfuge. If subterfuge is even the right word for it.

I raise a shaking hand and knock. As she approaches, I can see her outline in the frosted glass filling my reflection. She's whistling now; I recognise it as one of her songs. A catchy chorus part she wrote when she was sixteen. I whisper the words that go over the tune, "I am not one of you. I am not one of you." It's almost too much too much to bear. My heart hurts. I take a deep breath, pretend to be cool. Breathe out slow and shaky, pretend that this is just another day. My skin prickles all the way to the roots of my hair as I hear her reaching out to open the door.

I will be her Eli. One that is wrought from joy and despair. Love and envy. Death and life.

All just parts, like waves drawn back into the ocean. A named ship that is made of new wood. Standing at this door, I am her, too.

And what are we but the sum of our parts?

# Acknowledgements

For my wonderful wife, Marie, who listens to all of my story ideas (no matter how silly they are) and tells me when they don't make sense and gets excited when they do. This one is for you.

I would especially like to thank Jaclyn Arndt for her amazing editing skills; I am forever indebted to you and your incredible work. It was always a joy to receive your edits as well as your often hilarious comments and interesting trivia on the manuscript.

Special thanks to my beta readers and rather excellent friends, Sarah Linders, Alex Laurel Lanz, Lyle Enright, Stefan Sokoloski, and Callum Colback, for cheering me on, motivating me when I needed it, letting me bother you at weird hours with strange questions, and for your insightful, generous, and utterly invaluable feedback. Apologies and thanks to Jamie Snow, who read the earliest readable draft of this book and offered some very kind and helpful feedback.

Thanks also to Alex Laurel Lanz for her amazing typesetting work. Amanda Seagroatt for showing me that everything must flow just right. David G. Clark for listening to me moan. Lauren Butler, Dillon Campbell, Kat and Glen Cross, Jon Warner, and Anna Anderson for being fans. Also to Stephanie Victoire, my oldest writing buddy.

Thank you to all my brilliant and wonderfully talented friends at *TL;DR Press*, whose feedback, encouragement, and support is always amazing and sincerely appreciated. Everyone on this list has my eternal gratitude.

And finally, thanks also to you, dear reader.

# About the Author

**Joe Butler** lives and works in London, but dreams of living and working elsewhere. His writing has been featured in *Pilcrow & Dagger*, *Story Bits*, *Bandit Fiction*, *New Orbit,* and the *Corvid Review*. He also won the 2018, Bandit Fiction, Six Word Story competition.

He is a co-founder, along with Alex Laurel Lanz, Andi Curis, Brad McNaughton, Camden M. Collins, Callum Colback, David G Clark, Lila Krishna, Penfold, and Sarah Linders, of the charity publisher TL;DR Press. Since its inception in 2017, the press has released a number of literary collections to benefit various charities, including Médecins Sans Frontières, the Endometriosis Foundation of America, the Pilcrow Foundation, the Kempe Foundation, the True Colours Fund, Girls Write Now, and the Association for Science Education.

You can find more of Joe's work, including The Haunted Hotel project, an ongoing guerrilla ghost story project, and audio versions of his short stories, at www.writelikeashark.wordpress.com. You can also find him on Twitter as @writelikeashark